The SEAL and The Singer

Jesse Slade

Written by: Jesse Slade
Published by: Jesse Slade

THE SEAL AND THE SINGER
First edition: March 2022

Dedication

For Becky and Catherine, my biggest champions. You always listen, always encourage, and always make me laugh. What would I do without you?

Acknowledgment

Thank you for reading the SEAL and the Singer.

There are a few people I need to thank that made this endeavor possible.

To John, for making me remember there's more to life than work and telling me (more than once) to go for it. Without you, I probably wouldn't have attempted this, and if possible, I love you even more for that.

My beta reader, Tony, who got the first look and was so kind with his suggestions and criticism and ended up providing inspiration for "Smoke".

To Becky and Catherine, who have had my back for the last million and a half years!

To my editor, Alan, who tried to keep me from being repetitive, corrected my awful punctuation and kept me on my toes.

To Navy SEALs everywhere. You guys are the real badasses. Thank you for what you do.

To my dogs and writing buddies, Kate and Ziva, who lent sympathetic ears when I was frustrated, wagged their tails enthusiastically when I felt like I was getting it right, and danced around the house with me when I wrote Alex's concert scenes.

But most of all, thank *you* for reading.

Chapter 1

Cole

Commander Reynolds had called an emergency meeting, and I sat with my five SEAL teammates, waiting for him to come and give us the intel briefing on our next mission.

While we waited, I looked around the room at the five men who were not just my teammates but my closest, most trusted friends. I'd do anything for them, just as they would do anything for me.

My eyes landed on Tony "Smoke" Marcucci. Smoke was the team's medic, and because he spoke seven languages, he also acted as our linguistic expert. Smoke was laid back most of the time, a notorious flirt with a good sense of humor.

He was popular with the ladies and never failed to turn almost any meeting with a woman into something more. Like the rest of the team, Smoke enjoyed playing the field and wasn't looking to settle down. Of all the men on the team, Smoke was probably my closest friend.

Grant "Midas" St. John was our electronics and computer expert; there wasn't much he couldn't do with a keyboard, not all of it strictly legal. Not that any of us cared about that when he got results that often gave us essential intel that saved our lives.

Midas came from a wealthy family, which is how he got his nickname, and never had to work a day in his life if he didn't want to, but that didn't keep him from being one hell of a SEAL or make him treat us differently because he was rich. Midas worried he'd never find a lasting relationship with a woman because he could never be sure if she wanted him for him or his money.

My eyes next landed on Patrick "Jax" Morgan, who was the best of us with explosives. He got his nickname because everyone thought he bore a striking resemblance to Charlie Hunnam, who played Jax Teller on *Sons of Anarchy*. Wherever we went, Jax always got women's attention first because when they saw him, they thought he *was* Charlie Hunnam.

Although, women didn't seem to care once they knew he wasn’t the famous actor, which meant he didn't have to work hard for dates.

Like Midas, Jax worried that he couldn't be sure a woman wanted him for him or because of his looks, but it didn't stop him from looking or accepting what women offered him.

Bradley "Bruiser" Beckett didn't have the best childhood. From the little he'd shared with the team, it had been pretty bad at the hands of his abusive aunt, who raised him.

As a result, he didn't trust anyone outside the team, especially women. To say he had issues with women was an understatement.

He didn't laugh or smile much and often came off as abrasive, rude, or offensive because of how he spoke his mind. Of all of us, Bruiser was the best at any kind of close combat hand-to-hand fighting.

Derek "Boomer" Givens was the newest and youngest member of the team at twenty-five, and while we were still getting to know him, he'd proven himself over and over as a great addition. He was also the biggest of us at six-four and the best swimmer on the team.

Boomer considered himself a ladies' man but was actually somewhat awkward when it came to women. He was quick to laugh, loved to dance, and had the worst singing voice of anyone I'd ever heard.

We found that out after he'd had a few beers and jumped on stage on Karaoke night at our favorite bar. Since that night, we always encouraged him to sing on Karaoke night because it never failed to make us laugh.

These were my teammates, my closest friends, my brothers. I'd saved their lives, and they'd saved mine. There was no other group of men I trusted more.

My attention shifted when Commander Reynolds entered the room and immediately started passing out folders to each member of the team.

He wasted no time telling us about our next mission while he paced the room, "You're being sent on a rescue mission, greenlit by the President. Last Saturday, Alex Walker was kidnapped from a private party."

"The singer?" Boomer asked.

"Yes."

I flipped through the file, glancing at the information, stopping to look at the picture of her. About the same time, someone wolf-whistled.

"Knock it off!" the Commander barked before he continued, "This mission is extremely time-sensitive.

Intel has her being taken as part of a sex trafficking ring, specifically to be sold to the highest bidder."

The Commander looked pained. It seemed like he could barely get the words out, which wasn't like him, making me wonder why he was reacting so out of character.

He took a deep breath before continuing, "As you know, it's not unusual for hostages to be sold and resold through various pipelines, so we need to move fast before she's moved, and we lose her.

"You're authorized to eliminate any threat to her or you. You get in, find her, and get out. Our current intel has her in one of two possible locations in Peru. Maps and all other intel are in your packets. You're wheels up in an hour."

I studied the photo of Alex Walker; she was staring straight into the camera, obviously laughing at the time the picture was taken. She was wearing jeans and a plaid shirt, her auburn hair hanging over one shoulder in a thick braid.

Even without make-up, she was mouth-wateringly beautiful. I felt a jolt looking at her picture, realizing I was attracted to her. Of course, looking at her, what red-blooded straight man wouldn't be?

As the team walked out to get ready to head for Peru, Bruiser asked, "Did the Commander seem off on this one?"

"Yeah, he seemed agitated, almost panicked. Seemed like he had to get control of himself a couple of times," Midas responded.

"Maybe he's a fan," Jax guessed with a laugh.

“I’m a fan,” Boomer told us, and we all looked at him. “What? She’s really good, and have you seen her?”

"She's a spoiled rich girl; she'll probably expect special treatment," Bruiser grumbled.

"Something seems weird about this one, doesn't it?" Smoke asked as we walked down the hall. "The Commander seems almost desperate that we get her back."

"Maybe she's CIA," Jax reasoned. "Think about it we're being rushed in; it's basically a snatch and grab; get her, get out. We're greenlit by the President to eliminate anyone who threatens her or us. They're not fucking around here; it seems like overkill for one singer."

Looking at Jax, Midas nodded, "A woman who looks like her, she could get information out of almost any man. And being famous, she could get in and out of places other people can't."

"That would explain why this op seems so urgent and why the President is involved. If the kidnapper knows or finds out she’s CIA, the agency wouldn't want to risk her being tortured into giving up information," I responded, worried that if it was true, she probably *was* being tortured.

"CIA actually makes a lot of sense," Smoke stated.

"She'll probably expect us to kiss her famous ass, and if she’s CIA, she’ll think she’s in charge,” Bruiser complained.

"We don't get to pick who we save. We get in, get her, and get out. If she's a pain in the ass, we'll make sure to set her straight, but no one deserves to be sold as a sex slave. Hopefully, we won't have to spend too much time with her," I said as we started gathering our gear.

All five of my teammates nodded in agreement.

While we packed our gear, I worried about what violence she might have endured since her kidnapping that might change the happy, carefree woman in the photo, especially if she is CIA and her kidnapper knows that and is torturing her for information.

Hang on, Alex, we're coming for you.

Chapter 2

Alex

I was being held in a stall in a barn, the only light coming from a small window near the ceiling. I knew it was a barn because of the familiar sounds and smells.

I wasn't exactly sure how I got here or what I was doing locked in a barn, but it was obvious I was in a lot of trouble.

I'd woken up here, disoriented and confused. That was days ago, but I had no idea how many; my perception of time was off. But every day had been a day too long in this nightmare.

I'd been doing quite a bit of thinking since I woke up here. How could I not wonder how the road of my life brought me to this shithole? Which led to thinking a lot about my best friend, Gabe.

I met Gabriel Carmichael when we were fourteen. That was the year my grandfather died, and my dad inherited his ranch, and we moved. Gabe and I met on the first day of school. We just clicked and have been best friends ever since. He was my brother, my best friend, my rock.

Gabe is an extremely talented pianist, more than talented, like a piano savant. A musical genius. After graduating high school, Gabe went to Julliard to fulfill his dreams, and I stayed in Virginia, deciding to raise cattle and train horses on the family ranch.

After three years of fame, travel, and exhaustion, Gabe started his second career scoring movies and writing songs and had been much happier since.

Four years ago, he met and married a former world champion MMA fighter known as Chance 'The Slayer' Winchester, who started the company 'Give Him A Chance' after he retired from fighting.

Give Him A Chance started with a phenomenally successful men's underwear line and then added a popular line of shorts, sweats, and t-shirts. Between the two of them, they could only be described as rich as rich can get.

Gabe and Chance were a bit of an odd couple. Chance, the brawny, dark-haired, brown-eyed, tattooed former fighter, and Gabe, the tall blonde with blue eyes, who looked like he should be riding off into the sunset on a surfboard. But they were good together, and that's all that mattered.

A few years ago, Gabe called and told me he'd written a song, the first song he'd ever written. He asked if I'd come and sing it so he could hear what it sounded like. While Gabe might be a great musician, he would never be considered a great singer, and I could carry a tune.

Of course, I said yes. I sang it, Gabe made some changes, and we recorded it. When we listened to it, it sounded surprisingly good. I actually had a hard time believing it was my voice. Gabe asked if he could use it, and I said yes. He had me sign a release, and that was that.

Looking back, I should have asked more questions or more to the point; I should have asked *a* question. At the very least, I should have wondered what he meant when he asked if he could use it. But I didn't.

Gabe wrote more songs and each time asked me to sing them, and I did. He recorded them and asked if he could use them. Not once did I say no or ask what he was doing with them. It just didn't matter to me.

But I *should* have thought about it. *Should* have questioned it. I could not have imagined singing those songs would send my life spiraling in a whole new direction.

Thirteen months after I recorded that first song, Gabe called me. He was so excited; I'd never heard him like that. He said the song had been nominated for several major awards, including best original song. That one comes with a golden statue; you know the one I mean.

It took a while for him to catch me up, to make it clear that he put the first song I recorded into one of the movies he scored, and it was a hit. A really big hit.

And that sums up Gabe's musical ability quite nicely; the first song he writes gets nominated for every major award out there. It was also the moment my life changed. The moment he told me I was going to have to sing at those awards shows.

To say he had to work at convincing me to not only sing in public but to sing on a world stage is an understatement. I absolutely, positively, unequivocally was not going to sing in public.

But because a best friend can get you to do just about anything, even things against your better judgment, eventually I reluctantly agreed, and "Treasure You" won every major award that year. It also catapulted me into a world I didn't want to be a part of.

Because I had no desire to be a singer, and I sure as hell didn't want to be famous, I made a bunch of crazy outrageous demands no one in their right mind would agree to. I said I'd only work with Gabe, wouldn't sign with any sort of agent, manager, or record company, that Gabe would have to act in that capacity or no deal.

I would only perform a limited number of concerts; I wouldn't do a 'tour' because I wanted to continue being a rancher and didn't want to be on the road all the time. I just kept throwing out the craziest things I could think of. I figured Gabe would say no way, and I could go back to my life with a clear conscience.

But that plan backfired when Gabe started his own record label and agreed to every one of my screwball demands, and the bastard did it with a smile on his face.

Yeah, okay, I'm an adult, or at least a decent facsimile of an adult; I could have just said no. I *should* have just said no, but I made a critical error, one that I wish I had a time machine to fix.

And that was how I became accidentally famous. It sounds like the plot of some cheesy novel, but that's exactly how it happened.

I admit, I do like the singing, and *duh*, the money doesn't suck, but the rest of it, I don't like at all. And I've always felt guilty about it. People work for years chasing their dream of being a singer, of being famous, and I'd fallen headfirst into it and didn't even want it. And now here I was with a bad feeling my fame had something to do with my current situation.

There were bars on the door and back wall of my "prison cell", but the side walls had been left alone.

Every night since I'd woken up here, I'd been working on loosening the boards on the wall so I could escape.

It was slow going because I was being watched almost constantly, and I had to make sure my captors didn't notice what I was doing until I could make a hole big enough to fit through. Quietly dislodging boards from a wall without tools wasn't as easy as it sounds.

But I was highly motivated. The time to escape had become critical; I'd heard the men holding me say I was being handed over tomorrow to the man who bought me.

Someone had *bought* me. It was so sick and twisted; I was having trouble processing that information, but here I was, so I couldn't refute it.

I pushed that thought out of my head before it grabbed hold and caused panic. Well, more panic. Tonight, I needed my brain firing on all cylinders because I was going to escape or die trying. And I *was* willing to die trying; I'd rather be dead than be someone's sex slave. Just the thought of it caused an involuntary shiver to run through my body.

Luckily, I'd finally loosened enough boards and made a space large enough to fit through; I'd just been waiting until what I thought was the middle of the night, so some or all the guards were sleeping. It was dark and felt late, but I wasn't sure, and I had no idea how many men were guarding me tonight or any other details or even where the hell I was. I had no weapon, no supplies, no shoes, and was only wearing a bra and underwear.

Not the best of circumstances. Okay, who are we kidding? Those are the worst of circumstances. But those were issues I'd deal with later. First things first, I needed to get out of here undetected.

I slid the boards aside as quietly as possible and started through the hole. It was a tight fit, but I wiggled and squirmed until I was on the other side, standing in an empty horse stall.

I stood listening, my heart beating wildly in my chest. I didn't hear anyone talking, so I slowly crept to the stall door and quickly peeked out, looking left and right before pulling my head back inside. There was only one guard, sitting in a chair, with his back to me, and snoring like a freight train.

I took a moment to take in my limited view from the safety of the stall. I noticed a pitchfork leaning against the wall across the barn. There was also a jacket hanging on a hook, and the stall directly across from me had a horse in it that had stuck its head out and was watching me.

If I weren’t in a life-or-death situation, I would have done a little dance. Things were looking up, three problems solved; at least I’d have a weapon, some clothes, and a ride out of this nightmare.

I was terrified, it felt like I had jet fuel running through my veins, but if I didn't move, I had no chance of getting out of here.

Chapter 3

Cole

Smoke, Midas, and I were scouting one location while Jax, Bruiser, and Boomer scouted the secondary residence. Our location was a huge compound and included a large house and a barn. We decided I'd check out the barn, then meet up with Smoke and Midas before we entered the house to continue our search.

Dawn was an hour or so away; I didn't have time to waste. I needed to check out the barn and get back to Smoke and Midas so we could search the house while most of the occupants were still sleeping.

There was a copse of trees between the house and the barn, and I left Smoke and Midas and headed through them, using the trees for cover.

When the barn came into view, I was about six hundred feet away. It was a large structure, two stories tall, with open land as far as the eye could see in front of it.

I kept my distance and stayed in the shadows to avoid being seen. The lights were on in the barn, making it easy for me to see the single armed guard sitting in a chair, facing my way, sleeping. My instincts said there was something worth protecting in this barn; I couldn't think of a reason anyone would need an armed guard for their livestock.

I was on the move to get a closer look inside and hadn't gone far when I saw a stall door swing open. I watched as Alex Walker slowly emerged, looking left and right before she ran across the barn. She was dirty, dressed only in a blue bra and barely-there matching panties, a long auburn braid hanging down her back.

I watched Alex grab a jacket and what looked like a long strap off the wall. Then she opened one of the other stalls, stepped inside, and disappeared from my sight.

"Package located. Keep eyes on the tangos until I secure the package, then we'll meet up and get the fuck out of here," I said into my radio.

"Roger that," came the reply over my headset.

As I moved closer, I noticed the guard waking up. He moved and looked around as he stretched his arms over his head. I stopped, pulled my rifle into position, took aim, and shot him in the head.

The force caused his body to jerk backward, and the front legs of the chair lifted off the ground. For a split second, I thought he might topple over, but then the chair righted itself. The guard slumped over and looked like he was sleeping again.

Once the guard was taken care of, I was back on the move toward the barn. I watched Alex poke her head out of the stall and look around again. When she didn't see anything, she stepped into the barn, carefully closing the stall door behind her. She was wearing the jacket now, which was several sizes too big for her. She picked up a pitchfork that was leaning against the wall and was sneaking up on the now-dead guard.

Standing in front of the guard, I saw her startle, and she spun around looking out the barn doors, pointing the pitchfork into the night. She'd obviously noticed the guard had been shot. I wished I could have kept her from seeing that, but there wasn't anything I could do to prevent it.

She dropped the pitchfork and quickly turned back around and bent over the guard for a moment. She was blocking my view, so I couldn't see what she was doing and when she turned around again, she had the guard's pistol and was pointing it out of the barn into the darkness.

This complicated things. If she saw me, or I startled her, she could take a shot at me. Any shot from that gun would alert everyone in the vicinity, likely bringing the guards from the house, and all hell would break loose.

I had no doubt she'd leave that barn. I didn't want to scare her or have to forcibly subdue her, but I would if I had to. Better to have her come to me without firing that gun so I could let her know we were here to rescue her.

Alex ran back to the stall she'd been in earlier and opened the door. She quickly looked left, then right before she reached forward, and a horse came out following her. *Shit.*

She could ride away, and we could lose her. I started moving fast toward the barn again. The horse had no saddle, and I assumed she'd walk until she found something to stand on so she could climb on its back.

With the guard's gun in her hand, she stopped at the barn door, the horse standing next to her. She looked around before she put the gun in the right pocket of the jacket. Then threw the reins over the horse's head, grabbed the horse's mane, and gracefully and what looked like easily hopped up onto the horse's back. Once she was settled, she took the gun back out and broke into a run out of the barn.

She was moving at a good clip, the gun moving back and forth in her right hand in time with the motion of her head. I watched her lift her left arm straight in the air and flip the bird as she rode away from her captors. I couldn't help but smile at the unexpected gesture. Based on what I'd seen so far, Alex Walker was strong, smart, and brave.

Gun in one hand, flipping the bird with the other, she was riding with no hands, and she easily got on the horse without a saddle or help. It was obvious she knew something about horses. I briefly wondered how she knew how to do that, where she'd learned it.

As she rode away from the barn, I heard what sounded like 'ha,' and the hoofbeats sped up. *Shit. Shit. Shit.* As fast as she was traveling, she could ride right past me. She could be recaptured, die of exposure, starvation, or dehydration before we caught up to her again.

Before she got too close, I lowered my night vision goggles and stepped out into the path of the horse. I had no idea if she or the horse would see me before it was too late, but I had to stop her before she rode away and out of reach.

Chapter 4

Alex

When I saw the guard had been shot, my mind filled with rapid-fire questions. He'd just been shot because I'd heard him snoring only a few minutes ago, but who shot him? I hadn't heard a shot, so someone obviously used a suppressor. Where was the shooter now? If they were on my side, why would they shoot the guard and not make themselves known? Was this a trick?

I didn't have time to stand there and think about it, to analyze things; whoever shot the guard could try to kill me too. So, I grabbed the guard's gun and turned around to see if I was about to be under attack.

I didn't see anyone, not that I expected to; it was dark outside. I'd taken the time to put a bridle and bit on the horse and went and got him out of the stall.

I was scared before, but now my fear of being caught had ratcheted up to an extreme level; my heart felt like it was going to beat right out of my chest. I was so close to freedom; if I got caught now, it might actually kill me.

As I rode away from the barn, I couldn't see clearly because it was still dark out, but after about fifteen seconds, I thought I saw a shadowy figure ahead of me, standing directly in the path of the horse.

I could barely make it out, but it was big, a man, and his arms appeared to be held away from his shadowy body. I thought about riding right by him, but if he was a threat, he needed to be dealt with, so I slowed the horse and moved to the right of him, out of his reach.

I stopped when I reached him, which might end up being a mistake, but I was keeping my distance and pointing the gun right at him. I wasn't completely stupid.

He didn't make a move toward me, but I didn't know if that was because he wasn't a threat or because I was pointing a gun at him. Even this close, there wasn't enough light to see much more than his shape, but he looked huge.

His voice was calm, almost soothing, and he spoke English, which I hadn't heard since I'd been kidnapped, "Ms. Walker, I'm an American Navy SEAL. I'm here to get you home."

I lowered my head, the breath of relief I exhaled almost painful. I'd never heard sweeter words in my entire life.

I wasn't home free yet, but at least I wasn't alone anymore. Emotion was threatening to overtake me. I felt like I was about to simultaneously laugh and cry because he was there to rescue me. It struck me I might actually make it out of this hellhole.

Taking a deep breath and trying to pull myself together, I put the gun back into the pocket of the jacket and looked at his shadowy shape, "Sorry about the gun. Get on, and let's get out of here."

"No. You get down."

"We don't have time to argue, so I'm just going to lay it out. These assholes will come after me. I was a special order; the buyer is coming today. This horse will get us a lot farther, a lot faster than we can move on foot, especially since I don't have shoes. So, suck it up and get on so we can get the fuck out of here."

Because I couldn't see him, I had no idea what his reaction to my words was. I didn't really care. Even though he was there to rescue me, if he didn't want to get on, I'd have no problem riding away and leaving him standing there. I wanted to get away from this horrifying place, so with or without him, I was leaving.

Chapter 5

Cole

I wasn't sure about this idea, but we needed to get out of here, and she was right; the horse would be faster. So, I reluctantly walked toward them.

"This is going to be a little tricky because of your rucksack, but I'm confident you can do it...you *are* a Navy SEAL. Failure is not an option," she told me.

I wasn't surprised she was a bossy little thing. I'm sure she was used to barking orders and always getting her way. That was fine for now, but she wouldn't be calling the shots here.

It took some doing, but I managed to get on, and as soon as I was sitting behind her, she started telling me what to do, "Scoot forward, right up next to me. You can lay your rifle on my leg, so you don't have to hold it up. Put your left arm around my waist."

She had the experience, so I did what she told me, and she started walking the horse.

"Is your ass all the way on?"

"Hard to tell." I was tense and rigid behind her, and she must have known it.

"Try to relax; you're fine. It's just like riding a motorcycle."

I had the feeling she was joking, trying to get me to relax. I huffed out a short laugh before I told her, "No, it's really not."

"You ready?"

I answered honestly, "Not even a little bit."

She ignored my comment, "Okay then, here we go."

She made a clicking sound with her tongue, and the horse started trotting, and my ass started bouncing.

I wanted to tell her to stop, that we'd walk, I'd carry her if I had to. There was no way I was going to last long this way. I felt her leg muscles move next to mine, and the horse started galloping. Even though we were going faster, the bouncing was less. Not great, but better.

Using my radio, I informed the team I had Alex, "Package secure. I repeat, package is secure."

She surprised me when she said over her shoulder, "Hell yeah, the package is secure and currently riding the fuck out of dodge."

The comment made me smile; at least she wasn't panic-stricken and freaking out.

Just as she finished talking, Smoke came over my earpiece, "Tangos are seriously stirred up over something. If you're not already on the move, get going. We're moving; we'll meet you at the extraction point."

"Roger that."

Hearing me, Alex asked over her shoulder, "Everything okay?"

I didn't want to scare her, so I told her, "Everything is fine, just keep us moving."

"They're coming, aren't they?"

She was smart enough to pick up that there was a problem, even though I hadn't confirmed it.

She let go of the reins, putting her hands on my thighs, and squeezed a little, "Put your heels down and your weight in your butt. Try to keep your muscles relaxed," she told me over her shoulder.

I did what she told me because I didn't want to fall off this damn horse but relaxing seemed like an impossibility.

She must have felt the movement beneath her hands, "Good."

I wondered how she was riding this fast with no hands. As close as our bodies were, she didn't feel tense at all.

"You need to hang on before you fall off."

I heard her snort as if my comment was ridiculous to her, and she didn't pick up the reins, just continued with her instructions, "If you need to, put both your arms around me. Rock your hips in time with mine."

It took me a minute and more instruction from her for me to find the rhythm, and while I was still uncomfortable and bouncing, it was a hell of a lot better.

"Good job, cowboy! Now, just stay upright and hang the fuck on," she told me as she picked up the reins again and urged the horse to go even faster.

I realized she'd guessed there was something going on with her captors, but she took the time to make sure the ride was better and safer for me before she had the horse going faster, and honestly, I not only appreciated it but was impressed she wasn't just thinking about herself. It surprised me because most people wouldn't have done it, and I hadn't expected it from her.

We rode in silence, the only sound the horse's hoofbeats until the sun was coming up, and she slowed the horse to a walk and turned her head, her left hand casually resting on her left thigh.

"Problem?" I asked her.

"No. The horse is tired; I'm giving him a break. Plus, I wanted to watch the sunrise. I wasn't sure I'd ever see that again. It's a pretty one too."

I don't know why, but I squeezed her a little wanting to comfort her and let her know I understood, and she wasn't alone anymore.

Now that the sun had come up, I could see her bare legs were filthy and bruised. I could just make out bruises on the inside of her thighs in the shape of fingers, and the sight of them simultaneously concerned me and enraged me. Handprints on her thighs were not a good sign, and I worried about what she'd been through while she'd been held captive.

"Ms. Walker...."

"Alex."

"Alex, are you CIA?"

"What? You think I'm CIA?"

She started laughing, which I wasn't expecting, but I liked the sound. She had a great laugh, and she seemed extremely entertained I'd asked her if she was CIA.

When she got control of herself, she asked me, "Why would you think I'm CIA?"

"Just the way this op came down."

She still sounded amused, "Well, I'm not CIA. But I guess if I were, I wouldn't be able to tell you."

Chapter 6

Alex.

I was a little surprised when he squeezed me. Of course, he could have done it because he was concerned about falling off, but for some reason, I wanted to believe otherwise. Our position was intimate but comforting, which was odd since he was a complete stranger, but he was a SEAL, so I trusted him.

He was solid behind me, even if he was still a little too rigid. If he didn't relax, he was going to be sore later. I had the impression he'd either never been on a horse or didn't like them.

His arm around me felt good, made me feel safe. When I looked down, I could see how big his hand was; it spanned half my belly, and I could feel the heat and weight of it through the jacket I was wearing, which was reassuring.

“What's your name?"

"Master Chief Cole Montgomery."

"Nice to meet you, Cole Montgomery. Where's the rest of your team?"

"On the move now, but they were in other locations, looking for you."

I nodded. "Are you one of Uncle Mal's guys?"

"Who's Uncle Mal?"

"Oh, sorry, Commander Malcom Reynolds."

"Commander Reynolds is your Uncle?"

"Not biologically, but yeah, I've known him a long time. My dad and Uncle Mal were best friends on the same team for years."

He moved his head like he was trying to see my face, "Your dad is a SEAL?"

"Yep. My brother too."

He sounded surprised, "No shit?"

"No shit."

"What's your dad's name?" He asked me.

"Charlie Walker."

"Mad Dog Walker is your dad? He's special ops royalty."

I couldn't help but smile, "He would have really liked that."

"Would have?"

"He died."

"I'm sorry, Alex, I didn't know."

"Of course not, how could you?"

"What about your brother?"

"Marcus. They called him Mutt. He died too. What's your nickname?" I asked him, wanting off this subject.

"What makes you think I have a nickname?"

I thought he sounded amused, but I couldn't tell for sure.

"Every SEAL I know has one. Even if you're new, it's doubtful you wouldn't have one, and I don't think you're new."

"You know a lot of SEALs?"

I laughed a short laugh, "A few. So?"

"Reaper."

That amused me, "Awesome!"

"Why awesome?"

"Is it ironic like a really big guy being called Tiny? You're Reaper because no matter how hard you try, you can't kill anyone."

"No, not ironic."

"Then it's awesome because when you've been kidnapped and sold as someone's sex slave, you want a guy named Reaper to have your back when you're escaping," I said matter-of-factly.

His voice in my ear was low and sultry. Sexy. I bet that voice was good at talking women right out of their clothes. I was shocked by that thought, wondering where the hell it came from. I was on the run from kidnappers, and I was thinking about Mr. Sexy Voice sitting behind me, who was just there to do his job. *What the hell is wrong with me?* I really should have my head examined; apparently, being kidnapped made me loopy.

"How long have I been gone?" I asked him.

"Eight days."

"Eight days? Feels longer. Where am I?"

"Peru."

"Peru! What the hell am I doing in Peru?" I didn't wait for an answer because I didn't think he knew the answer, "You shot the guard in the barn, didn't you?"

"Yes. He woke up, and I didn't want him to hurt you."

I wasn't expecting how that made me feel. It should have bothered me that he killed someone to keep me from being hurt, but instead, it made me feel safe and protected and, if I was honest, a little squishy inside.

"Thank you for doing that."

"Are you okay to tell me what happened? The more details we know, the better."

I knew what he was asking. Once I knew he was a SEAL, I knew I'd eventually have to give him details, and I'd rather tell one person than a whole room full, so I nodded and started telling him about the bizarre events of the past week.

"I had a concert in L.A. on Saturday. There was a VIP after-party I didn't want to go to. Refused to go to, actually. Not my thing. But my best friend, Gabe, knew what buttons to push to get me to agree. On the way to the venue to do the concert, I reluctantly agreed to go.

“I wasn't being a party girl because partying with strangers just isn't me. I did dance with Gabe and his husband, Chance. I did talk to people, but mostly I was at the end of the bar people-watching."

"Were you drinking?"

"Yes, but not to excess. I got up to go to the bathroom. I used the bathroom and came out. Two really well-dressed men were standing there. I figured they were on their way to the bathroom too, and it was just bad timing that I was coming out when they were walking by.

“I was surprised by them, came to a stop and said, “Oh, sorry”. I expected them to move and continue down the hallway like normal people, but they just stood there looking at me.

“As weird and creepy as it is, it's not unusual for men to just stare at me. I don't understand it, but it seems to happen a lot.

"I wasn't freaked out, but I was getting a tingle something wasn't right. I said, “Excuse me,” thinking they'd move, but they didn't. That's when my Spidey sense said danger, and I took a step backward.

“They didn't move, so I took another one. Then I opened my mouth to yell for help when one of them grabbed me lightning fast, put one hand over my mouth, and yanked my hair, so my head went sideways. The other one stuck something, I'm guessing a needle, into my neck, and it was lights out.

"When I woke up, I was in a cargo plane, or at least that's what I think it was. I could see big wooden crates and other stuff. I was in a metal cage I barely fit in."

I felt him gently squeeze me again as if he were trying to comfort me, and surprisingly, the gesture did help bolster me, so I took a deep breath and continued with the story.

"I could hear two different voices, both men speaking Spanish, talking about how I wasn’t awake yet, so I didn't move. Not that I could have moved much anyway."

"You speak Spanish?"

"Yes."

"Go on."

"They were worried I wasn't awake, and I should be and were wondering what they should do because they needed me knocked out when they took me off the plane. That led me to believe wherever we were landing wasn't private.

“I could feel we were descending, and they were getting more and more concerned. I guess they decided to risk an overdose because they came and stuck me, and it was lights out again.

“When I woke up, I was in that barn. The stall had been semi-converted to a cell. I was sick, like, ‘I drank way too much next day hangover sick’. I threw up, then dry heaved for a while, and my head was seriously killing me. I tried to stay awake, but I couldn't. I don't know how long I slept, it could have been hours or could have been a day.

“Three guards were assigned to me, but maybe once a day another man showed up, the boss. He didn't talk to me; he'd just stand there and stare at me."

"What made you think he was the boss?" Cole asked me.

"The guards deferred to him, and he wore fancy clothes. While they were on duty, the three guards would open my door and sit there talking to each other. They’d also talk to me, but I pretended I didn't know what they were saying."

"That was smart," he told me.

"Some of it scared the shit out of me, and I'd hide my face because I was afraid they'd figure out I could understand them. What I picked up was I was specifically targeted; it wasn't random. Someone paid them to take me...someone bought me."

Chapter 7

Cole

I hated this story, hated hearing that someone had taken her, drugged her, put her in a fucking cage in the belly of a plane and thought they could sell her as a sex toy.

I was surprised when she told me she didn't understand why men stared at her. I'd seen her picture, I understood it. I didn't like it but I understood it. But it couldn't be possible that she didn't know why men stared at her. All beautiful women knew why men stared at them.

Her voice cracked when she told me someone bought her, and I squeezed her, and she leaned some of her weight into me and put her left hand over mine. It made me feel good she trusted me enough to do it. I couldn't explain why, but I liked it.

I heard her take a deep breath before she continued the story, "Today's a new day, so I guess the night before last, my guards were talking about how I was going to be picked up soon. They were drinking and complaining that they weren't allowed to have sex with me.

“Long story short, they said the boss would be gone the next morning, so they decided that would be a good time to gang rape me. Said it wasn't like the buyer would refuse me because he really wanted me.”

I didn’t know what to say or do to take that memory away from her, and she still had the rest of the story to tell. I did not want to hear her tell me she’d been raped, and I especially didn’t want to hear the details of her being gang raped, but as much as I wanted to, I didn’t say anything to stop her from telling the rest of her story.

"I'd been working on an escape since I got here. I was removing the boards on the wall but had to do it so they wouldn't hear me or notice what I was doing. It took longer than I expected.

“I worked like crazy that night, but the hole still wasn't big enough. I could have just smashed through it, but it would have made too much noise, and I figured they'd probably put me somewhere more secure where I had no chance of escape.

“Anyway, the three guards came in that morning, guess that was yesterday, and that's when I lost my clothes. They took my shoes, those were gone when I first woke up, but I still had my dress.”

“They took your shoes so you couldn’t run.”

She nodded. "That makes sense. I was not on board with being gang raped, so I fought back. The three of them got me on the ground, ripped my dress off, and one of them held my upper body down, but I was pitching a fit, so one of the others told him to shut me up. He tried to put his hand over my mouth, but he missed, and one of his fingers ended up over my mouth, so I bit down on it as hard as I could and wouldn't let go.

“He was screaming and started pulling...that was a mistake. One of the others was squeezing my face while pulling the other one's hand, and that didn't work, so one of them popped me in the face, and that made me let go. But when I saw it last, his finger was kind of hanging there.

“Then there were two. The bossy one wanted the other one to hold me down, but he was afraid I'd bite him too. The bossy one shifted off me, and the other one was right there, so I nailed him in the balls as hard as I could with my foot. That left the bossy one, the sadistic one."

I needed her to get through this in her own time, in her own way, but I was really hoping this story wasn't going where I thought it was. I didn't like what I'd already seen and heard and wanted to tell her to stop talking, that she didn't have to say anymore, that I didn't want to hear anymore. She was almost naked and had handprints on the inside of her thighs, and she was about to tell me how they got there.

"He straddled me, and I had no wiggle room. He started choking me. When he got bored with that, he started hitting me, grabbing me, pinching me all over. He seemed to get off on it. That went on for what seemed like forever. Then he took out his knife and started cutting me."

I went completely rigid behind her. I hated where this was going, especially when she laced her fingers through the top of my hand as if she needed the connection. I wasn't sure she even realized she’d done it.

"Luckily, the boss showed up shortly after the knife came out, and he was pissed. He was yelling and smacked the sadistic one around some. Then he just stood there staring at me. I told him I was going to need stitches. He stared some more and left.

“A little bit later, he came back and threw one of those travel sewing kits at me. I heard the boss say to the sadistic one my new owner was coming the next day and how was he supposed to explain the damaged goods, then he hit him some more.

“They locked me in and left. I sewed myself up, but I wouldn't want to do that again; it hurt more than I thought it would. It was totally unsanitary, and I’ll probably get an infection from the thread, but the way I see it, it’s a lot better than being gang raped. But with everything I heard, I knew last night was my only chance to get out of there.

“I knew Gabe would freak when he couldn't find me at the party, and he'd call Uncle Mal. I knew Uncle Mal would come for me sooner or later. Uncle Mal and the rest of my dad's team would look for me until their last breaths, and I was right because here you are."

As much as I didn’t want to, I needed to see what was done to her, "Alex, I need you to stop this horse and let me look at your injuries."

"I'm okay,” she replied in a firm voice. “I promise you can look, poke, and prod, but when we're farther away. Really, I'm alright. I'm sure it doesn't look good, but I wouldn't do anything to risk you getting me out of here."

Her fingers tightened around mine as if trying to convey the truth of her words. In the distance, I could see a fence, likely the end of the property.

"I don't like it, but I'll make a deal with you; we ride to that fence; we have to leave the horse there anyway.

We'll take a break, I'll look you over, and if you're physically able, we'll head out on foot. The Commander sent clothes for you, so you don't have to worry about being barefoot. Deal?"

She didn't hesitate, "Deal. While I was locked up, I exercised as best I could, figured I'd need to be able to move, so I am physically able. I'm a good runner. I might be a little slow right now, but I'll keep up, you won't have to worry about me."

Alex Walker was not what I expected. She kept surprising me. Instead of giving up, she'd not only fought back but did what she could so she could run when she needed to.

She hadn't let herself believe she wouldn't escape her captors. It took incredible strength to do what she'd done.

It was at least a minute before she spoke again, her voice soft and trembling, "Thank you for coming for me, Cole. I know this is just a regular mission for you and your team, but it's something completely different to me."

Hearing her say my given name was odd. It had been a long time since anyone other than my dad had called me Cole, but I liked the way it sounded coming from her.

I'd been about to tell her I *was* just doing my job, but something about her words touched me, so instead, I simply said, "You're welcome, Alex."

As we approached the fence, we noticed a small stream glittering and bubbling between two grassy banks in front of it, "Oh hell yeah," Alex said as we stopped. "Okay, cowboy, use me for balance, swing your right leg over and just slide off."

I did with a soft groan and took a couple of steps, turning my back on her, needing to adjust myself. I was surprised by how sore, so many of my muscles were, and it wasn't just my muscles that were sore. I stood there wishing I had an icepack for my balls. How and *why* would people ride horses when it made you feel this way?

Trying to stifle a giggle but not able to do it, Alex said, "Sorry about your boy bits," as she hopped off the horse like it was nothing.

The giggle stopped me in my tracks. When was the last time I'd heard a woman giggle like that? The sound was pleasing, and I was shocked how much I liked it.

"My boy bits?" I asked, responding to her comment.

She giggled again, "I was trying to be tactful."

"You failed."

She laughed a real laugh, and I turned around to look at her, but her back was to me as she tied the horse to a small tree right next to the stream, the horse immediately lowering its head and drinking. I loved the sound of her laugh, and the fact that she could laugh after what she'd been through said a lot about her.

I walked a short distance away, took off my pack, sat down on a fallen tree and watched her strip off the jacket and lay it across the horse's back.

When she walked into the stream, her back was to me. I couldn't see her face, but I could see bruises on her shoulders, across her back, her thighs, and her ass.

She was wearing some sort of thong, and I tried not to stare, but other than the bruising, she had a perfect backside, and I couldn't seem to take my eyes off it as she walked into the water. I mentally chastised myself for being a reprobate and forced myself to look away.

"Don't take too long," I told her.

"Understood," she called back.

I watched as she dropped her head to wash her face, and pulling the braid over her shoulder, she washed her neck. I could see a blue mark on the back of her neck, a tattoo, but I couldn't make it out because it was small, maybe an inch tall. A butterfly or flower, I guessed.

The water was only knee deep and was probably cold, but she didn't seem to care. Alex knelt in the water and washed, and I appreciated that she was being quick.

When she was finished, she wasn't exactly clean, but it was a hell of a lot better. I wished I could let her have a real bath with soap, but there just wasn't time.

When she walked out of the stream, the horse was happily munching grass at the water's edge. She patted him on the neck and grabbed the jacket. As she walked toward me, she carried the jacket modestly in front of her, with her head down. She didn't seem afraid but may have realized that she was mostly naked in front of a man she didn't know.

She was obviously in shape, muscular, but not overly so. I assumed that part of her lifestyle meant constant dieting and exercise, so she looked good on stage. She was probably one of those women who ate a carrot and called it a meal.

I watched her walk toward me. I could see more bruises on her arms and legs. She had a body that would tempt a saint, utterly feminine and softly rounded in all the right places. She was taller than I expected, probably around five-nine. Those long muscular legs were distracting, and I could imagine them wrapped around me while I was inside her.

It was completely fucked up that I was thinking about her this way. Where did that inappropriate thought even come from?

Even though it was a dick move, it didn't diminish my appreciation. But I'd be glad when she had some clothes on. When she got close enough, I gave her a chamois I carried in my pack; she thanked me and used it to dry off.

I would never settle down. I wasn't relationship material; no woman would ever get that out of me. I didn't bother dating women because I didn't need to. My looks helped me get laid, and being a SEAL was great for my sex life.

Women were good for a night, and it was *always* just one night. Their faces and bodies blurred together, and I couldn't even remember the majority of their names.

I was used to women being fake, brazen, vain, but Alex seemed anything but. I instinctively knew she was not a one-night-stand kind of woman, and sex with her would just complicate things.

Besides, she had just been kidnapped, I was part of her rescue; the last thing she needed was me hitting on her. While I was intrigued, I would have no problem leaving her alone, no matter how appealing she was. But I did mentally kick myself; it was completely fucked up that I was thinking about her this way.

Once she had dried off, I handed her the pack of clothes the Commander sent for her, but she still wouldn't look at me, was hiding her face from me, and I was starting to get concerned about that.

"Um, could you turn around for a second? My legs are fine; I can change and get my pants and shoes on just in case we have to boogie out of here, then you can check me out."

Chapter 8

Alex

He turned around, and I quickly stepped out of the skimpy blue underwear and into white cotton. Then I pulled on my army green cargo pants before I sat down and started putting on the shoes and socks he'd brought for me.

"You can turn around," I told him.

I shoved the blue panties into one of the pockets at the bottom of my pants, not wanting to leave evidence I'd been here.

Cole crouched down in front of me. He didn't say anything; he just waited for me to look at him.

"Please don't freak out; I swear I'm fine," I said before I lifted my head.

Seeing him for the first time was a shock; I hadn't thought about what he might look like while we were riding. When I saw him, I involuntarily gasped. Even though he was scowling at me, he was the most beautiful man I had ever seen. Not even kidding a little, the most beautiful man I'd *ever* seen.

I let my eyes roam over every inch of him; I couldn't help myself. He was big, I guessed around six-two or three, his hair was black, like a raven's feathers, blue-black in the sunlight, long enough that it brushed his shirt collar; it was wavy and a bit wild, which just made it sexier. He had a short, neatly trimmed beard, and I had a sudden urge to touch it to see if it was soft.

His shoulders were broad, his chest was huge, his biceps muscular and straining against his shirt with his movements. His eyes were ocean blue, surrounded by mile-long eyelashes.

Those eyes were currently staring at me in a way that made me think he could see straight into the heart of me. His sheer masculinity was overwhelming my senses. He was beautiful, rugged, and powerful—a warrior.

It wasn't like I'd never been around handsome alpha men before; I was raised by alpha men, most of which were seriously good looking, all of them in good shape. But this man was different, and I was afraid if he touched me, I might spontaneously combust.

Is this what attraction felt like? How could I be attracted to him? I was never attracted to anyone. I didn't have time for men, and the sexual experiences I'd had didn't go well; in fact, they went pretty badly, and I wasn't in any hurry to repeat that.

Men, dating and sex had never been a priority for me; I was completely uninterested in sex, at least until this man, who made me want to brush the dust bunnies off my lady parts and let him have a go at them.

I couldn't take my eyes off him. I felt like a jolt of electricity had hit me, and my entire body broke out in goosebumps. I wondered how that was possible.

"What is it? Are you alright?" He asked, concerned hearing my gasp.

I just stared back at him.

"Alex?"

"Hmmm?"

"Are you okay?"

"Uh-huh."

He gently prodded around my eye and cheek, his face right in front of mine. There was some pain when he touched around my left eye, but I barely noticed it because his touch felt electric, like I'd been tazed. It felt like intimacy, not examination to me.

I felt off-balance. *What is wrong with me?* The man was doing his job examining me, and I was getting turned on, which had never happened to me before, if how I currently felt was any indication, and even more disturbing was I didn't want him to stop. *Seriously, Alex, get your shit together.*

Chapter 9

Cole

She looked and sounded befuddled. I'd never seen anything more adorable, and I couldn't stop the twitch of my mouth.

She was staring at me and her eyes, which from her photo I thought were just green, distracted me. This close, I could see they were like emeralds shining in the sun with a slight burst of yellow around her pupil, her irises outlined with the thinnest line of black.

Her long eyelashes and elegantly arched eyebrows only managed to highlight them. They looked like the eyes of a jungle cat or little undiscovered planets. They were the most unique eyes I'd ever seen.

I knew the look of an interested woman, and Alex Walker was eating me up with her eyes. But there was something else, something I couldn't put my finger on, something that looked like confusion mixed with curiosity. There was something innocent about her that I didn't understand.

Shrugging off my thoughts, I got to work examining her. All around her left eye, her left cheek, and neck were bruises in every shade of purple and blue, and her left eye was bloodshot and a little swollen.

There were bruises on her jaw and chin where someone had violently grabbed her face, and there was some dried blood she didn't get washed off from a cut over her left eye.

It looked horrific and made my heart ache, knowing the pain she had to have felt receiving those bruises. The pain she must feel now. But more than that, I was incredibly pissed and *hated* that someone had dared to beat the shit out of her.

I wanted to take her pain away but knew that wasn't possible, and that fact pissed me off. I wanted to go back and kill the men who had touched her and hurt her, but I couldn't, and *that* pissed me off. The sight of her felt like a fist to the gut. I felt the need to gather her into my arms and hold her, but I couldn't explain why.

"I don't think anything is broken. There's a little cut here. This might sting," I told her as I used an antiseptic wipe over her left eyebrow to clean the cut, then wiped the blood off her face.

"Can you tilt your head back for me?"

She did, and I gently touched the bruises on her neck that were clearly the impressions of someone's hands.

With her position, I noticed a tattoo that was between her belly button and her waist, above the waistband of her pants that said, 'Fight Like A Girl.' About half an inch tall, the lettering looked like it had been done by an old-fashioned typewriter.

I was about to touch it when I realized what I was doing, and while my fingers only hovered over the tattoo, I watched her stomach muscles flutter as if I were touching her.

I could see three cuts on her chest over her left breast. Two of the cuts had been sewn up. The third one, the smallest of them, was slightly oozing blood. I cleaned the wounds, applied antibiotic cream, and placed a large bandage over them.

Her sexy blue bra barely covered her; I couldn't help but notice her breasts were bruised, and I was pissed all over again that someone had dared to touch or put bruises on those beauties.

I looked away, forcing myself to look at the three cuts on her left bicep. When I touched her arm, she lifted her head. The cuts were surrounded by bruises that looked like handprints, each cut bigger than the last, and all three of them had been sewn up with thread.

"Those were harder to sew since I could only use one hand," she told me.

I again cleaned the cuts and put antibiotic cream on them before I bandaged her arm. Looking at her and tending her wounds, my jaw was clenched tight, seeing the damage that had been done to her.

"You might as well say what's on your mind. If you keep clenching like that, you're going to crack a molar."

I didn't hesitate, "I want to kill the bastards that did this to you."

She nodded and whispered, "Me too."

She'd taken a beating, fought three men to avoid being gang raped, been beat up and sliced with a knife, sewn herself up and relayed her story to me, and she hadn't screamed or yelled or shed a tear. This woman had a core of steel.

"As soon as we have time, this thread will have to come out, and I'll need to re-stitch you, so these don't get infected."

"Well, that sounds like the best time ever," she said sarcastically.

I couldn't help but smile. I asked her to turn sideways so I could check her back. I didn't really need to, I'd clearly seen her back while she was in the stream, and while I saw the bruises, I didn't notice any cuts, but I was curious about that tattoo and wanted to see it.

I moved her braid over her shoulder and saw the small anchor tattoo on the back of her neck just below her hairline. I could only stare at it. We had the same tattoo; hers was a tiny version of my own.

I didn't know why that would affect me the way it did. Without thought, I rubbed my thumb over it, the rest of my hand gently wrapping around her neck. She shivered, and I saw goosebumps spread over her exposed skin.

Her breathing hitched, "I got it when I was sixteen, so I had to hide it from my dad and the guys," she said softly.

My own voice was soft when I told her, "I have a bigger one just like it."

It was a moment before she said anything, "I don't even know how to respond to that."

Chapter 10

Alex

When he was finished examining me, I thanked him and asked if he could turn around again. I put on a white cotton bra, and pulled on a tank top and a long-sleeved camo t-shirt. Then I tied the stolen jacket around my waist and shoved the blue bra into the pocket with the underwear.

I watched as Cole started looking through his pack, "Ah, the magic rucksack."

"Magic?" He asked, not looking up from what he was doing.

"Yeah, you never know what a guy might pull out."

He turned and cocked an eyebrow at me.

I felt my cheeks flush with heat and turned my head away, "Do you have an extra drink of water in there?"

"Of course, I have water for you."

I smiled at him, "I figured you did but didn't want to just demand a drink. That would be rude."

He handed me water a protein bar and opened his hand to show me several pills, "Antibiotics and over the counter pain killers unless you want something stronger."

I took the pills out of his hand, trying to pretend I didn’t notice the zing I felt when my fingers touched his palm. “No, these are good, thank you.” I took a drink and swallowed the pills he’d given me.

He stared at me before he reached forward to tuck an errant strand of hair behind my ear. The gesture seemed intimate and caused me to suck in my breath, and he was looking at me intensely in a way I didn’t understand.

When he removed his hand, I tried to appear like he wasn’t affecting every cell in my being; I opened the protein bar, “Do you want half?” I asked him.

He looked at me like I sprouted a second head before he shook his head, “No, thank you.”

I took a bite of the protein bar and made a face but didn't say anything.

Cole smiled at me, "They don't taste good, but you need the protein and calories."

"It's *really* awful. No wonder you didn’t want half. We should talk to someone about improving these," I said, taking another bite. "How far do we need to go?"

"About eight or nine miles now."

Knowing SEALs always made contingency plans, I asked, "And that's plan A, right? How far to plan B?"

"We probably won't need plan B."

I chuckled, "So there's no plan B? Seriously, how often does plan A go off without a hitch? Humor me."

He looked like he was considering whether or not to tell me before he answered, "It would be another ten miles or so."

"That's not bad. Which letter is you and I end up walking across the border?" I smiled at him, “Is that plan Z?”

Chapter 11

Cole

I palmed her cheek and rubbed it with my thumb; I just couldn't seem to stop myself. There was something about this woman that pulled at me, that fired up all my protective instincts.

I hadn't wanted to tell her we might not get picked up at the initial extraction location, and if we didn't get picked up, we'd have to go ten more miles. But she seemed to know it was a possibility and just took it in stride and accepted it.

She unconsciously leaned into my palm, "Please don't be sweet to me or I'll go all girly, and that would be so embarrassing," she said softly.

"No one ever accused me of being sweet before." I was fighting a strong desire to kiss her. "What does "go girly" mean?" I asked, dropping my hand.

I immediately felt the loss and wanted to put my hands back on her.

"I'll be a big crybaby. It'll be ugly and messy and probably loud."

"You can let that out if you need to; I think I can survive it," I said, smiling at her again.

"Yeah, well, I might not, and it doesn't help either of us in any way."

Changing the subject, I told her, "I saw you in the barn. I was on my way to come get you, but when you took the guard's gun, I thought you might fire it if you saw me, and if you fired it, that would have alerted the guards at the house."

"Probably a wise decision; I admit I was pretty jacked up then."

I couldn't allow her to keep the gun, there were just too many risks involved. I looked at her and told her gently, "Alex, I need you to give me that gun."

Surprising me, she sprung to her feet and started moving away from me. It appeared she was trying to put distance between us, and for the first time, I saw fear in her eyes.

Her hand slipped into the pocket of the jacket, and I had no doubt it was wrapped around that gun. I stood up slowly but didn't move toward her, and she backed up as if she were afraid of me, and I hated that.

Alex walked backward toward the horse. I knew if she got on that horse and rode away, I wouldn't find her quickly, and this entire op could be FUBAR, but it was the fear filling her eyes that made my chest constrict.

"Alex...." I started, but she interrupted me.

"No! You'll have to fight me to take it away," she said angrily.

I could easily take the gun from her, but I didn't want to have to do it that way. I wanted her to give it to me of her own free will. I needed her to trust me; trust was a huge factor when rescuing kidnap victims.

We had a long way to go, and if she didn't trust me, it would make things more difficult and could put her at more risk. But more than that, I didn't want to force her and make her afraid of me.

She took a deep shaky breath and in a calmer voice, told me, "I've been shooting since I was nine. SEALs, one of which is your Commander, taught me. Do you think they didn't teach me how to properly use a firearm? Someone *bought* me. Do you know what that feels like?"

Her voice cracked, a look of agony on her face, "They're coming for me, and we both know what my life will be if they get their hands on me again. Since I saw those two men in that hallway, I haven't felt safe, and it's worse now because I know exactly what's in store for me if I'm recaptured. I need to be able to protect myself."

She took a step toward me, her eyes filling with tears, "Choose a target, I'll prove it. I'll take it apart and put it back together, but please don't take it away or make me give it to you. Please, Cole," she begged.

I watched a single tear roll down her cheek, and she wiped it away immediately. That single tear affected me more than if she'd been sobbing. She hadn't cried while telling me what happened to her, hadn't cried while I tended to her wounds. She was breaking my heart and considering I didn't have a heart, that was saying something.

I took a cautious step toward her, and she choked back a sob. When she didn't back up or move away, I walked closer until I was standing right in front of her.

I hated to do it, but softly, gently, I told her, "Alex, I will not let anything happen to you. I promise you're safe with me. I'm sorry, but you need to give me the gun."

She seemed disappointed in me, and that bothered me, but she took the gun out of her pocket and handed it to me, then spun around and walked back to the horse, and I was afraid she might get on and ride away.

Chapter 12

Alex

I was wiping away the tears that were now freely flowing out of me. I wouldn't let the macho asshole see me cry. I was going to survive with or without him. Right now, I needed him because I didn't know where I was going and had no food or water.

I hated that he thought I was helpless, that I couldn't be trusted with a weapon, and it made me angry that he would treat me that way. I focused on that anger, and it dried up my tears, and after a few minutes, I walked back, keeping my distance from him.

When I came back, the look on his face told me he realized I'd been crying. I knew he wouldn't have known if he hadn't seen my face because I never made a sound. He looked upset by it, but I didn't care.

"We should get going. Are you ready?" he asked me, his voice soft and smooth.

"Are we taking the horse?"

"We can't; there's no way to get it over the fence."

"Yes, there is."

"How?"

"I'll jump him over it."

"No."

"Yes. This is my area of expertise; the fence is short, it's not a problem."

"How is this your area of expertise? You're a singer."

"No. I'm a rancher who happens to sing."

He narrowed his eyes at me, and I knew he didn't believe me, but I wasn't going to try and convince him.

"No, it's too dangerous," he finally said.

I turned around, shaking my head, walking toward the horse.

"Where are you going?"

I spun around and faced him, not even trying to hide how angry I was, "I'm going to let the horse go so he doesn't die, is that okay with you?"

I didn't wait for an answer, just turned back around, untied the horse, and sent him off with a smack to his butt.

Cole put on his pack and headed for the fence, and I followed him. He easily went over and turned to help me, holding out his hand. I looked at his hand then up to his face before I climbed over the fence on my own, hoping my face telegraphed how annoyed I was with him.

I walked behind him, taking out the protein bar and nibbling it here and there until it was gone. I also drank the water he'd given me. I kept up with him but couldn't see where we were going because his size blocked my view.

Several times, he stopped and appeared to listen, and when he stopped, I stopped. When he hopped over a large fallen tree in our path, he turned around and again offered me his hand, and I again refused it without a word, climbing over on my own.

"You okay?" he asked once I'd gone over the tree.

"Yep."

He stared at me, and I stared back. If he thought I was going to say more, he was wrong. When he realized I wasn't going to say anything else, he turned and started walking again.

I had no idea how far we walked or how long we walked. I no longer seemed to have any concept of time. When Cole stopped again and started looking around, I stopped and looked around too, but I didn't hear or see anything.

"Let's rest here," he said, taking off his pack, and I immediately sat down, happy to be off my feet.

Cole gave me more water and a new protein bar. He took my empty bottle and put it in his pack. I thanked him, opening the water, and taking a drink before putting the bottle in my pocket and taking a bite of the protein bar.

Cole sat down next to me. I wouldn't give him the satisfaction of moving, even though that's exactly what I wanted to do. I sat silently, but I could see him watching me out of the corner of my eye. I felt like he wanted to say something to me, but he didn't.

We took a short rest, then we were up and walking again. And that's how the day went. We walked, we rested, and we took off again. This time when we stopped, I told him I was going to use the bathroom.

I did my business, noticing the quiet. The only sounds were the birds, the bugs, and the breeze rustling everything around me. Just as I was about to head back,

I heard a noise in the distance and thought an animal was coming through the trees until I heard faraway voices speaking Spanish.

I headed back quickly but quietly. Cole was already on his feet; I pointed to my ear and mouthed eight o'clock, pointing in that direction.

The sounds were closer now. Cole listened, picked up his pack, grabbed my hand, and walked quickly, deeper into the trees, dragging me behind him.

He pulled me behind a large tree and pushed me up against it while he shrugged his pack on and held his rifle up. My heart was hammering in my chest, and I couldn't move because Cole had me pressed into the tree trunk and was covering me with his body. I couldn't move him any more than I could move the tree.

The sounds got closer, and we could clearly hear several men speaking Spanish. I listened and gasped at what they were saying. Cole tilted my head up to face him and cocked an eyebrow at me. I shook my head at him; I did not want to tell him what I'd overheard those men saying.

He stole a look around the tree then looked back at me, "We're moving," he whispered.

I nodded at him, and he grabbed my hand and moved us deeper into the jungle.

After we'd moved a good distance away from the tree, he turned and looked at me and whispered, "We're going to run. Are you up for it?"

I nodded at him. He stared at me as if he didn't believe me, but still holding my hand, he started running, pulling me behind him.

Once we'd gone a safe distance away, I pulled my hand. He stopped, but he didn’t let go, "I can't run if you're dragging me behind you," I whispered.

He looked at me, and if I had to guess, I’d say he looked pissed. "Let go, I'll be right behind you," I hissed at him.

We didn't have time to argue, and he knew that as well as I did. He huffed out a breath before he let go of my hand, turned, and started running again.

Cole seemed to change directions pretty regularly, running some sort of zigzag pattern. I didn't have a clue where we were or where we were going. I hoped he did, but we could be going in circles for all I knew.

I hadn't lied when I told him I could run; I’d been running nearly every day for most of my life. I was scared, and while he might not like me, I was sure Cole wouldn't let anything happen to me if he could help it. I don’t know how I knew that, but I did.

With that thought in my head, I focused on my breathing, putting one foot in front of the other, and keeping up with him. Concentrating on Cole in front of me, I managed to get into the zone where there was nothing but the running.

He finally stopped running but kept walking. I pulled out my water and took a drink, following behind him. He turned around and looked at me. I was hot, just as sweaty as he was, and my breathing was rapid, but I gave him a thumbs up.

He reached back for my hand, but I jerked mine away from him before he could touch me. He shook his head and scowled at me before turning and continuing on in front of me.

We walked in silence, and I followed where Cole led. It felt like forever before he stopped again and looked at me, "We'll take a break here, and hopefully, it'll be a longer one."

"Shouldn't we have reached the extraction point by now?" I asked him as I sat down, leaning my back against a fallen tree.

"There was some kind of issue with our transportation, we have to go to the secondary pick-up point, and since we've been evading the people chasing us, we're farther away than we should be."

"Guess that means plan A didn't work out after all," I said smugly as I turned my head away from him.

I had no idea what time it was, but it felt like the longest day of my life after the longest week of my life. I hadn't slept much in the past week and wondered if I'd ever been this tired in my whole life.

Cole could drag me through the jungle all day, and I wouldn't say I was done, I wouldn't quit. I wouldn't tell him that with every step, my face throbbed more, my cuts throbbed more, my body ached more.

Besides, people were chasing me; I'd relax once I was out of this country. But it couldn't hurt to close my eyes just to rest them for a minute.

"Alex?"

"Hmmm?"

"Time to wake up."

"Not sleeping," I said groggily.

I was so comfortable; I didn't want to move. Cole chuckled, which I felt more than I heard, and I had the thought that was weird.

I slowly opened my eyes and found myself tucked into his side, my arm over his chest, his arm around me, holding me close.

I immediately jerked away from him and shoved against his chest, "Get off me!"

Chapter 13

Cole

I couldn’t help smirking at her, "You're the one who’s on top of me."

Her face turned scarlet, and she jumped to her feet, and I couldn't help but wonder how far down that blush went. When was the last time I’d seen a woman blush like that? It was adorable and unexpected.

"I'm going to the ladies’ room," she said in a huff.

"Don't go far," I called after her.

She must have heard the amusement in my voice and flipped me off without looking at me as she walked away, and I couldn't help but chuckle.

I got it; she was mad I'd taken the gun from her. She refused my help, and any time she looked at me, she flashed emerald fire out of her eyes. If looks could kill, I’d be a sizzling pile of ash. She’d get over it.

It had been obvious she was falling asleep, so I sat right next to her and gently tipped her my way, and she immediately curled against me.

I knew she wasn't afraid; she was embarrassed. Hard to justify sleeping on me when she was trying to pretend she hated me. Despite her anger, she trusted me enough to relax and sleep.

I liked the feel of her in my arms, the way she'd flung herself over me, her body lush and compliant against my chest. I was having trouble maintaining control around her.

I wanted nothing more than to lay her down, strip her clothes off and fuck her until she was screaming my name. But instead, I kept my hands to myself and let her sleep as long as possible before waking her up.

So far, everything I'd seen and heard from Alex attracted me, but I wasn't here to pick up a woman, especially a woman I was responsible for rescuing, who considered my Commander family and was famous on top of that. If I could just stop the thoughts that kept occupying my head, I'd feel a lot better.

Chapter 14

Alex

I went farther than I should have and did my business; I wanted to hide so I wouldn't have to face him. How embarrassing. I practically crawled into his lap and took a nap. *What the hell was that about? How did that even happen?*

But man, he was so comfortable, and he felt so good when I woke up. *You're an idiot, Alex.*

How was I supposed to face him when I had slept right on him? What if he gloated about it? I didn't have a defense; I woke up on top of him. *Where's a giant hole in the ground when you need one?*

When I came back, I couldn't look at him. Luckily, he didn't bring it up. He acted as if it hadn't happened, and I was more relieved and grateful than I could say.

He already had his pack on and asked if I was ready to go again. I nodded at him but couldn't look him in the eye, so I didn't notice him grinning at me.

The next time we stopped, he set his pack on the ground next to my feet and told me, "I need to talk to my team. Stay here."

I didn't say anything, just watched him walk a short distance away and turn his back to me.

I sat down, ate some protein bar, and listened for any out of the ordinary sounds. I could hear the deep timbre of Cole's voice but couldn't make out the words.

I watched him. I couldn't see much of him because of his cammies and his gear and vest. I knew he was muscular, I had felt him against me on the horse, when he had me pushed against the tree and when I woke up practically in his lap.

He was solid. Big and beautiful with a serious 'don't fuck with me look'. But when he smiled, it changed everything about his face. He was gorgeous, but when he smiled, he was deadly.

I wasn't afraid of him. I probably should be, but I wasn't. I felt safe with him, not that I'd ever tell the big-headed caveman that bit of news. I thought it was obvious he didn't like me, but he'd been decent to me, even if he was an intolerable jerk. *An intolerable jerk with a beautiful face, perfect ass, and muscles for days.*

I stared at his legs. Long, muscular, and even with all his gear on, I could see his muscles rippling and rolling with every movement. The man was power and grace.

And his ass, you could bounce more than a quarter off that ass. With him in front of me, I had been staring at it most of the day and wondered if it felt as good as it looked.

He was like an eclipse. I shouldn't be looking right at him, the sight of him could burn the retinas right out of my eyes. I wanted to climb him like a tree, and I'd never felt that way about any man. I wanted to look away, but my traitorous eyes refused, it just wasn't possible to rip my eyes from him; all I could do was stare.

I bet he's really good in bed. I wonder what his beard would feel like against my skin. Yep, I'm just sitting here thinking about the big, beautiful jerk rubbing that beard all over my naked body.

I felt like all the oxygen had suddenly been sucked away and wondered if there was such a thing as a spontaneous orgasm. *Fuck on fuck toast. I literally need someone to slap my face right now. I wonder if it would be weird if I slapped my own face?* What the hell was wrong with me? I really wished Gabe was here so I could ask him what was happening to me.

"Are you looking at my ass?"

I jumped a mile and let out a long whoosh of breath I didn't even know I was holding. A strangled sound came out of me, but it sounded more like a moan, even to my own ears, and my heart started hammering in my chest.

"What? No!"

My voice came out too high-pitched and squeaky, and it felt like my face was on fire; in fact, if it got any hotter, it might melt off my skull.

I shook my head and slammed my eyes shut as if that could make me disappear from his sight. *If only.*

"Your words say no, but your face says you're lying," he said as he swaggered toward me, flashing his perfect teeth with that damn smile on his face.

I turned my head and glared up at him. I knew my face was still scarlet, but I lifted my chin defiantly, "You're an ass."

"I am an ass, or you like looking at my ass?"

He was smirking at me, and if it was possible, my face got redder.

I looked away, resisting the urge to punch him, "You're a conceited butthead."

"Did you just call me a butthead? I'm just asking because I haven't heard anyone use that term since I was in eighth grade," he said with a smug grin.

I gave him a double thumbs-up, "Good one, chucklehead."

He had the bad manners to throw back his head and laugh. *Laugh.* I wanted to freakin' kill him.

"Bite me," I snarled.

He grinned at me, "Is that an offer?"

"I will throat punch you," I snapped, and he had the audacity to start laughing again.

My eyes narrowed to slits, and I hoped my face was telegraphing how much I loathed him. He didn't seem to get my message, walking and standing in front of me, still looking amused and thankfully changing the subject.

"We're going to have to spend the night. The team will meet up with us tomorrow. We're going to rest here for a little while but need to go a few more miles to get closer to the extraction point before we stop for the night. Are you up for that?"

I didn't look at him, "Yes."

He crouched down right in front of me, and I tried not to look between his legs, but he was right there, *it* was right there, and I couldn't seem to help myself.

When I looked up at him, he was grinning at me, "Caught you lookin'. Again."

Kill. Me. Now.

My face was on fire, and I couldn't hide it. *Is it possible to die of embarrassment? If it is, he won't have to rescue me because I'll be dead in about three seconds. That is if I don't kill him in the next three seconds.*

I wanted to bolt, but instead, I stared back at him with my best 'I really really hate you' look, although I had a feeling I wasn't pulling it off very well.

"We need to get something straight, if you're hurt, I need to know. If you're hungry, I need to know. If you're tired, I need to know. If you can't do something, I need to know. You can't lie to me. If you don't talk to me, if you're not honest with me, this mission could be fucked."

I glared at him, "You think I'd do anything to fuck this up? I've told you the truth, you didn't believe me. I want to live. I want out of this hellhole. I'm not keen on being someone's sex slave.

"You walked, I followed. You ran, I kept up. You said stop, I stopped. You said eat, I ate. Said drink, I drank. So, what's your complaint? It's not my fault if you think I'm a liar. That's on you.

"You want to treat me like a defenseless girl, that's your choice. You don't believe what I tell you, that's your choice too. Shit goes sideways because you don't trust me, that's all you, buddy."

He stared at me for a long moment before he asked, "What were those men saying that scared you?"

"Nothing good."

"Alex?"

I stared at him, angry he was going to make me tell him, "There's a monetary bonus from someone named Del Norte for whoever finds me and brings me back, and as an added incentive, that guy gets to rape me first. Happy now, nosey?"

"No, I'm not happy. I want to kill every one of the motherfuckers that did this to you or think they can touch you.

“Understand this; I'm not going to let anything happen to you. I was wrong. I underestimated you. You're strong and brave, and you've done an amazing job today. I'm sorry."

He actually sounded sincere.

"Will you give me back the gun?"

"I can't do that," he told me, shaking his head.

I stood up and walked away from him. I’d almost caved to his pretty words, but he was still treating me like a damsel in distress if he wouldn't give me a weapon to protect myself.

Fine, if Mr. Macho wouldn't give me the gun, I’d find another weapon. This was just an obstacle; I’d find a way around it.

He could scowl at me and treat me like a defenseless woman, but he'd soon learn I wasn't some simpering, cowering girl.

I was raised by Navy SEALs who didn’t know what to do with a little girl, so they raised me like one of them. I’d been taught to fight in all sorts of ways and was good with fighting sticks. There were plenty of sticks just lying around, so I started looking for one I could use.

While I looked, I wondered what was wrong with me. Why was I acting like this? Cole had me acting completely out of character, and honestly, he had me feeling different than I’d ever felt, and I didn't understand any of it at all.

Maybe it was because he expected me to trust him, but he didn't trust me. Or because I actually did trust him even though he didn't trust me. Or maybe it was because he was the first man to make my lady parts sit up and take notice. Whatever it was, I felt...off.

I knew I was acting childish but just couldn’t help myself. I didn't understand why I wanted to throw myself at him one minute and kill him the next.

I almost felt bad for being bitchy to him, but he pushed all my buttons, and it felt like he was doing it on purpose, so I was having trouble feeling sorry for him.

Chapter 15

Cole

When Alex told me what she'd overheard the men saying, she looked away from me, but not before I saw the fear in her eyes. I wanted to reach out and comfort her in some way, but I didn't, convinced she wouldn't welcome the gesture.

When I teased her about looking at my ass, she was embarrassed, and her face went crimson. If she were a cartoon, steam would have been coming out of her ears.

She was so feisty. And she was right, I'd pushed her, and she'd done everything I'd asked of her, done it without complaint *and* done it well.

I sat there, watching her. She seemed to be thinking hard and looking for something on the ground. I watched her pick up a stick, look at it, and toss it aside. She did that several times before she picked up a stick about three and a half feet long and an inch and a half in diameter. The bark was peeling, and it looked like some sort of hardwood.

I watched her hold the stick against her bent knee as she tried to break it, but she couldn't do it. I was about to tell her I'd break it for her when she walked back with the stick and sat down away from me.

She removed the bark and ran her hands along the stick. Then she used a rock almost like sandpaper, rubbing it against the stick in certain places, and after each time, she'd rub her hands over the stick, feeling it.

My curiosity getting the better of me, I finally asked her, "What are you doing?"

I wished it were otherwise but wasn't surprised when she didn't answer me or even act as if she'd heard me. I shook my head, got up, and walked away, but I kept her in sight, watching her.

When she saw I'd left, she stood up with the stick and held it in her hands as if she were gauging the weight and length of it. Then she started spinning it, passing it from one hand to the other, spinning it fast enough it made a whooshing sound.

I came back into the clearing behind her. She must have heard me because she spun around, holding the stick with both hands over her right shoulder. Her arms were back, one foot behind her, her knees slightly bent.

She was in a fighting stance, ready to strike. When she saw it was me, she stood up straight, and I cocked an eyebrow at her as if asking 'what the fuck', which is exactly what I was thinking.

Staring at me, she spun the stick in her hands to the left of her, in front of her, then to the right of her. Passing it from hand to hand, spinning it faster than she had before. She never took her eyes from mine before she stopped and held the stick unmoving in her right hand by her side.

I watched her, fascinated. Watching her spin that stick, passing it from hand to hand without looking, took skill and a lot of practice.

I stood there, staring at her. Those emerald eyes pinned me with anger, but damn, if I didn't like how fiery she was, I liked her spirit.

But there was no more teasing, no more smiles. I couldn't say why, but I liked both sides of her, the soft, sweet woman who was quick to smile and the angry little spitfire who shot green daggers out of her eyes. Together they made a hell of a woman.

Her voice was laced with sarcasm, "What? You want to take this away from me too? Oh my god, you're right, I could break a nail or get a splinter." She lowered her voice, "Or crack the back of your head open."

While she said it low, she meant for me to hear her. I narrowed my eyes at her and stepped closer, stopping right in front of her. She refused to back up even though I could tell she wanted to.

I took a deep breath, "Alex...."

"Save it." She interrupted, "I don't want to hear whatever macho shit is about to come out of your mouth."

"Even if it's an apology?"

Now it was her turn to narrow her eyes at me, "Another fake apology to try and trick me? Pass."

I let out a long sigh. She put her free hand on her hip and, in an exaggerated imitation, huffed out her own long sigh.

I was trying not to smile. "You're giving me a headache."

"Good. I hope it hurts."

"You're infuriating."

"You irk me. You're *irksome*."

“And you’re a brat I’m about to put over my knee.”

Her eyes went wide, and she gasped, “You wouldn’t dare.”

“You sure about that, angel?” I said, smirking at her.

Although now I had the image of her naked ass stuck in my head.

She blushed but narrowed her eyes and stared at me, then lifted her hand and very deliberately gave me the finger. I couldn’t keep myself from smiling at how adorable she was all rankled and how easy it was to get under her skin. I shouldn't be enjoying this, but I was. I couldn’t remember when I’d ever smiled this much with a woman.

No woman had ever been so snarky to me, most were trying to get me into their bed. I could see her attraction to me under her anger, it was obvious. She was easy to read; Alex Walker wore her emotions on her face, and being able to read her thoughts and expressions was refreshing and intrigued the hell out of me.

She’d had the dreamiest look on her face when I'd caught her staring at me, and it had been obvious what she’d been thinking. The way she jumped at being caught, the sexy little moan she made, the way her cheeks flushed with color, the way she tried to recover but failed so miserably. I couldn't remember the last time I'd seen a woman blush so much, and it just made her more appealing.

She was comfortable enough to be sassy with me. She didn't look at me with fear. She alternated between looking at me like I was a lollipop she wanted to lick and an emerald eyed alley cat who wanted to scratch my eyes out and damn if I could figure out which I liked better.

Chapter 16

Alex

He took a step forward, standing in my space and stared at me. I didn't understand why he was looking at me so closely, like I was a filet mignon, and he was starving, but he couldn't eat it because he knew it was full of E-Coli.

The way he was looking at me felt like it was scorching me where I stood, and it felt like electricity was zinging through me, causing rhythmic pulses of need between my legs.

I watched as something in Cole's eyes changed, they went darker, and his pupils dilated. I felt like the air around us was electrically charged, as if a spark would ignite the air. I watched as a muscle in his jaw twitched, and my eyes dropped to his mouth. His beautiful, perfect mouth.

My lips parted, and he looked down at them as I involuntarily ran my tongue across them. Suddenly, everything faded away, our location, the danger; it was just him in front of me and nothing else.

"This is your one chance to say you don't want this."

I wasn't sure what he was talking about, didn't want what?

His head dipped, and I realized he was going to kiss me, and I gasped just before his mouth touched mine. Taking advantage of my parted lips, he didn't ease into the kiss, his tongue plunged into my mouth, teasing mine. I was hesitant at first, mimicking his movements, then I melted into him, my body reacting...fiercely.

I was lost in sensation, his tongue teasing and torturing. I pressed myself against him from mouth to thigh, his hands on either side of my head, holding me to him, moving my head where he wanted it while he devoured me, our tongues stroking and caressing against each other in perfect rhythm, a dance of advance and retreat.

He took what he wanted. His mouth demanding, savage, owning me, and I took all he gave, giving it back as good as I got. I let out a moan of pleasure, and he growled in response and hauled me tighter against him, one hand on my ass, one hand tangled in my hair at the nape of my neck. My arms slid around him, my fingers digging into the back of his head.

When he pulled away, I whimpered in protest. I was panting, his hands still holding me against him, my fingers still digging into him.

I felt like I'd been woken up, and I hadn't even known I'd been sleeping. I could feel his erection against me, his breathing was as labored as mine, and I hoped that meant I wasn't the only one affected.

Chapter 17

Cole

I looked down at her. It took a moment before she slowly opened her eyes and stared back at me with a stunned expression on her face as if she didn't understand what had just happened.

The undamaged parts of her face had a rosy glow, her lips were wet and swollen, her eyes, like dark green sea glass, sparkled with lust, and she was breathing hard, but then, so was I.

She was soft and submissive in my arms, and I thought she looked well and properly kissed. I'd kissed the sass right off her mouth, and her perfect ass under my hand was not disappointing.

I rubbed my thumb over her lower lip, "You're trembling."

"Wow," she said in a barely audible exhale as if she hadn't heard me, and I grinned at her.

I wanted nothing more than to kiss her again, to lay her down, strip off her clothes, and fuck her right here. But I reluctantly let her go, knowing if I didn't get some space between us, I would do exactly that. I was also not prepared to analyze why I kissed her in the first place.

"Ready?" I asked as I picked up my pack and shrugged it on.

Alex stood there, glued to the spot, staring as I took a few steps away.

I turned around, but she hadn't moved, "Are you coming or are you just going to stand there all day?"

I watched her blink a few times as if she were coming out of a trance. She distractedly nodded her head and took a few steps.

"You forgot your stick," I told her.

She stopped, bent over and absently picked it up.

I hadn't meant to do it but couldn't have stopped from kissing her if my life depended on it. It was instinctive and impulsive. I didn't do impulsive. Impulsive could get one of my teammates or me killed. And I'd kissed her in a way I'd never kissed a woman before.

She was so responsive it caused a visceral reaction; she was full of lust and passion. I'd never been this hard from kissing a woman before. For me, kissing was a means to an end, something I tolerated to get to the good stuff, but kissing Alex *was* good stuff.

I'd never met anyone like her. She was soft and feminine but feisty and strong. She was a contradiction, and that was fascinating. There was an innocence to her, and that intrigued me.

But nothing could happen between us, and kissing her, while more than enjoyable, had been a mistake. One that couldn't be repeated. Despite not wanting to, I had let her go and walked away.

Chapter 18

Alex

I walked behind him, my thoughts on that kiss. *Why did he do that?* That kiss affected my entire body. *Who knew a kiss could be like that?* I briefly wondered how many women it took for him to learn to kiss that way. I licked my lips and could swear I tasted him there.

My lady parts were in a frenzy, beating out a rhythm like a drum and the gush of wetness between my legs made me wonder if he'd disintegrated my underwear.

My nipples were so hard I was surprised they didn't poke right through my shirt. I'd never felt like this before.

Little baby Jesus with a firecracker, this is so bad.

Then he just walked away, and I knew he'd been messing with me, and I'd fallen for it hook, line and sinker. That stung more than I wanted to admit because I'd never been kissed like that, and it made me feel things I'd never felt before. But he was obviously just playing with me.

Why would he do that? What a dick. Do not start thinking about his dick, Alex.

I was developing feelings for him, not that I'd ever tell him that. It was dangerous, and I knew it. He was a threat to my heart, the first man to make me want him, the first to make me feel something.

But I was a job to him; I knew that too. Plus, I'd only known him about a minute and a half, so why the hell was I kissing him? When this was over, he'd go back to his life, and I'd probably never see him again.

For the first time in my life, I was actually attracted to a man, and there was no chance of anything happening between us and that made me want to cry.

I should have known better. He was so far out of my league if I had a league, which I didn't. But if I did, he'd be out of it. He was probably used to beautiful, sophisticated, experienced women who didn't lose their minds when they met him, saw him, or thought about him.

It was doubtful he dated a lot of dorks; he definitely didn't seem like a dork dater. I knew I didn't have the experience for a man like him, but that knowledge wasn't stopping the way I felt.

I was so lost in my thoughts; I didn't realize he'd stopped until I walked right into him and bounced off. The force of me hitting him didn't even jostle him.

Seriously, it's like the man is carved out of solid rock.

I would have fallen on my ass if he hadn't grabbed my arms to steady me.

"You okay?"

"Of course," I said indignantly, trying to look and sound as if I hadn't just walked into him because I was daydreaming.

I watched his lips twitch. In my mind, I was punching him right in the mouth. Also, in my mind, I was jumping on him like a trampoline.

Once I was steady on my feet, he let go and said we were going to take a break. He told me to stay where I was while he took a look around.

I welcomed the distance from him. I *needed* the distance from him. He disappeared into the trees, but I wasn't expecting him to come rushing back about fifteen seconds later.

Chapter 19

Cole

I came into the clearing quickly, "We need to go."

"Again? Where the hell are they coming from?" Alex whispered, jumping up as I grabbed her hand, pulling her along behind me, being careful to make as little noise as possible.

I could hear the men who were following us, and this time it sounded like a group of them. I once again maneuvered her against a big tree, and stood right in front of her.

I put my hands on either side of her face and bent my head, so we were face to face, "Stay here. If anyone comes, you run that way," I whispered, jerking my head to the left without taking my eyes from hers. "I'll find you."

Alex shook her head at me, "No. We stay together. I'm safer with you. Give me a gun, and I can help you," she whispered back.

I tucked that same runaway strand of hair behind her ear before I told her, "I can't. I need to know you're safe, then I can concentrate on what needs to be done.

“If anyone comes, you run, Alex. I'll come for you. I. Will. Find. You." I told her, enunciating every word to make my point.

I knew she was afraid; her breathing had sped up, and I could see her pulse racing in her neck, the fear in her eyes, and she had a hold of my biceps as if I were her only lifeline, but she finally nodded and whispered, "Please stay safe. You are not allowed to get hurt."

She was killing me. She was obviously afraid but wanted to help me and was worried about my safety. When had that ever happened before?

I stared into those emerald eyes for a moment before I nodded and, for reasons I couldn’t possibly fathom, quickly kissed her forehead. Then I turned and left her standing there so I could eliminate the threats against her.

*****

It took longer than I would have liked to take care of the men following us. Once they realized I was there, they ran away in different directions.

One of them managed to get farther away, and it took me longer than expected to catch up to him, but I couldn’t let him get away so he could come back later.

It wasn’t hard to dispatch them, they weren’t well trained, and I was pissed they were after Alex and intended to hurt her, which helped my motivation.

I hurried back to where I'd left Alex, but she wasn't there. Instead, I found a man on the ground who appeared to be regaining consciousness and had a nasty bloody gash on the side of his head.

Fuck.

"Where is she?" I barked at the man; my gun pointed at his face.

The man said something in Spanish, but I didn't understand him. I wouldn't get any useful information from him, so I shot him. I didn't feel bad about it; Alex had obviously hit him, which meant she'd felt threatened by him, and I had no doubt the man would have hurt her or collected the 'bonus' of raping her if he'd had the chance.

I took off in search of her. The farther I went, the more worried I got. I found plenty of signs to follow but didn't know if they were from her or the men searching for her. Was I wasting time following the wrong trail?

I should never have taken her gun away. What had she gone through? Was she hurt? Out here dying somewhere? Did she get recaptured? Was she being tortured? Raped?

I was kicking my own ass for leaving her alone; I was a couple of miles from where I'd left her by that tree. She couldn't have run this far...could she?

I was about to turn back the way I'd come when I heard a man scream in the distance. My heart flipped over in my chest, and I took off running in the direction of the sound. I was scared. Not for myself, but for Alex, and that was something I'd never experienced before.

Chapter 20

Alex

Within a minute of Cole leaving me standing there, a man came through the trees, scaring the crap out of me. When he saw me, he leered at me, holstering his pistol, his intentions clearly written in his lecherous, partially toothed smile.

I didn't wait to find out what he wanted from me; I swung my stick like a bat hitting him as hard as I could in the head before he got close enough to touch me.

He went down in an unconscious heap; his forehead split open and bleeding. Once he was out, I bent down, quickly stripping him of his gun and holster, his knife, and his backpack. I searched his pockets, taking his phone.

I hooked the knife in my waistband on the back of my right hip, took his picture with his phone, and shoved the gun, holster, and his phone into the backpack. I put the backpack on, grabbed my stick, and took off running.

I ran as fast as I could, in the direction Cole told me to go, adrenaline coursing through me and pumping my legs. I had no idea how far I'd run, but I needed to stop. I was gasping for air, and my lungs were burning. My legs were screaming at me, my feet, my face, and my cuts were throbbing, my heart was beating quadruple time, and I had a painful stitch in my side. I stopped running but kept walking.

What the hell am I doing running willy-nilly through the jungle without any idea where I'm supposed to be going? This was not a good plan. Cole is never going to find me. Is he even alive? Should I turn back and look for him?

I had no idea how to control all the adrenaline shooting through my bloodstream and slamming through my heart and wondered if I'd survived to this point only to have a heart attack. That would really suck.

It took a few minutes, but once my breathing returned to normal, I started muttering to myself in a low voice, "Just run that way, Alex, and I'll find you. Yeah, run, now I'll just die tired. I'm so kicking your ass when you don't find me, and I'm lost out here with no idea where I'm going. He probably did this on purpose to get rid of me. You better show up, Cole Montgomery.

"Great, I'm already crazy enough to start talking to myself. That didn't take long. Where the hell are you, cowboy?"

There were so many men looking for me. How was I supposed to survive and stay one step ahead of all of them? What if I got turned around and went right toward them? I was trying not to panic, but this seemed like the perfect situation for panic. I hated to admit it, but with every passing second, I was more and more afraid.

Noises snapped me out of my musings. Hearing men speaking Spanish, I darted behind a big tree. *If I don't have a heart attack today, it'll be a miracle.*

They were discussing that I had to be around somewhere since they'd been following my trail. *Damnit, I wasn't even paying attention to the trail I was leaving.*

The men were talking about wanting to be the ones to find me so they'd get their money but, more importantly, the opportunity to rape me. Although that's not the term *they* were using.

They were talking and laughing about how they wouldn't have to wait; they could rape me here, in the jungle, have some fun with me before they brought me back and raped me again in front of their buddies.

Their conversation was painting a pretty clear, disgusting picture, and it scared the shit out of me. I shook my head, trying to ignore their commentary and get the images they described out of my head.

One of them went silent, but the other continued talking, and I didn't move because he sounded so close. They must have stopped right on the other side of the tree I was hiding behind. The sound of my blood whooshing through my veins was loud in my ears, making it hard to hear anything else.

That's probably why I never heard one of them sneaking up on me and didn't know he was there until he grabbed me from behind. His arms were like iron bands around my upper torso.

I would have screamed, but his hold was so tight it forced the air from my lungs, and the only sound that came out sounded like a strangled squeak. The force of it also made me drop my stick.

The man who had a hold of me stunk of body odor and seriously rank breath. He carried me around the tree before loosening his grip, and I was able to drag air into my lungs again. He ripped the backpack off me before clamping his hands on my biceps. I winced at the pain of his death grip on the cuts on my arm.

My heart was beating like a jackhammer. Another man was standing in front of me, pointing a gun at my head. Luckily, they didn't search me, but I couldn't move my arms, and the knife on my hip was now squashed between me and smelly man.

The man with the gun walked closer and gripped my face so hard it caused a distorted pucker, and when he moved his head toward me, I had a bad feeling he was going to put his disgusting mouth on me.

I forced my head and upper body back into smelly man's chest as hard as I could and head-butted the other man as his face came at me.

I didn't get much leverage but based on how much it hurt, it was still a decent hit, and it pissed him off pretty good. He stumbled back a step, rubbing his forehead.

"You shouldn't have done that," he said in Spanish right before he pulled back his arm and punched me in the face.

My head slammed back into smelly man's chest from the force, a direct hit to my left eye. *Yeah, that frickin hurt.* I could feel blood starting to drip down my face, so I assumed he split my face open.

"I like it when my women fight," he told me in Spanish.

He backed away and pointed the gun at my head again. I had an idea, but the man needed to be close, but not too close. At the moment, he was too far away, and he had the gun pointed at me.

Ignoring the frantic beating of my heart, I spoke to him in Spanish, with a confidence I didn't feel, "You hit like a girl. Turn me loose, and I'll show you how to throw a real punch."

That got his attention. He holstered his gun and started toward me, looking at me like I was a five-course meal, and he hadn't eaten in days.

Just a couple more steps.

When I thought the distance was right, I took a deep breath and, in a quick movement, pulled my legs as far up to my chest as possible. I shoved all my weight back into smelly man while at the same time kicking out with as much force as I could, hitting the man in front of me with both feet.

I was aiming for his face, but somehow one foot caught him in the chin, and one foot caught him in the chest. It didn't matter, his head snapped back, and he fell backward, hitting the ground.

As I'd hoped, the momentum caused smelly man to fall backward too, and he released his grip on me as we hit the ground in a heap. I landed on top of him with an *oomph* and scrambled to my feet as quickly as I could before smelly man could get a grip on me again.

Raising my right leg high, I stomped on smelly man's left knee as hard as I could. He howled in pain and was screaming, calling me a bitch, yelling he needed a doctor. *Good, hope that hurt.*

While his knee might be toast, his hands still worked, so I immediately bent down and grabbed smelly man's gun and skirted out of reach of his hands. But the other guy was back on his feet and yanked me by the hair, making me drop the gun as he flung me sideways, and I fell on my hands and knees. Lucky for me, my stick was right there, so I snatched it up.

The man jerked me to my feet by the hair, and I used the stick to jab him hard in the belly, making him let go. I turned around and lifted the stick in both hands, and slammed the right side of it against his head.

Sliding my hands so they were closer together, I stepped around his right side and, in a quick fluid movement, whacked him with the stick on the left side of his rib cage with one side of the stick, then up to the back of his head with the other side, causing him to stumble forward. But he immediately turned and faced me again.

He grabbed the stick in the middle, trying to pull it away from me, and I used my right knee to deliver three quick jabs to his ribs, a trick Chance had taught me. The man let go to get away from me, so I planted my right foot in his belly, shoving him, causing him to stumble backward.

Following him, I spun around him again, slamming him with my stick across the right side of his back, then the left side in quick succession. Then I swung up and hit him hard across the back of the head again as I darted away.

He turned, coming straight at me in a demented rage, and grabbed the stick in the middle again, pulling at it, his anger making him strong enough to take it from me this time.

I let go of the stick and grabbed his left forearm with both hands, and held on, dropping backward, using my body weight to take him with me toward the ground. I drew up my legs, my feet on his belly and using my legs for leverage, I flipped him over my head.

He landed on his back, and I scrambled to my knees and punched him as hard as I could between his legs, yelling at him in Spanish in a voice I barely recognized, "You like it when women fight back, huh? Well, how you like me now!?"

Both his hands went between his legs, and he yelled in Spanish, "You crazy fucking bitch!"

I pulled the knife from my hip and jammed it as hard as I could into his thigh with what could only be called a war cry and twisted the blade before pulling it out. He let out a bloodcurdling scream, clutching his now bleeding leg.

He looked terrified as I grabbed his gun. I was having trouble controlling the emotions raging through me, and it took everything I had not to stab him repeatedly while screaming uncontrollably.

I was gasping for air, and my voice was shaky, "Give me your backpacks and weapons," I barked.

I had the gun pointed at smelly man, and the knife pointed at the other man, but my hands were shaking so badly if I had to use either weapon, I probably couldn't.

"What?" He asked in Spanish.

"Give me. Your backpacks. And weapons," I repeated, moving the knife, and pointing it between his legs with my shaky hand.

Watching me closely, they both took off their packs, their knives and holsters and tossed them toward me.

Chapter 21

Cole

I arrived in time to see Alex in the middle of fighting a man with her stick before throwing him over her head to the ground, punching him in the junk, taking his gun and screaming at him.

There was another man on the ground who seemed to have a leg injury, and I assumed Alex had inflicted that injury causing the scream I heard.

She yelled something in Spanish at the man she flipped over her head, and he yelled something back. She pulled a knife from her hip and stabbed him in the leg in reaction to whatever he said to her.

Where the hell did she get a knife?

While the little I'd seen was impressive, at the moment, she appeared out of control, and I was honestly afraid in her current emotional state, she'd kill those men, and I didn't want that on her conscience.

I kept my distance and called her name, not wanting to startle her. She didn't react or respond, so I stepped closer and called her name again.

Once she heard me, she whirled around, pointing the knife in my direction. She had a wild look in her eyes, and the hand holding the knife was shaking uncontrollably.

It seemed to take her a couple of seconds to realize it was me, but when she did, she stood up and ran for me. I could see blood on her face and on the front of her shirt. Just before she reached me, she dropped the knife and gun and threw herself into my arms.

I held her off the ground, tightly against me. “Fuck, angel,” I said in an agonized voice.

Nothing felt as good as Alex felt at that moment, safe and alive in my arms, and I held her tight, soaking up the feeling. I could feel her shaking against me, and she started to cry.

My voice was ragged as I whispered, “I’m here. I got you, baby. You’re safe.”

I didn’t know if my words were more for her ears or mine. She clung to me tightly, holding on for dear life. I held her and let her cry herself out while I whispered she was safe. I didn’t want to let go of her, but after her tears dried up, I set her on her feet, gently peeled her off me and palmed her face.

Staring down at her, I asked, “Are you alright?" My voice full of unfamiliar emotion.

“They were looking for me. They were going to take me. I had to do it, I had to, they would have taken me. They would have hurt me.”

She sounded panicked and guilt-ridden as if she’d done something wrong.

I hugged her to me again, “I know. It’s okay, you did what you had to do. I’m sorry you had to do that, but you didn’t have a choice, you didn’t do anything wrong.”

She nodded against my chest before pulling back and looking up at me, “I’m having trouble letting go of you,” she whispered, gripping my wrists, tears streaming down her face mixing with the blood, "I thought I lost you. I was so scared. Are you whole?”

"I'm good,” I told her, but I was again surprised that she was concerned about my well-being. Most people in her situation would only be concerned with themselves.

“Swear it. Swear you’re okay.”

I knew she needed to hear it, “I swear I’m okay. You’re bleeding again, why?” I asked her as I brushed her tears away, my voice angrier than I’d meant it to be.

“All these guys like to hit. I’m okay.” She nodded, “I’m okay.”

But I had a feeling she was saying the words to convince herself, not me.

Gently turning her head, I looked at her face. Her left eye was more swollen than it had been, and there was a new cut over her left eye, the source of the blood.

Rage swept through me, “I need to go take care of these two, I want you to go stand over there and don’t look this way,” I told her, pointing.

“Wait,” she said, walking back toward the men with me on her heels.

She picked up their backpacks, their holsters and knives and a gun that was lying on the ground away from the men. Then she turned and said something in Spanish to them before walking away.

After making sure the two men who attacked her wouldn’t be doing it to her or anyone else ever again, I made my way back to her, “How did you get this far?"

She was finishing transferring things from their backpacks to a third one and looked up at me, "You told me to run, I ran. You didn't say how far to go or how long to run. You just said run," she told me as she stood up.

I rested my forehead against hers, "I'll be more specific next time."

"No," she said forcefully. "No, next time." Throwing her arms around me, she told me, "I'm so sorry, Cole. I've been such a bitch and a pain in your ass. I wouldn't have blamed you if you had just left me. Thank you for coming. Thank you for not leaving me."

I held her tight, "You haven't been a bitch or a pain in the ass. I'm proud of you. You eliminated the threats against you. You were thinking critically even though you were scared. You kept your shit together, just like you've done since this all started. You didn't give up. You fought back, fought to live."

Her voice was muffled against my chest, "Are you just saying that so I'll trust you?"

I pulled back and looked at her, "No. But you did trust me. I told you to run, you did. You trusted I'd find you."

"Honestly, I was cursing you pretty good when it took you so long. I was going to kick your ass if you didn't find me."

I grinned at her, "How were you going to do that if I didn't find you?"

"Yeah, I was working on that one myself. It was a dilemma." She rested her forehead against my chest, "Man, what a day, huh? I don't know how you guys do it, this shit is exhausting."

I kissed the top of her head before I released her. She picked up and shrugged her backpack on. Taking her hand, I started walking, telling myself she needed the connection, but if I was honest, I was the one who needed the connection to her.

She wasn't just brave; she was a little badass with serious skills. I had to admit she was like watching poetry in motion. But I was still upset that she fought two men and had been hit again. That she'd been put in a position where she'd been hurt and was scared. I was pissed at the men who'd done this to her, but I was angrier at myself for not being there to protect her.

We walked in silence for a while until we came across a decent place to camp for the night.

Once we were settled, I told her, "Let's take care of your cuts while there's still enough light."

Alex nodded, and I started with the new cut on her face. It wasn't very big but had bled quite a bit. When I was done wiping the blood off her face and cleaning the wound, Alex stripped off her shirt and tank top and laid on her back.

The one cut on her chest that hadn't been sewn up was still oozing blood, and the stitches on her arm had been ripped out. The cuts on her arm were bleeding, and new bruises were forming on her arms. The sight of it made me angry all over again.

I prepared and gave her a shot of anesthetic to numb both her arm and her chest.

"I'm going to sew up this other cut, it's bleeding from all the physical activity," I told her while we waited for the anesthetic to take effect.

She smiled up at me, "You sure do know how to show a girl a good time, cowboy."

I smiled back at her and ran my knuckles over her cheek. Woman or not, she was one of the toughest people I knew.

After a few minutes, I gently prodded her and asked if she could feel it. She shook her head, so I got started removing the thread on her chest and stitching her back up properly.

“Talk to me,” she said.

“What do you want to talk about?”

“I don’t care, just distract me.”

"I'm sure your boyfriend or husband will be glad to have you home."

"I've never had a boyfriend."

I looked at her in shock, "How is that possible?" I thought she had to be kidding, but it didn't look or sound like it.

For some reason, I was glad to hear she didn’t have a boyfriend waiting for her at home.

She shrugged, "I was twenty-two last time I had a date."

"Don't take this the wrong way, Alex, but are you a virgin?" While unbelievable, it would explain a lot.

"I'm whatever is right next to a virgin. I've had sex twice."

"Twice?" It wasn’t possible to keep the shock from my voice.

"Both times were anti-climactic, in every way. I didn't get what all the fuss was about. Mostly it was awkward, disappointing and if I'm totally honest, I was bored. So, I went on with my life and never felt like I was missing anything. What about you?"

"What about me?"

"Are you a virgin?"

I stopped what I was doing and looked at her, "You think I'm a virgin?"

"I think you might be, yes."

She managed to keep a straight face for about three seconds before she started giggling. I loved that giggle; the sound was so fucking sexy and never failed to go straight to my cock.

"You should have seen the look on your face. You looked so insulted," she said, laughing.

I shook my head at her.

"C'mon, that was funny. Guess it would be hard to be a virgin when you look like," Alex waved a hand in front of me, "that."

"What's 'that'?" I asked, imitating her wave and going back to stitching her up.

"I know you know what I'm talking about. Like you don't know how freakin' hot you are."

"You think I'm hot?" I asked, smiling again.

She went still as if she just realized what she said, "No."

"Want to try that again?" I asked.

"Um...not really. Why are we talking about this?"

"You brought it up."

"It's that shot. You drugged me and made me blabber."

I couldn't help myself and started laughing, "It was anesthetic. All it did was make you numb," I told her without looking at her.

"Wow, way to have my back, Montgomery." It was a moment before she spoke again, "I'm going to pretend none of that just happened. So, what about you? Do you have a wife or girlfriend waiting for you at home?"

"No," I told her without further explanation.

I finished sewing one of the cuts and repeated the process with the next one.

"Cole?"

"Yeah, angel."

"Do you think they put a tracker in me?"

"Why would you ask that?"

"They keep finding us like they know where we are. We were way ahead of them using the horse. It seems like you've had us zigging and zagging, and it feels like we've covered a lot of ground, but they keep finding us, how are they doing that? How are they that lucky? The only thing I have from that night is my underwear, so unless there's a tracker in that, it has to be in me."

I didn't want to worry her and definitely didn't want to tell her a tracker was a possibility or that I'd also been wondering how they kept showing up. Wondering how they'd caught up so fast or that I was concerned there were so many of them looking for her. Instead of telling her any of that, I decided to distract her from the topic.

"I have a confession," I told her.

She grinned, "Uh-oh."

"I'd never heard of you before this mission."

She flashed me a huge smile. Even though at the moment she could only be described as a hot mess, she was still a beautiful woman, but when she smiled that megawatt smile, she was magnificent.

"Really?"

I nodded, concentrating on what I was doing.

"That's awesome."

"Are you being sarcastic?" I asked her, somewhat confused by her reaction.

"No. I never wanted to be famous. I just did a favor for a friend, and it snowballed out of control. You can't imagine how often I wish I was just some anonymous, regular girl that no one notices.

"When you're famous, everyone you meet wants something from you. Even when you get to know someone and think you can trust them, the next thing you know, you're pulling their cutlery out of your back. The fact that you don't know who I am means I'm just Alex to you, I'm not *the* Alex Walker. So yeah, that's awesome."

I never thought of it that way. Never considered how hard it would be to never go anywhere without someone recognizing you and wanting something from you. But she had one thing wrong, even if she weren't famous, she could *never* be a woman no one noticed.

After I was done stitching up her chest, I bandaged her, she sat up, and I moved on to her arm. When I was done, I told her to let me know if she needed painkillers once the anesthetic wore off.

Alex put her tank top and shirt back on, and I started setting us up for the night. She asked if there was anything she could do to help. I told her no, but she again surprised me by asking.

I prepared us each an MRE for dinner, and Alex shared some of the snacks and water she'd collected from the bad guys' backpacks. Based on the way she dug into the MRE and snacks, I was rethinking my opinion that she was constantly on a diet. Of course, it could just be that she hadn't been fed well and was hungry.

"Is Alex your real name, or is it short for something?" I asked her while we sat and ate.

"Alexandra, but no one ever calls me that unless I'm in big trouble," she said with a laugh.

"How old are you?" she asked.

"Thirty-one. You?"

"Twenty-six. How long have you been a SEAL?"

"Nine years. You said you were a rancher before."

"Yeah."

"How does a famous singer become a rancher?"

"That's backward; a rancher accidentally became a singer."

"So, you have cattle?"

"A small herd of Scottish Highlands, about three hundred head now. I selectively breed them, concentrating on genetics. Other ranchers buy them to breed with their herd. I also train horses since it's hard to make a living just off cattle these days. The money is in the horses, especially trained cow horses."

"So, you really are a rancher."

"That's my real life, who I really am."

“So that explains how you know how to ride. How big is your ranch?"

"Fifteen hundred acres. The land has been in my family for generations."

"Wow. How long have you been doing that?"

"Dad bought me two cows and a bull for my seventeenth birthday, and my herd started from there. Do you have family, siblings?”

“It's just me and my dad, Wyatt. He lives in Colorado. He's got his own construction business.”

She nodded, “Did you always want to be a SEAL?”

“No. I joined the Navy right out of high school. A few years later, I met a couple of SEALs in a bar and, after hearing some of their stories, decided to give it a try.”

Alex started laughing, “Did they explain the training or just tell you glory stories? Because if they didn’t explain the training or hell week, it must have been a shock once you were in the middle of it.”

“It *was* a shock. Although even if someone tells you, the stories and the experience are two vastly different things.”

“But you made it. Most guys don’t. And now I’ll bet you can’t imagine doing anything else.”

“No, I can’t. I love it. Being a SEAL is a part of me.”

Alex nodded, “Every SEAL I know feels like that. It might not start out that way, but it’s a calling.”

We got into a rhythm of asking each other questions. I was surprised how much I found out about her and how much I shared with her.

Her mom died in a car accident when she was three. She didn't eat seafood and only ate eggs if they were cooked in something, in her words, like a cake.

Her middle name was Harlow. Her favorite TV show was *Supernatural,* and she chastised me for never having heard of it.

Her favorite Christmas movie was *Die Hard*, which surprised me. It also caused a lively debate on whether or not *Die Hard* was, in fact, a Christmas movie. She remained steadfast it was and told me if I didn't think so, I needed to watch it again.

"You're taking this almost too well. Why is that?" I asked her.

"I don't know, pretending?"

"Pretending? What do you mean by that?"

"We have these crazy paintball competitions. Each team looking for the other, get them before they get you, trust your team. They're extremely similar to this, except for the real bullets and people really trying to kill us.

"Also, they're fun, and this isn't. So, I'm pretending that's what this is, it's just a paintball competition. When that isn't working, I'm pretending we're trying to survive the zombie apocalypse."

I looked at her trying to figure out if she was kidding or not, and she shrugged one shoulder.

"Paintball competitions?"

Her entire face lit up, "They're so much fun. You have to come and play with us. My door is always open. Consider yourself and the rest of your team officially invited any time you want."

"You don't even know my teammates."

"So?"

"Why would you invite people you don't know to your house?"

Once again, she surprised me, "They're SEALs. My house is open to any SEAL any time. Besides, you trust them, why shouldn't I? I'll even teach you how to ride, cowboy."

She smiled at me, "Speaking of...how are your boy bits?"

"I'm glad my discomfort is amusing to you." I smiled at her, so she knew I was teasing her.

Still smiling, she told me, "It's not, but you were walking funny there for a minute."

She started laughing at the memory.

"My boy bits are fine now, thank you."

"Look at that, you rode, you lived."

We sat in comfortable silence, both lost in our own thoughts. I'd never opened up to a woman like this before or gotten to know a woman this way. I never had the desire to.

But surprisingly, with Alex, the more I found out, the more I wanted to know. But the biggest surprise was that I was actually enjoying myself.

I got the impression she worked hard, and it was impressive that she worked to accomplish her goals on her own starting when she was seventeen and didn't stop even after she became famous and could do whatever she wanted. She seemed to love ranching but only tolerated being a famous singer.

She didn't avoid my questions, didn't try to talk herself up to impress me, didn't fish for compliments. She was open, honest, real, and funny.

And she was not at all what I'd expected. She wasn't spoiled or whiny or demanding. She continually offered her help. She hadn't complained. She was strong and brave. Feisty. She wasn't afraid to voice her opinion, but ultimately, she followed my instructions, even when I could see she didn't want to.

Alex had been kidnapped and tortured and was being chased through the jungle by men who wanted to do unspeakable things to her. I could see how scared she was, it was written all over her face and in those expressive eyes, and was evident by the way she gripped my hand.

But she wasn't paralyzed by her fear, and when shit hit the fan, she hadn't hesitated to do what needed to be done. She was in pain but didn't complain about it or let it slow her down, and through all of it, she still laughed and smiled, still had her sense of humor.

She was resilient. What she'd been through would have broken most people. How someone acted in a crisis said a lot about who they were as a person, and Alex Walker had stepped up to the plate and knocked it out of the park.

Finding her beaten and mostly naked in that barn was seared into my brain. Even if it hadn't been, her face was a constant reminder and knowing the people responsible were still out there only fueled my anger.

Something about her had sent my protective instincts into hyperdrive. I wanted to keep her safe and kill every motherfucker who dared to consider putting his hands on her. I'd never felt this way about a woman I'd rescued before, or any woman for that matter.

We'd been sitting side by side, and she shifted and turned around, so she was sitting facing me, "Do you have any tequila in your pack?"

I looked at her and raised an eyebrow.

"For medicinal purposes," she said smiling.

I smiled back but shook my head.

"How about a breath mint? Or a rubber band?"

"That I can do."

"Really? Which one?"

I didn't answer, just poked around in my pack for a moment before I gave her a piece of wintergreen candy and held up a rubber band. She smiled and popped the candy in her mouth and moaned once the flavor hit her tongue.

"Can you just hold on to that for a second?" she asked, indicating the rubber band.

She had used the same thread she sewed herself up with to make a hair tie and removed it, unbraided her hair and started finger combing it, "This mint is heaven, thank you, and I can't believe you had a rubber band...see, magic rucksack."

I knew her hair was long, but once it was unbraided, it was longer than I expected. It was thick and kinky from being braided and wasn't all one length, but looked like it had layers, which explained why she always seemed to have wayward strands that wouldn't stay contained.

I wanted to fist that hair, bury my face in it. She watched me, attempting to interpret the way I was looking at her, "What?"

"I've never seen you with your hair down," I answered as I reached for a strand, rubbing it between my fingers.

"You want to braid it for me?" She asked softly, hesitantly.

I immediately spread my legs and patted the ground in front of me. She shifted until she was sitting between my legs with her back to me.

I started at the nape of her neck and ran my fingers through her hair. Alex sighed. I wasn't in a hurry to braid it, just wanted to keep running my fingers through it.

When I didn't think I could get away with it any longer, I finally started to braid it and tied it off with the rubber band.

"Thank you," she said softly.

"My pleasure," I said, my voice husky in her ear.

Alex started to move, but my hands stopped her, and I started rubbing her shoulders.

Alex moaned, "That feels so good."

I was immediately rethinking this idea with every moan of pleasure that came out of her.

"I'll do you next," she said, and a low rumble came from somewhere deep inside me in reaction to that comment.

After about five minutes of listening to her little moans of pleasure, I leaned forward, my voice sultry in her ear, "If you don't stop moaning like that, this is going to go a whole different direction."

Alex went still as a statue, but I heard her breathing increase.

"I suck at boy girl stuff, but are you...flirting with me?"

"Would it upset you if I was?"

Alex slowly shook her head, her voice a breathless whisper, "No. You make me feel something I've never felt before, and I feel like I'm getting a vibe off you that you're starting to like me, even though you don't want to. But I don't have the experience to know if that's real or not."

She put her hands over her face, hiding, "Never mind, you've probably had just about enough of me. Can we please just pretend I didn't say that. I'm such a dork."

She was so vulnerable and unsure about herself. She didn't play games, just put out there what she was feeling. I pulled her into me, wrapping my arms around her, her back to my chest.

She didn't fight against me, instead, relaxing into me, holding onto my arms. She'd admitted she was extremely inexperienced and shocking as the thought was, for some reason that inexperience was drawing me to her.

But Alex was too innocent for me. Clean and pure, too light for my dark, which was just another reason why I should stay away from her. I was fire and darkness; I'd contaminate her and burn her up, and if I extinguished her light, it would be the worst thing I'd ever done.

It was reckless, but I wanted to be the one to unleash her, to show her what she'd been missing. I had a feeling Alex would be all passion and lust in bed, an aura of sex emanated from her.

Despite all the warning bells and the thoughts in my head, I told her, "You're not a dork, and I haven't had enough of you. If I'm being honest, the opposite is true."

Alex turned around and faced me. Still sitting on the ground between my legs, she put her feet on either side of my hips, resting her legs on mine, and my dick jerked in response.

My hands moved to her face, my thumbs rubbing across the apple of her cheeks. I lowered my mouth to hers, kissing her lightly, not able to resist. She opened to me immediately, and I slid my tongue inside. Alex wrapped her arms around my neck, her hands in my hair, pulling me to her and kissing me enthusiastically.

I let her control the kiss at first, then took over. My tongue tangling with hers, she moaned, and I growled in response, pulling her closer, hauling her up by the ass until she was in my lap straddling me, never breaking our kiss.

I ended the kiss before I wanted to. She tasted like wintergreen, and I wasn't sure I'd ever be able to taste wintergreen again without thinking of her. Alex rested her head against my chest, her arms around my waist, and I lazily rubbed her back.

"Cole?"

"Yeah, angel?"

"After we get back to civilization and I'm clean, and I've brushed my teeth for an hour, do you think you might kiss me again?"

My hold on her tightened, "I think that could be arranged." *Why did I say that?*

I should be putting distance between us, not promising to kiss her again.

What the fuck was happening to me?

After several minutes she spoke again, "Cole, I'm scared."

I held her tighter, "I know, angel. I'm not going to let anything happen to you. Trust that I will get you home."

"I know you will, but I'm still scared."

Even after she was home, she wouldn't be safe. Someone went to a lot of trouble to bring her here. I didn't know who was behind this, but I knew they were out there waiting for her, hunting her. But no one was going to hurt her again, not on my watch. Whoever was after her would have to come through me to get to her.

Even with all my gear, fully dressed, she felt good in my arms, she fit against me perfectly.

As if reading my mind, she told me, "No one has ever held me like this. It feels nice. It feels safe."

I had no idea how it was possible no man had ever held her before, but it felt amazing knowing I was the first. It made me feel good when she said she felt safe in my arms. I knew the moment she fell asleep, her breathing evened out, and she melted into me.

I was not, had not ever been a cuddler. I did not cuddle. I never understood the appeal of cuddling. But the way she fit perfectly against me, her soft in contrast to my hard, felt good. I couldn't help but imagine what she'd feel like in my arms if we were both naked, skin against skin and that thought went straight to my cock.

I shouldn't be having these thoughts. I shouldn't have to remind myself I was on a mission, that she was just a job and was off-limits.

Off. Fucking. Limits.

I just couldn't seem to get that to stick in my mind or make my overactive dick believe it.

Chapter 22

Alex

I woke up on the ground with Cole leaning over me. I was instantly wide awake and started to panic, my heart beating wildly.

Clutching his vest, I whispered, “What’s happening?”

He gently brushed the hair off my face, “I’m sorry. I didn’t mean to scare you. Everything is fine, it’s just time to wake up.”

I relaxed again. “Cole, even if you have to lie, tell me we’re getting out of this place in one piece.”

He palmed my face and stared down at me, “I promise we’re getting out of here, and you’re going home.”

He kissed my forehead, his lips lingering there for a long moment. Before I knew what he was doing, he stood up, taking me with him as if it were the easiest thing in the world.

I let out a very unladylike groan from the movement. “I’ve had just about all the kidnapping and rescue I can stand. Do I look as bad as I feel?"

"No," he answered immediately.

I grinned, "Liar. But I appreciate the lie.”

I had a feeling I looked like a troll that had just emerged from years in her cave.

“Do I smell as bad as I think?" I asked, smiling at him and stretching.

He didn't answer right away, and I thought he might not. "Yeah, you do."

I looked at him and started laughing, “Now *that* I believe.”

“Are you really hurting?” he asked me seriously.

“I feel like I was hit by a truck going a hundred and fifty miles an hour, but I’ll be okay. It’ll be better once I move around some.”

I really hoped I wasn’t lying.

I took a few minutes to stretch my sore muscles while Cole watched me.

“I’m off to the bathroom,” I told him, before walking away, wondering if I’d ever been this sore before. My whole body ached. Even my hair hurt.

When I came back, he made us breakfast of another MRE, and we sat and ate while I tried not to lay down and go back to sleep. I hoped we wouldn’t have to run through the jungle again today. I wasn’t sure my body could take it.

“You know, it’s alright with me if you go save the world alone today. Just come back with an Uber and get me when you’re done.” I grinned but was only half-joking. Okay, I wasn’t joking at all.

After we were done eating and getting ready to go, Cole told me, "I have a surprise for you later, if that helps motivate you this morning."

He held his hand out, and I put my hand in his without hesitation, he laced our fingers together and turned and started walking.

"Wait, what's the surprise?"

He didn't answer.

"That's not fair; you can't just say something like that and walk away. Are you just trying to distract me? Or do you really have a surprise?"

He didn't turn around or stop walking but said over his shoulder, "There's a surprise."

"Well, good on you, because now I am distracted."

I heard him chuckle.

"You're mean. You're a mean, mean man, Cole Montgomery."

He didn't say anything but squeezed my hand. I couldn't see him, so I didn't know he was smiling.

The day passed much like the previous one. We walked, we rested, and we walked more. Luckily, we hadn't had to run yet today.

When we stopped to eat lunch, Cole gave me the surprise he promised, a little pound cake from an MRE. I offered to share it with him, but he refused, saying it was all mine.

"You're very easy to please," he told me, watching me happily eat the cake. I wasn't sure that was true, but I liked that he thought so.

Since I'd been kidnapped, I'd only been given enough food to keep me alive, and none of it tasted very good. So, I savored the tiny treat and thought it might be the best present I'd ever received.

Chapter 23

Cole

It was hot and humid this afternoon. During our last break, Alex stripped down to her tank top and rummaged through her backpack, putting on two holsters, giving her access to two guns. She also still had the knife on the back of her right hip.

She looked like the little warrior she was. I shouldn't have let her do it, but I knew it made her feel better, and now that I knew more about her, had seen her in action, I didn't have a reason not to trust her with weapons.

It was late afternoon, and we were going to have to spend another night out here, and I had been on the lookout for a good place to stop.

We were standing, discussing our current location, when we heard another group coming toward us. The concerning thing was they somehow managed to get extremely close before we heard them.

There wasn't time to move, so I pushed Alex behind me to protect her and raised my rifle. Alex moved and stood next to me; a gun raised in each hand.

Without looking at her, I told her gruffly, "Alex, get behind me, now."

"In a minute," she responded, knowing I couldn't do anything without lowering my weapon, which I wasn't in a position to do.

Standing shoulder to shoulder, guns drawn, we waited for the latest threat to appear.

I was relieved and smiled when I saw it was the rest of the team finally catching up to us, which explained why I didn't hear them until they were on us. But Alex didn't know who they were, and she was still a little tense from yesterday's encounters.

I lowered my weapon and put my hand on her arm, "It's okay, it's the rest of my team, and you're in big trouble for putting yourself in danger this way."

She turned and faced me, "What was I supposed to do, let five guys shoot you in the head while I just stood there?"

"You could have been shot."

"*You* could have been shot. Then what? You could just say thanks instead of being a butthead again," she said as she holstered the guns while my teammates watched, looking more than a little confused by what they were seeing.

I lowered my voice, "And you're being a brat again. You remember what happens to brats?"

She smiled at me, "Yeah, I remember."

I couldn't help but smile back at her, "So, you want to meet the team or what?"

She gave me a lopsided grin, "Are you gonna stop barking at me long enough to introduce me?"

I laughed and shook my head at her before walking toward the team with my hand on the small of her back.

Except for Bruiser, the rest of the team was grinning at us.

"Alex, I'd like you to meet my best friends and teammates," I told her as we stopped in front of them, "This is Smoke, Midas, Bruiser, Jax, and Boomer. Guys, this is Alex."

"Hi. Nice to meet you," Alex said.

She got chin lifts from Midas, Bruiser and Jax.

Smoke looked at her and smiled, "Well, hello there, killer."

Boomer stuck out his hand, and she shook it, but he didn't let go, smiling wide at her, "I'm a huge fan."

He looked like a love-struck puppy; I was surprised he didn't have little hearts for eyes.

"Thank you. I'm a big fan of Navy SEALs, so I guess that makes us even," Alex told him with a smile.

"I saw your show on the Navy base in San Diego last year, it was awesome," Boomer told her, still holding on to her hand.

"Boomer," I warned, but he ignored me.

"That was a fun show, enthusiastic crowd. Hey Boomer?"

"Yeah?" Boomer sighed.

"Do you think I could have my hand back now?"

Boomer laughed nervously, "Oh, sorry. I just can't believe I'm meeting you."

He finally dropped her hand, and I suddenly understood what Alex had been talking about last night when she said she wished for anonymity.

"What happened to her face?" Jax said, frowning.

Alex answered before I had a chance to, "It met the wrong end of a fist."

Smoke looked at her and frowned, turning to look at me, "Her face and arm, are those her only injuries?"

"She's got more bruising and other lacerations. They've been cleaned and stitched up, and I've been giving her antibiotics."

"Hey, hi guys, I'm right here, you can ask me yourself, and I'm fine, by the way," Alex said.

“You have no business having a weapon, you need to hand those over to us before you hurt someone,” Bruiser told her.

Alex stared at him for a moment, “Why? Because I’m a girl?”

“To be blunt, yes, and you’re not trained.”

Alex huffed out a laugh, “Unfortunately, Magic 8 ball says, ‘outlook not so good.”

Several of the team laughed, and I couldn’t help but smile that her sass was back and wasn’t surprised she would put up a fight for her weapons after everything that had happened yesterday.

“I’ve probably had as much or more training than any one of you. I have just as much right to have a weapon as you do. You’re welcome to try and take them from me, though.”

Bruiser narrowed his eyes and glared at her.

“Your scary SEAL face won’t work on me; I was raised by SEALs way scarier than you.”

I put my hand on her arm, “Alex, I need to talk to the team.” Now wasn’t the time for her to get into it with Bruiser.

She nodded and took off her backpack, “I’m going to go to the bathroom while you guys talk about me behind my back,” she said, smiling at me.

I liked that I didn’t have to argue with her or explain. Liked that she didn’t demand to be included, that she understood and accepted without a fight.

I grinned at her, "Don't go far."

She rolled her eyes at me, "Really?"

I was still smiling as I watched her walk away.

"How's it been with the princess package? She doesn’t seem that bad," Midas said when we were alone.

“Are you kidding? Didn’t you hear how bossy she was?” Bruiser responded.

"She's not a princess or a package. And she isn’t bossy. Don't talk about her like that." The comment came out angrier than I meant it to.

"What were we just watching? What’s going on here?" Smoke asked.

"Nothing."

Smoke smiled at me, "Want to try that again, brother?"

"She's not a spoiled princess, she's tough as nails, and she shouldn't be insulted like that. That's all."

"Only you could pick up a chick in the middle of the jungle," Bruiser grumbled.

I narrowed my eyes at him, "Choose your next words carefully, Bruiser."

“Oh shit, it’s like that, huh?” Jax said.

“No idea what you’re talking about.”

Smoke belly laughed at my response, "Uh-huh. Where’d she get the weapons?”

“She took them from assholes who attacked her yesterday.”

“She has no business having a weapon. We need to take those weapons away before she kills one of us,” Bruiser complained again.

"She could have shot us and didn’t," Smoke told him.

"She knows how to use a gun, although she’s also pretty deadly with a stick. Her dad is Mad Dog Walker; she was raised by SEALs, including Commander Reynolds. She’s already had to fight three tangos; she knows what she's doing. I wouldn’t let her have a weapon otherwise,” I told Bruiser.

“A stick?” Boomer asked.

"Stop. Back up. Maybe you should start at the beginning," Midas said.

I’d just finished giving the team a brief rundown of what had happened, leaving out our kiss and all the details of our night together when we heard the now telltale sounds of men stomping through the jungle.

“It’s a group, coming from different directions; they’re trying to box us in,” Jax said.

I looked for Alex, who had been sitting at the base of a tree, but she wasn’t there anymore. I was alarmed until I saw her peeking around the tree looking at me, obviously having heard the sounds too. I held up a fist, the signal for stop. She nodded and disappeared behind the tree.

We silently disappeared into the jungle. Fanning out, Smoke, Bruiser and I went west, Jax, Midas and Boomer went east. With adrenaline coursing through our veins, we were ready for the fight.

The men became aware of us when some of them suddenly started crumpling to the ground. While our rifles had suppressors, and they likely didn’t hear anything, there was no mistaking the men on the ground had been shot.

They panicked seeing their dead friends, and that started a hail of gunfire as the remaining men scattered in different directions while trying to shoot behind them as the team gave chase.

The sound of gunfire was loud and echoed through the jungle. They were firing aimlessly. It was obvious they didn't know where we were because we didn't make our positions known to them.

We made quick work of taking out the nine men before hurrying back to where we'd left Alex.

Chapter 24

Alex

Cole came around the tree and palmed my face in both hands after I holstered my guns. His thumbs gently rubbed my cheeks, and he was looking at me intensely. I really liked it when he did that; he could do it all day as far as I was concerned.

Before I could stop myself, my arms went around his waist. He didn't complain, didn't ask why, he just held me in his strong arms until I pulled away, and he looked down at me, "You okay?"

"Yeah."

"C'mon."

"I don't know about you, but I'm tired of these assholes and their clusterfuckery," I told them as Cole, and I walked up.

The team laughed, even though I wasn't kidding. "How are there any left? The jungle must look like the last scene of *Reservoir Dogs* by now."

They all turned and looked at me.

"What?" I asked the twelve eyes staring at me.

"We should double time it out of here before more assholes show up," Midas told us.

“Can you run?” Bruiser asked me, well barked at me was more like it.

“Yes. Besides, we haven't run for at least twenty minutes. It's like we're slackers.”

Cole laughed and squeezed my hand before letting it go, “You sure? Not too sore?”

“I’m okay.”

He bent and picked up my backpack and was surprised at how heavy it was. He took the time to open it and look inside, “What the hell. Snacks, bottles of water, another gun, extra clips, *two* more knives.”

I shrugged, “Some women like shoes.”

"Marry me," Smoke said to me with a wide smile, two dimples puckering his scruff-covered face.

Cole glared at him and looked like he was about to say something.

"Sorry, you have to be this tall to ride my ride," I told Smoke, lifting my hand above his head.

“This is too heavy for you,” Cole told me.

“I’ve had it since yesterday. It’s not too heavy.”

“I’ll transfer some of this to my pack.”

“It’s fine,” I said, taking the backpack from him.

“Alex.”

“Not the time to go caveman, cowboy.”

He stared at me, and I stared back. I knew he wanted to demand I let him take some of the contents, but to his credit, he finally nodded and helped me into my pack before he shrugged on his own.

“If this gets too heavy, you let me know.”

“Okay.”

“Alex, I mean it.”

“I know. I will, promise,” I responded.

We took off, Midas, Bruiser and Cole in front of me and Smoke, Jax and Boomer behind. After what felt like forty miles, but was probably only one, we stopped running but kept walking while the team started looking for a place to stop for the night. Every muscle in my body was aching, but I kept that information to myself.

When they finally decided on a spot, we took off our packs and got comfortable. Cole turned and looked at me, "Smoke is a medic; he's going to take a look at your stitches."

I sat down next to Smoke, and Cole sat on the other side of me. I pulled the top of my tank top down, exposing the wounds but nothing else. I wasn't about to strip down to my bra in front of all of them, although I did wonder why I didn't have a problem stripping down in front of Cole.

The entire team was paying close attention.

"Why was she sewn twice?" Smoke asked Cole as he looked at my chest wounds.

"She was sewn with thread, it needed to come out," Cole told him.

"They sewed you up with thread?" Jax asked me.

"I sorta had to do that myself."

The team looked from me to Cole, and Cole gave them a curt nod. The team looked surprised and angry at his confirmation.

When Smoke was done with my chest, I sat up, and he removed the bandage from my arm.

Chapter 25

Cole

After Smoke finished looking over Alex's wounds, we all settled in and made a dinner of MREs.

"MRE roulette. What did you get?" Boomer asked Alex.

"I don't know, it looks like some kind of mac and cheese," she answered, showing him.

"None of them are good, but that's my favorite one," Boomer told her.

Alex held it out to him, "Trade me."

"No. I can't. I didn't mean I wanted it."

"Don't be a weenie, just trade me."

Boomer laughed, "Are you sure?"

"I wouldn't have offered if I wasn't."

"Thanks, Alex, that's really nice of you," Boomer said bashfully.

Those little hearts were back, swimming in Boomer's eyes, and I was torn between wanting to roll my eyes at him and punching him in the face.

Alex opened her backpack and started piling up the snacks she'd collected, sharing them with the team.

"Check it out, Bruiser, she's got those peanut butter crackers you can't get enough of," Midas said.

"Where did you get all this?" Jax asked her.

"The bad guys' backpacks. Take whatever you want. Does anyone need water?" She asked, taking the package of peanut butter crackers out of the pile and holding them out to Bruiser. He stared at her but didn't take them.

Alex set the crackers on Bruiser's leg and went back to eating her dinner. She waited until the team chose snacks before taking something for herself. A few minutes later, when Bruiser opened the crackers, she smiled a little satisfied smile.

She was kind and thoughtful. Generous. Trading her dinner with Boomer because he liked hers better, making sure Bruiser got the crackers he liked even though he hadn't been very nice to her. Sharing snacks and making sure the team got what they wanted first. Giving everyone water she'd been lugging around in her pack, asking for nothing in return.

The team laughed and joked around like we normally did when we were together. We were brash and foul-mouthed as usual. Alex wasn't saying much, she just sat observing, and I was worried she was put off by our behavior.

Leaning into her, I whispered, "You're awfully quiet, you alright?"

She turned and looked at me, "I'm fine. Just listening. It's comforting. Familiar."

"Alex, are you CIA?" Jax asked her bluntly.

"Why does everyone think I'm CIA?" She asked, looking at me.

"Are you?" Bruiser asked harshly, glaring at her, and I shot him a look letting him know he needed to watch his tone.

Bruiser's attitude didn't seem to faze Alex, "You're really starting to warm up to me, aren't you?" she quipped with a straight face.

The rest of us were caught off guard and started laughing while Bruiser stared at her, looking perplexed, but I saw the slightest ghost of a smile and a softening of his eyes.

"Why do you think I'm CIA?" she asked him.

"This op was greenlit by the President. No offense, but you're just a singer," Midas said.

"Ah, that explains it." She shook her head, "No, I'm not CIA."

"Why does the op being greenlit by the President explain things to you?" I asked her.

"Uncle John was on my dad's team."

"Uncle John, like Uncle Mal?" I asked.

"Exactly."

Understanding, I nodded at her.

"Is anyone else lost by this conversation? She sure sounds like CIA," Smoke said.

"She's not CIA," I told him.

"So, Reaper, you and Alex rode out of that barn on a horse. I would have paid to see that," Boomer said, sounding amused.

Alex started giggling and couldn't stop.

"That bad, huh?" Midas asked.

Alex managed to regain control of herself long enough to say, "No. He did good," but she immediately started laughing again.

I leaned over and whispered in her ear, "My boy bits?"

Alex laughed harder, put both hands over her mouth, and nodded.

"You're cruel, woman," I said, smiling at her.

"I'm so sorry," she said, unable to control her laughter.

“Is that why you call him cowboy?” Smoke asked, which just made Alex laugh harder.

Jax looked at me, "What the hell is going on?"

"What happened on that horse that has her laughing like that?" Midas asked.

I watched her, that laugh, the sound of it, how it changed her appearance. Alex, laughing, relaxed, without worries or fear, was a remarkable sight.

The rest of the team noticed the connection I had with her. It happened that way sometimes, and when it did, the team encouraged it. But this was different. This was more than a kidnap victim trusting one of us more than the others. In all our years together, none of them had ever seen me act like this with any woman because I never *had* acted like this with any woman.

A little while later, Alex laid down, and it wasn’t long before I noticed she was asleep. I wasn’t surprised. She had to be sore and tired. These were my best friends, and I knew they were going to have something to say about my behavior toward her.

"Something you want to tell us, Reaper?" Jax asked.

"What do you mean?"

He jerked his head toward Alex, "You and the woman, something happened," Jax clarified.

"He won’t admit it, but he likes her,” Smoke said.

I shot him a look, but Smoke just smiled and shrugged.

"You sure you want to play with this one, Reaper?" Midas asked.

"Yeah, she's not a one-night stand woman, she's a relationship woman, and you don't do those," Jax said.

"It's easy to see how she looks at you. If it's just sex, you could hurt her, and she doesn't deserve that," Boomer remarked.

"Plus, she's famous, how would that work? What would you even have in common with her? She knows the Commander, if shit went sideways, that could fuck you up. No chick is worth that, even one who looks like her," Bruiser piped in.

"You might want to back off now before she becomes too attached," Boomer said.

"I've never met anyone like her. She's strong and brave, kind, and funny. She's not jaded, she doesn't play games. That's rare. She intrigues me. But I know nothing can happen between us."

"She might be completely different when she's at home. She could be one of those crazy psycho women," Bruiser said.

“She’s not a psycho,” Smoke snapped at Bruiser, surprising me.

Smoke turned and looked at me, “It’s not hard to tell what she thinks or feels. Either she says it, or it's written all over her face, and she doesn't take your shit, which is fun to watch. If you don't want her, I'll take her."

I glared at Smoke, "The fuck you will, she's mine."

Why the fuck did I just say that, and why did I sound like a barbarian? She wasn't a thing; she was a human being.

I hadn’t meant to say it, especially after I had already declared nothing could happen between us. But the thought of her with anyone else was unacceptable. I couldn't explain why I felt so possessive about her. I wasn’t surprised when I looked over and saw all my teammates except Bruiser grinning at me.

"Seems Reaper has finally met his match," Smoke said, still grinning.

"This could be interesting," Jax said.

"Or a huge disaster," Bruiser replied.

"I don’t know, she might be good for him," Smoke told Bruiser.

Having had enough and not wanting to dwell on why I felt so possessive of her or why I had declared her mine, I told the team, "Something is off about her kidnapping. Men in fancy suits drugged and kidnapped her from a private party, which is risky.

“She overheard the guards saying she was targeted, a special order, why bring her to Peru? She was separated and kept in that barn. Why? And she wasn't raped or tortured until three asshole guards made plans of their own."

I felt sick saying those words out loud.

"Someone is trying really hard to keep her from leaving here, there's a lot of manpower out searching the countryside for her, and they’re extremely tenacious," Smoke added.

"Exactly. The manpower, the tenacity isn’t normal. It’s overkill. Someone really wants her, and they've spent a lot of money to get her. She won't be safe even when she's back home," I responded.

We spent the next hour trying to figure out what was going on with her kidnapping but couldn’t seem to connect any of the dots with the limited information we had.

*****

After everything we’d been through, the two hours it took us to get to the extraction point the next morning were surprisingly anti-climactic. I’d expected some sort of resistance, and the team was on high alert, but in the end, we were able to just run and jump into the helo and take off.

Of course, it was possible after all the men we’d taken out, there just wasn’t anyone left to prevent us from flying out.

Once we settled in and were flying away, I sat next to Alex and put a set of headphones on her head, adjusting the microphone until it was in front of her mouth.

It wasn’t long before we heard the pilot in our ears, "Ms. Walker, Commander Reynolds is anxious to talk to you. He's coming through now."

Alex took a deep breath; we could all see she was getting emotional. I laced our fingers together, and she squeezed my hand before she started talking, "Uncle Mal?"

"Alex?" The Commander’s voice was filled with emotion. "Jesus, I've never been so fucking glad to hear your voice," his voice cracked, and he cleared his throat. "Are you okay?"

"I'm fine. Tired. I knew you'd come for me; I knew it."

"Fuck yes, we were coming for you."

"Thank you for sending the team to get me," she said, wiping tears from her face with her free hand.

"Everything went okay?"

"Walk in the park," she told him.

The team laughed and shook their heads, and I squeezed her hand again.

"Did you think it would be otherwise?" She asked him.

"No. The helo will take you to the airport where you'll catch a plane home. Once you land, there will be transportation waiting for you. I want the team to stay with you until we debrief all of you and we figure out what our next move is. And I want you in the ranch house, so everyone is close just in case."

Alex shook her head, "Uncle Mal, tell Gabe it wasn't his fault," she choked back a sob and covered her mouth with her hand as if she could hold it in.

"I will, but I doubt he'll believe me. We were scared shitless."

Alex nodded. "Me too," she said in a small voice.

"Gabe gave me your phone, and it'll be on the plane; you can call him. You're sure you're okay?"

"Yes. The team is taking good care of me. I'm in the best hands possible, and you know it. Don't worry."

"I'll stop worrying when I see you for myself. I love you, sweetheart."

"I love you too. See you soon."

"Hell, yes you will," the Commander said before the transmission disconnected.

I wrapped her up in my arms as she started to lose control, then almost as quickly, she sat up straight and pulled the emotions back. She wiped her face, shaking her head.

"Hey, it's okay to let it out. You've been through a lot, no one will think less of you," I told her honestly.

She took a couple of deep breaths, "I'm okay. Let's go home."

I liked the way that sounded but was worried about her not letting her emotions out. At some point, the way she'd been holding those feelings back was going to catch up with her, and she was going to crash...hard.

She looked at the team, "I don't even know how to begin to say thank you to you guys for coming and getting me and having my back...but thank you."

"Just doing our job," Bruiser told her.

She looked directly at him, "Even so, thank you."

After a moment, she turned around, facing me, our thighs touching, her hand on my chest.

"There's so much I want to say to you, cowboy. Thank you for keeping your promise, for keeping me safe, for being the baddest badass of all the baddasses. There's no one else I'd rather run through the jungle dodging bad guys with."

I couldn't help smiling at her and put my hand over hers where it still rested on my chest, "I enjoyed meeting you as well."

She smiled at me, "In case you were wondering, I haven't forgotten what we talked about."

I had every intention of taking her up on the offer to kiss her again, but I wasn't going to tell her that in front of the team, "You know everyone can hear you, right?"

"I don't give a twirly fuck as long as *you* hear me."

There was laughing in our ears as I rested my forehead against hers and chuckled, "I hear you, angel."

“What’d they talk about?” Boomer asked.

Jax looked at Midas, "Twirly fuck? That's a new one for me."

"I'd never heard clusterfuckery. Killer has a mouth on her," Midas responded.

Alex smiled wide, hearing everyone and turned back around until she was sitting next to me again, and I put my arm around her shoulder. I liked having her next to me. I liked the way she felt against me.

She leaned against me, putting her arm over my chest, and I tightened my hold on her, not paying attention to the looks the team were giving me and ignoring the voice in my head telling me I shouldn’t be doing this.

Chapter 26

Alex

The helicopter landed, and we walked a short distance to a private plane. When I got a good look at it, I smiled.

"What is it?" Cole asked.

"I know this plane," I told him as I started walking to climb the airstairs.

Cole stopped me with a hand on my arm, "We go first and check it out."

I nodded, and Cole sent Jax and Midas into the plane while the rest of us stayed at the bottom of the stairs. Cole, Bruiser, Smoke and Boomer surrounded me, standing alert, watching for any signs of danger while we waited.

Not long after, Midas popped his head out the door, "Clear."

We all climbed the stairs and got on the plane. This was Chance's plane, and I'd been on it many, many times. One thing was certain, once you flew on a fancy private plane, you never wanted to fly any other way.

The interior had two bathrooms, a bedroom, and thick plush carpet on the floor. It also had ten captain's chairs and a couch, all made of buttery soft cream-colored leather.

Justin, the pilot, was standing to the side of the door watching us and smiled when he saw me, "Hi Alex, sure am glad to see you in one piece."

"Hi Justin, it's good to see you too. Justin, these are my friends, Reaper, Smoke, Jax, Bruiser, Midas and Boomer."

Looking at all of them, Justin gave them a chin lift and got one in return from each member of the team. I couldn't help but smile at them and their manly greeting.

"Mr. Winchester made sure we were fully stocked," Justin told me, tapping the top of an expensive bottle of tequila with one finger.

"He also left some personal items for all of you. Settle in, we'll be taking off shortly."

"Thank you, Justin."

"Gentlemen," Justin said to the team as he closed and locked the exterior door and went into the cockpit.

There were two large blue bags and one smaller pink one sitting on the floor. The pink bag had a note on it,

"Mal said the team was going to the ranch. We didn't know if they needed supplies, so we packed some for them just in case. Had to guess on sizes. Thought you might need a few things too. See you soon, sweetie. So glad you're okay. Love you, Chance."

After I set the note down, Boomer picked it up and read it, "Chance. Mr. Winchester. Chance Winchester? This is Chance Winchester's plane?"

I nodded, "Uh-huh."

The plane started moving, taxiing out onto the runway. The team was pulling things out of the blue bags. There were lots of Give Him A Chance products, underwear, t-shirts, sweats, and shorts.

There was also a bunch of personal hygiene products, soap, toothbrushes, toothpaste, razors, shaving cream. It looked like enough for an army.

I picked up my phone that was sitting on one of the tables with my driver's license. I shoved my license in my pocket and dialed Gabe's number.

I put the call on speaker while I started pulling things out of the pink bag, trying to find a toothbrush and toothpaste.

My bag had a brush, a comb, a bra and underwear, jeans, sweats, a t-shirt, shorts, scrunchies, and a box of condoms. I rolled my eyes when I saw the condoms, leaving them in the bag. Obviously, Gabe still had his sense of humor. About the time Gabe answered the phone, I finally found a toothbrush and toothpaste.

"Hello?"

"Hey there."

"Alex? Oh my god, gorgeous, are you okay?"

"I'm fine."

Gabe immediately started balling, and his tears triggered my tears.

"I'm so sorry," he told me.

I straightened, wiped my face, and took a deep breath. "Stop it, or we'll both be blubbering. This was not your fault; you feel me?"

"If I hadn't talked you into that party, it wouldn't have happened."

"Then they would have got me somewhere else. It wasn't your fault. Somehow they got into that party. They had to be on the list. Call Uncle Mal and tell him to get that list and check it out."

"He's already on it. Chance and I sent him the pictures we took, and Oscar sent him photos too. Are you really okay? Are you hurt?"

“I'm okay.” I started speaking Italian, “You're on speaker. I do have something to tell you.”

I didn't notice the shocked looks on the team's faces when I started speaking Italian or how they were all looking at Smoke.

Gabe responded to me in Italian, “Since you're speaking Italian, I assume it's important, but you don't want anyone else to hear it.”

“I met someone.”

“You met someone. You got kidnapped, and you met someone. Is that what you're saying to me? Only you.”

“He kissed me, and it was wow. But better. Like holding a live wire, but in a good way, if that makes sense.

“My lady parts were on high alert, like DEFCON one alert. But I'm so confused about him, you have to tell me what to do.”

“Wait. He kissed you? And you kissed him back? O-M-G! You kissed a boy, and you liked it! You acted like a girl! I'm so happy right now,” he screeched.

“Yeah, I did, but I can tell you this, there isn't one thing about him that's boy.”

Gabe let out a girly scream, “I'm having a heart attack right now. I am so happy! *Finally*.”

I shook my head, “Don’t be, I was just a job to him, and in a minute, he’ll go back to his life.”

"You are so adorably clueless. What’s he like?”

I sighed, “So dreamy.”

“I’ve literally never been this happy. You’re not dead, you’re coming home, and you finally noticed a man. Best. Day. Ever!”

I went back to speaking English, "Thank you for sending the bags and getting my phone and driver’s license back to me and thank Chance for the plane. I have to go, we're about to take off, but I just wanted to let you know I'm okay. I'll see you soon."

"Thank you for not being dead. I can’t wait to see you so we can talk about this.”

"Jerk,” I said.

"Bitch," Gabe responded.

I laughed, "Love you too, bye."

I wasn’t paying attention to the way Cole was looking at me or the way Smoke was smiling.

After I hung up, I started putting things back into the bag, keeping the toothbrush and toothpaste out when Smoke spoke to me in Italian, “You’re Italian is flawless, where did you learn?”

I whipped my head toward him and instantly panicked, responding in Italian, “You understood that?”

“I’m the team’s language guy, *and* I’m Italian, my last name is Marcucci. So, you think he’s dreamy, huh?” He asked with a huge smile on his face, making those adorable dimples pop.

“Well shit.” I narrowed my eyes and put my hands on my hips, “What do you want?”

He held his hands up, “Hey, relax, I don’t want anything. I won’t tell him. It’s been obvious since we met you how you feel. Honestly, we’ve never seen him like this before. But you should know he’ll fight how he feels because it scares him.”

“It scares me too.”

“Hey, speak English,” Bruiser protested.

When I looked up, Cole was staring at me, “You’re just full of surprises.”

I didn’t respond because Justin came over the speakers of the plane, his voice calm, "Attention passengers, this is your pilot speaking, we have multiple vehicles coming up our six, and our clearance is being called off by the tower."

The team looked at each other, and all started talking at once, moving to pick up their weapons.

“Fuck.”

“What the hell?”

“Son of a bitch.”

“Shit.”

“This isn’t good.”

“Be ready for anything. Alex, back of the plane, now,” Cole barked.

I got up and moved to the back of the plane while the team took up defensive positions. In case of what, I had no idea.

The plane’s engines were revving, and we started to move. The team was looking out the windows when Justin spoke again, "Buckle up people, take off is going to be hard and fast. Let's get this bird in the air and get home, shall we?"

"Who is this guy?" Jax asked.

"He's retired Air Force. He flew a shit-ton of missions in Afghanistan. His call sign was Skyhawk," I told him as my shaking hands tried to get my seat belt on.

I felt like I was in a never-ending nightmare. I was white-knuckling my armrest as we raced down the runway, and I felt when the plane lifted off the ground. I kept expecting to get hit by bullets or a missile or fighter jets to flank us and force us to land or bomb us out of the sky. We flew away from the airport on our way out of Peru, but the team didn't relax, so I didn't relax.

It took a while, but Justin eventually came back over the speaker, telling us, "We have entered Ecuadorian air space, feel free to roam about the cabin."

We all finally breathed a sigh of relief.

"Who the fuck is after her that would chase down a plane and could get the tower to call off clearance?" Cole asked, looking at the team.

"Our pilot could get in a lot of trouble for this," Midas said.

"He won't get in trouble," I told him.

"How's that?" Bruiser asked.

"I know people who know people, and those people know people. We'll have Justin's back. Besides knowing Justin, that was fun for him."

The team stowed their weapons again and started for the galley as if we hadn't been about to be shot out of the sky only seconds ago.

Justin wasn't kidding when he said Chance had made sure the plane was fully stocked. The fridge was full of pre-made sandwiches, beer, soda, and water, and the cupboards were stuffed with almost every snack known to man.

We all pulled out food, and the team grabbed beers. We sat, and I ate the first real food I'd had in more than a week. When we were finished, I went to brush my teeth, vowing never to take a toothbrush for granted again.

I was so exhausted; it was as if my entire body shut down, knowing I could finally relax. Even though the plane had a bedroom, I laid down on the couch and promptly fell asleep.

I don't know how much time went by, but it felt like I'd just closed my eyes when Cole woke me up, saying we were about to land.

Once we were on the ground, the team gathered up our bags and their gear and headed for the exit. One by one, they thanked Justin.

Before leaving the plane, I hugged him, "Thank you for getting us home."

"My pleasure, Alex. See you next time, hopefully under better circumstances. You take care of yourself."

"I will."

Justin smiled at me, and I left the plane with Cole and Bruiser following behind me.

When I reached the bottom of the stairs, I stood to the side, emotion getting the better of me. I was back in the United States, and it hit me all at once that I'd come close to never being here again. For the first time, I understood why people got on their knees and kissed the ground.

Not far from the plane was a black Ram 3500 heavy duty crew cab truck with the Walker Ranch logo on the front doors. Parked in front of the truck sat a 1969 cherry red Camaro super sport convertible that looked like it just rolled off the showroom floor.

Bruiser whistled, “Nice fucking car.”

I couldn’t help but smile, “I call her Delilah.”

They all turned and looked at me, like it was practiced, like the Olympic synchronized head turning team. I should have taken their picture just to capture the looks on their faces, mostly because for the first time, I saw Bruiser smile.

Cole looked at me, “This is your car?”

I nodded, “I have a thing for American muscle cars.”

“Seriously, marry me,” Smoke asked once again.

I laughed and shook my head at him and mouthed, “sorry”.

We walked toward the vehicles, and the team put all the gear into the back of the truck. Cole, Bruiser, and Boomer started walking toward the Camaro and Jax, Smoke and Midas got into the truck.

Cole sat in the passenger seat beside me and with Bruiser and Boomer in the back seat, I put the top down, and we headed home.

The simple act of driving home felt different. Hearing the normal sounds, seeing the normal sights. Even the air felt different. I was sore and tired, but I felt alive in a way I never had before. It was at that moment I realized I didn’t truly expect to make it back here.

“You have a ranch?” Bruiser asked, pulling me back to the conversation.

“Yeah. Dad inherited it from my grandfather but didn’t want anything to do with ranching and got rid of the cattle and most of the horses then he opened it up to

SEALs. Anyone who needed to decompress, or if they needed to get their head on straight.

"After an injury or a sideways mission. If they wanted to get away, they didn't have anywhere to go on leave, Thanksgiving, Christmas, whatever. I continued that after dad died but got into ranching when I was seventeen.

"Right now, there are three guys there, four if you count Duke, but there could be more if someone showed up while I was gone.

"You have SEALs living with you?" Cole asked me.

I nodded my head, "Most just come and go, but Duke struggled after losing his leg on an op. Dad brought him to the ranch, and he's been there ever since. Duke married Maggie about five years ago, and Maggie acts as our unofficial/official cook.

"Popeye was my brother Mutt's best friend. Popeye and Mutt went through BUD/s together and were on the same team. Popeye medically retired from the teams about six months ago due to an arm injury.

"Ryan lost part of his right leg on a mission and has been living at the ranch for about seven months, and Carl has a brain injury from the concussive force of an IED. He has trouble remembering and repeats what you say, which is a good thing because it shows he's engaged. He's been living at the ranch for about five months now. But he won't be leaving because of the supervision he needs."

I didn't see the way Cole, Bruiser and Boomer were looking at each other.

We continued to chat, and after a while, I finally pulled onto the ranch. I drove under the two huge posts with the big metal sign that said Walker Ranch with the WR brand. We drove down the road until we arrived at the front gate, and again, I was overwhelmed with emotion.

Before I could enter the code to open the gate, a voice came over the speaker box, "Alex? Where the hell have you been?"

I looked at the camera, "I've been at the corner of kiss my ass and none of your business, open the damn gate."

There was laughing in the back seat.

"I see we had nothing to worry about, you're still cranky as ever."

"Popeye!"

The gate opened, and I drove for several minutes until I turned left, passing my own house before turning left again headed for the main house.

"The bunkhouse should be empty, but I could be wrong. If anyone wants to stay in the main house, the two upstairs bedrooms should be empty. Two of you can come and stay with me at my house or not. I'll leave that up to you guys."

Cole shook his head, "The Commander wants you in the main house."

We reached the house and parked in front, and I turned and looked at Cole as I shut off the engine, "I'm going home, taking a shower in my own bathroom, and sleeping in my own bed tonight. I'll be perfectly safe on my own, but I'm making the concession of letting two of you stay with me. Take it or leave it," I told him as we got out of the car.

The ranch house was big, two stories high, six bedrooms, seven baths. It had a covered wrap around porch with chairs, stone pillars and a low stone wall surrounding the porch. There was also a big gym with six showers, a bathroom and a sauna in the basement and a huge rec room that dad added to the original house.

To the right of the house was the 'bunkhouse'. Once an actual bunkhouse, I'd recently torn it down and had it rebuilt. Now, it was a large two-story rectangular building with a kitchen and common space on the first floor and six bedrooms, each with a private bathroom upstairs.

Across the driveway, about six hundred feet away, was the huge barn with a series of paddocks on either side of it. A couple of hundred feet to the left of the barn was an enormous, covered arena, and there was a smaller arena about fifty feet in front of the barn that wasn't covered.

"Alex!" I heard from behind me.

We all turned around, and I saw Ryan coming from the barn.

"Hold up a second," Ryan called out and jogged over. When he got close, Ryan looked surprised, "Jax?"

"Falcon? Holy shit, what are you doing here, brother?" Ryan and Jax hugged and slapped each other on the back, looking happy to see each other.

"Jax and I went through BUD/s together," Ryan announced before he turned and faced me, "Fuck, what happened to your face? Why do you look like that?"

"Long story. Is the bunkhouse empty?" I asked Ryan.

"Except for Popeye," he responded.

"These guys are going to be staying with us. Can you set them up and show them around? That way, you and Jax can catch up," I told him.

"Smoke, and I will be staying with Alex," Cole said casually.

Ryan studied me, "Alex, is everything alright?"

"Everything's fine. Jax and the guys can tell you what's going on. Can you let Maggie know I'm back, and we'll have eight more for dinner?"

Ryan smiled at me, "Mal told us you and the team were coming home. Maggie's been cooking since yesterday; dinner should be epic tonight."

I smiled back at him and nodded as he and the four team members turned to go. They stopped at the truck to gather their gear, taking one of the blue duffels from the plane.

About that time, my Pitbull Zoey came barreling across the driveway and showed no signs of slowing down. I squat down, and she nearly flattened me, slurping my face, her entire body wiggling, obviously happy to see me.

Once Zoey calmed down, Smoke, Cole and I walked back to the truck. I dropped the tailgate, and Zoey jumped into the back.

"What happened to your dog?" Smoke asked me after we got into the truck.

"She was used as a bait dog in a dog fight ring. That's how she lost her ear and got all those scars, but she's the happiest dog you'll ever meet, and she's smart as a whip."

We headed for my house, which was about a two-minute drive. We could have walked, but I just didn't feel like it and figured they didn't either.

"What's going on over there?" Smoke asked, pointing at the house under construction in the distance as we pulled up in front of my house.

"My best friend, Gabe, is coming home, they're building a house. It should be done in the next month or so."

We went inside, and I told them where the laundry room was if they wanted to use it, then showed them to their rooms and went to mine, telling them to make themselves at home.

Zoey followed me and jumped on the bed and laid down, and I sat next to her rubbing her head, just letting it soak in that I was actually here, in my own house, in my own room.

After a few minutes, I unpacked the pink bag from the plane. With a roll of my eyes, I tossed the box of condoms in the drawer of my nightstand.

I went into the bathroom and stripped off my clothes and the bandages, and stood in front of the mirror. I couldn't help but gasp at the reflection looking back at me. I was filthy. No, worse than filthy, I was disgusting.

It looked like I'd gone several rounds with Mohammad Ali. My left eye was swollen and severely bloodshot, and I had a serious black eye. I had bruises in every shade of purple and blue on my face, neck, shoulders, arms, breasts, and legs.

My face was tender and throbbed, and the cuts that Cole had sewn looked like little caterpillars on my arm and chest. I also had quite a few scratches I had no idea how I'd gotten and more than a few bug bites.

I don't know how long I stood there looking in the mirror, turning my head this way and that, leaning forward to get a close-up view. My reflection was not pretty.

I brushed my teeth for a while and took the time to unbraid and brush my hair before I got into the shower. The hot water stung my bruised body.

I washed my hair three times before it finally felt clean, then I put conditioner in it and, avoiding the major wounds, scrubbed my body head to toe twice, which hurt like hell.

All the adrenaline that had kept me going was gone. My body was beyond sore and throbbing. Someone had drugged me, kidnapped me, taken me out of the country and sold me. I'd fought men, stabbed someone, almost been gang raped, been beaten, and cut, stitched up twice, and spent days running through the jungle trying to stay alive.

There was no more adrenaline to power me, no one to run from, no immediate danger. Without warning, all the emotions of the past week and a half came crashing in on me.

The tears came like a faucet had been turned on. The tears turned to sobs I couldn't hold back if my life depended on it. My legs felt weak, and I ended up on the floor of the shower, my knees pulled up and my arms wrapped around them, my sobs causing my body to shudder.

The screams that came out of me felt torn from my throat. The water rained down on me, and I cried like

I've cried only once before. I was in the shower for more than an hour, staying there until there wasn't another tear to cry.

When I was out of the shower and dressed, I found Cole and Smoke sitting on the couch in the living room with Zoey curled up next to Smoke, who was using her as an armrest.

I couldn't help but smile when I saw them; they were wearing Give Him A Chance shorts, and Smoke was wearing a Give Him A Chance t-shirt. They were probably wearing Give Him A Chance underwear too.

Chance is so smart, a marketing genius really; they were a walking, talking spectacular billboard of advertising. I was glad to see they had made themselves comfortable and weren't acting like guests.

This was the first time I'd seen Cole clean and not in his cammies. He was wearing shorts and was shirtless, showing off his big biceps, wide shoulders, twenty pack abs, tapered waist, and sexy as hell V muscles.

His dog tags were resting in a smattering of chest hair, and he had a happy trail that led to the promised land. His long legs were well-muscled and stretched out in front of him.

He had tats on his biceps, and I saw the large anchor tattoo that curved around his right side. It *was* exactly like mine, just much bigger.

I took my time studying every glorious inch of him. He was magnificent, and I felt like I couldn't catch my breath looking at him.

Fuck on a fuck sandwich. My brain is going to go into meltdown again.

I was definitely going to need more than a few minutes to recover from the sight of a half-naked Cole Montgomery.

Chapter 27

Cole

Alex's house was a single story, built in a 'U' shape. After the entryway, the large living room and big kitchen were open with a table and chairs next to the kitchen. The living room had a big couch and a couple of big comfortable looking chairs with a large flatscreen hanging on the wall over a fireplace.

The wall on one end of the living room was glass with French doors leading out to a large, covered deck and a courtyard that the 'U' shape of the house created.

The deck had a couple of small couches, chairs and small tables, ceiling fans and a decent size BBQ. The courtyard was Zen-like with flowers and small trees, some grass, and a brick path down the middle. There was a good size pool and what looked like a large pavilion in the distance past the courtyard.

It was a big house, but not a mansion. It was comfortable and homey, not fancy. It was warm and inviting rather than cold and sterile.

Alex took Smoke to his room on one side of the house, and when she returned, I followed her to my room on the other. The long hallway wall was entirely made of glass looking out into the courtyard, and I could see the opposite side of the courtyard was also glass.

"I don't see any curtains, what do you do if you want privacy?" I asked her as we reached the end of the hallway.

She flipped a switch on the wall, and the entire wall of glass turned from clear to frosted.

She turned and smiled at me, "There's a switch on either side of the hall. Pretty cool, huh?" She flipped the switch and the wall turned back to clear glass.

"Very."

Alex's room was at the end of the hall, and she indicated the room next to hers as mine. I'd finished my shower when I heard the first sobs coming from her room. Her bedroom door was open, and I wanted to go in there, gather her up and hold her close, tell her she was safe and that everything would be okay, but I didn't.

My hands fisted, and I paced, listening to her. She'd spent days controlling her emotions. Hell, she'd probably kept them in the entire week. She hadn't allowed those emotions out, but now she sounded as if her life was over, and while it was good she was finally letting it out, I hated that she was in there all alone, crying by herself.

The sound was pure agony, like a wounded animal in pain. I was even more concerned when her dog came running into my room whining and looking at me as if she were as worried as I was.

I couldn't go in there, and I couldn't stand hearing her pain. I had to get away from it. So I left my room with Zoey following me. Smoke was at the end of the hall, standing with his laundry, his face reflecting the concern I felt.

"Bring your laundry."

I nodded and went into my room and came back out and met up with him in the laundry room.

"Do you think she's alright?" Smoke asked me as we loaded the washer.

"I don't know. I hope so. This needed to happen, but it's not easy to listen to."

When I saw Alex again, I was glad to see with my own eyes that she seemed okay after hearing her in the shower, but I wasn't convinced she wasn't putting on an act. She was clean, and even though she was still bruised and battered, she looked completely different.

Her beautiful auburn hair was loose and free and still damp. It was several shades lighter than it had been, and I noticed it had lighter highlights that hadn't been there before.

It wasn't kinky and dull the way it had been in the jungle. It was thick and shiny, slightly wavy and hanging to her waist. I couldn't ever remember being this fascinated by a woman's hair.

When she got close enough, I could smell her; she smelled fresh and clean, but there was something else I couldn't identify. Whatever it was, it was hypnotizing.

She was wearing a well-worn gray NAVY t-shirt that molded to her body, NAVY standing out proudly because of her full high breasts. Those perfect tits.

She was wearing socks and jeans that drew attention to her long legs and that delectable ass. Her body was made for sin, which I knew all too well. She was the sexiest woman I'd ever met, and she didn't even know it, and that unconscious sexuality was extremely captivating.

Alex sat in one of the chairs, pulling her legs under her, "Just a warning, this isn't going to be like any debrief you've ever had before. I expect it will be more family dysfunction than a real debrief."

"What do you mean?" I asked.

"You'll see."

It wasn't long before the phone rang, and when Alex hung up, she told us the Commander was at the main house. I put on a t-shirt, and we all put on shoes and headed out with her dog following us.

The Commander and the team were out front when we drove up. Alex got out of the truck and walked straight into the Commander's arms, and he hugged her tight.

"Jesus, fuck, Jellybean," he said after seeing her face, turning her head, looking at her injuries.

"I'm okay, promise."

"I thought I told you to stay at the main house."

Alex grinned at him, "And I thought you understood after all these years, you're not the boss of me. Reaper and Smoke are there; I'm perfectly fine."

The Commander didn't argue; he just hugged her tight again.

"Rec room?" Alex asked.

The Commander nodded his head, "Yeah."

We followed Alex and the Commander inside. The house smelled of food cooking.

The living room was large, with a staircase leading upstairs. There was a hallway to the left leading to more rooms. As we walked, we passed a massive kitchen on our right.

No ordinary kitchen, it had industrial appliances, an enormous refrigerator with a matching freezer, a ten-burner stove with a pot or pan of something cooking on every burner, and two huge ovens.

There was an island in the center of it at least eight feet long. The island was almost completely covered with food, including at least five pies. The only occupant was a plump, middle-aged woman standing at the stove humming to herself.

We entered the rec room, and Alex closed and locked the door once we were all inside. The room was enormous. There was a small stage tucked in the back left corner with a baby grand piano, a drum kit, and a couple of guitars on stands, a door that said 'Armory' next to the stage, and a huge table and chairs that could easily seat twenty that had all sorts of snacks laid out on it.

There was a pool table, a poker table, and an enormous collection of DVDs on either side of a large fireplace with two comfortable looking chairs and a small table between them. One wall had a big window and door that led out to a large deck. There were photographs everywhere.

Six couches sat in the center of the room, three arranged in a 'U' in front of a freestanding wall maybe eight feet long that looked like it was there just to hold the massive TV, with three matching couches behind them in a 'U' facing the stage, coffee tables sat in the middle of them, and there were small tables and lamps at each end.

On the right was a bathroom and kitchen area with a counter and stools. It didn't have a stove or oven but had a huge fridge, a built-in microwave and a counter with a coffee maker and toaster oven.

There was a bar next to the kitchen area that looked well-stocked with several under counter beverage fridges. Everything looked like it was sized to service an army.

As the team was looking around, Alex went to the bar for beers, and I followed to help her. She grabbed a shot glass and poured a shot of tequila.

"Want one?" she asked me.

I shook my head, "No, I'm good."

Alex downed the shot and poured another one.

Leaning toward her, I whispered in her ear, "Jellybean?"

She held a finger up and whispered, "No. You do not get to say that name." She poked my chest with her finger for emphasis.

Smiling wide at her, I grabbed her finger and held it, "Little Jellybean."

She smiled back at me, "Stop it. Which part of no don't you understand, the N or the O?"

Neither of us noticed the way the Commander was watching us from across the room.

The Commander called to her from the table, "Are you okay to go through some photos of the night you were taken?"

I reluctantly let go of her finger.

Alex downed the second shot of tequila before she answered him, "Yeah."

The team sat at the table, and Alex and I brought the beers, passed them out and sat down. The Commander gave her a large stack of photos, and Alex flipped through them, pulling a stack from the top of the pile and setting them aside before she started looking through the rest of them.

While Alex looked at pictures, the Commander and the rest of the team sat around the table talking and digging into the snacks.

Sitting next to her, I started looking at the photos she set aside. They were of Alex on stage the night she was kidnapped. In all the pictures, she was wearing a short emerald green, skintight dress with short sleeves and a large cut out in the bodice that exposed the tops of her breasts and emphasized her cleavage.

She had black knee-high boots on her feet. Looking at the pictures, I could see she'd definitely lost weight since she was kidnapped because the dress showed every magnificent curve of her body.

There were about ten pictures of her backstage that were obviously professional photographs. All of them were stunning, but one picture, in particular, caught my eye. It was shot from slightly above her, the angle showcasing that beautiful cleavage.

She was standing in front of a white brick wall, one leg out in front of her, the other bent with the sole of her booted foot against it. Her arms were spread out from her sides with her palms against the bricks.

Her hair looked like it was blowing around her head and flowing over her arms and onto the bricks. Her head was turned slightly, looking up at the camera, her lips parted. The look on her face could only be described as seductive. She was spectacular. A low rumble came from somewhere deep inside me.

The sound got Alex's attention, and she glanced at the pictures I was looking at. She didn't look at me, still going through the other photos.

"That's one of Oscar's photos from before the show. Stupid publicity shots. They're ridiculous. I look like a clown. Just throw those away, they don't help us here."

She had completely misinterpreted my reaction. Not only was I not going to throw them away, but I didn't want the rest of the team or anyone else to see them for that matter.

The team was passing around some of the photos of her on stage.

Jax whistled, "That's some dress."

"Yeah, Gabe and I had an argument about that dress," Alex replied, not looking up from the photos she was looking through.

"What was the argument about?" Boomer asked her.

"I complained that it was like a second skin and screamed, look at me, I have boobs. Gabe said that was the basis of its appeal."

"I'm with Gabe on this one," Smoke told her.

I glared across the table at him. Smoke smiled and shrugged.

"Looks like you lost the argument," Midas said.

"I always lose the girly clothes arguments," Alex stated, matter-of-factly.

She was almost finished going through all the pictures when I realized she was making three stacks.

I turned and looked at her, "Why three stacks?"

"The ones I want to keep. The kidnappers, and the rest of them."

"The kidnappers are here?" I asked uneasily.

Alex handed me a stack of about fifteen photos and tapped her finger on two men clearly visible in the background, "These are the clearest pictures of the men who took me."

The whole table started to pay attention as we passed the photos around.

In all the pictures, the two men were near her, watching her. In some of the pictures, they were together. In some, they were separate, but they were never far away and always watching her.

There was a pounding on the door, and Alex got up to see who was there.

"Sorry I'm late," a voice called out, and when we turned to look, we all jumped out of our seats and stood at attention, saluting the Rear Admiral who had just walked in the room.

"Make them stop that, Uncle Doug," Alex told him.

The Rear Admiral saluted us as he snatched her up and hugged her, but we all remained standing.

"Is she hugging Rear Admiral Faraday?" Smoke whispered to me.

"I believe that's what we're seeing," I whispered back, watching them.

"Did she just call Rear Admiral Faraday Uncle Doug?" Jax muttered from across the table.

"That's what it sounded like," Midas answered.

"Uncle Doug, tell them to sit down and relax. Tell them you're just a regular guy today, and not Rear Admiral fancy pants everyone has to salute."

The Rear Admiral looked at her and smiled, “Rear Admiral fancy pants?”

“You know what I mean. Tell them. They’ve just spent days running through the jungle, they’re tired. Let them relax and drink beer, they earned it.”

He smiled at us, “Gentlemen, Jellybean says you should sit and relax and drink beer.”

We all sat down, looking at each other like we’d entered an alternative universe.

He turned back to Alex, “Better?”

“Much. Thank you.”

The Rear Admiral looked at her as they walked toward the table, "Are these your only injuries?"

"I have some cuts."

The Rear Admiral looked at all of us, "What kind of cuts?"

"Bastards cut her with a knife, sir," I told him.

"Show us," the Rear Admiral demanded.

Alex lifted the sleeve of her shirt. She hadn’t bothered to bandage her arm after her shower, and it didn’t escape my notice that she wasn’t saying anything about the wounds on her chest.

“Son of a bitch,” the Rear Admiral said gruffly.

“What the fuck? You need to see a doctor,” the Commander chimed in.

"Reaper’s been giving me antibiotics. I called and made an appointment to see the doctor, so let's not lose our minds,” Alex told them.

It was odd hearing her call me Reaper. I wasn’t sure I liked it; I’d gotten used to and liked hearing her call me Cole.

The Rear Admiral looked at the team, "We owe you a huge debt of gratitude."

"Just doing our job, sir," I replied.

Alex turned and looked at me, suddenly looking sad, and it was only then that I realized what I'd said and immediately wanted to take it back.

Before I could say anything, the Commander received a text and asked us to move to the couches in front of the huge TV. Alex picked up a couple of pictures and went to the bar and downed another shot before following us but couldn't get to a seat because when the team saw the President of the United States on the screen, we stopped and stood stiff at attention again.

"Stop it. Just sit down." Alex told us. "Uncle John, tell them to relax and sit," Alex called out.

Midas looked at me and mouthed, 'Uncle John?' I shrugged and shook my head in response.

"Yes, of course, please sit, gentlemen. Jellybean, thank god, we were so worried."

We were moving to take our seats, so Alex had to wait for us.

"Where are you?" the President asked.

"I'm here," Alex said as she scooted by everyone and took the empty seat I'd left in the middle of the couch between Midas and me.

"Oh, hell no," the President said, pissed, slamming his hand on his desk when he saw her face. He pointed at her, "I want the motherfuckers responsible for...that."

"I'm okay, Uncle John."

"Like hell you are."

"Bastards took a knife to her too, Viper," the Rear Admiral told him.

"What! Let's see it."

"Big mouth," Alex told the Rear Admiral as she turned and lifted the sleeve of her shirt.

"Mad Dog would have our balls if he saw this. Jellybean, is this Shadow's team?" The President asked Alex.

"Yes. This is Jax, Smoke, Midas, Reaper, Bruiser, and Boomer, pointing to each of us as she said our names. "Guys, this is Viper or John, pointing to the President. Shadow or Mal, pointing to the Commander and Raider or Doug pointing to the Rear Admiral." She looked at the President, "You should be proud of them; they're awesome."

"I am proud, but they're SEALs; it's not like they were going to fuck it up."

"Hooyah," Alex said.

"Hooyah!" The entire team, the President, the Rear Admiral, and the Commander, repeated loudly, making Alex smile.

The President grinned at her, "I hope you didn't give the team as much grief as you give us."

"I'm sure they'll be glad to be rid of me," Alex told him.

"Actually, sir, Ms. Walker was no trouble at all," I said.

"We consider Killer one of us, sir," Smoke told him.

"Can we dispense with the sirs and Ms. Walker shit? Tell them they don't have to do that today. Tell them to call you Viper, SEAL to SEAL. Or John," Alex told him.

"Killer?" The President asked, ignoring her.

The Commander looked at the President, "We're never going to hear the end of this."

The Rear Admiral laughed, "She's going to petition for a name change again."

"No. They can call her whatever they want, but she's our Jellybean. Mad Dog named her, that's not changing," the President told them.

Alex dropped her head back, "Please. Stop. Talking. I'm begging you."

I smiled and leaned closer, whispering in her ear, "Jellybean."

"Stop it," Alex whispered, smiling back.

Neither of us noticed the President, the Rear Admiral and the Commander sharing a look.

The President grinned at her, "You find a boyfriend yet?"

Alex rolled her eyes, "Here we go."

"She's still not even dating," the Commander replied.

"How are we ever getting grandchildren if you don't date?" the President asked her.

"Kill me now. You know you guys are still young enough to have kids of your own to torture, right?"

"Not going down that road."

"No, thank you."

"Not after what we went through with you."

"Oh my god, the gossip girls need a hobby. Did it ever occur to you that you're embarrassing?"

The President smiled at her, "No, not really."

"Well, you are, so save it for family time. You three are done talking now; we have company, time to shut up."

"This team brought you home; they are family now," the President told her.

"Trust me; they don't want you monkeys or this circus. Don't you have a country to run?"

The President smiled at her again, "Right. Let's get to it."

It took a while, but the seven of us ran down the events, starting with the kidnapping until we made our way out of Peru.

When we were finished, the President looked at each of us, "Gentlemen, you have our deepest gratitude. We're not an emotional bunch, but Alex is the heart of us. This could have gone another way, and we might have lost her, and that would have destroyed us.

"Shadow, keep me updated. Jellybean, your dad would be so proud of you. I'm beyond proud of you. I'm going to make time to get to the ranch to see you...and kick your ass on the field."

Alex laughed, "You wish."

"I love you, sweet girl."

"I love you too."

"Shadow, Raider, gentlemen," the President said with a nod and disappeared from the screen.

“Kick your ass on the field. Is that paintball?” I whispered to her.

Alex smiled wide and nodded, “Yeah. See, even the President thinks it's fun.”

Chapter 28

Alex

After Uncle John disappeared, everyone except Cole, Smoke and I got up. I didn't know why they stayed, but I stayed behind to make a call.

Gabe's face popped up on the screen, "Oh my god, gorgeous, look what they did to your face," his eyes starting to tear up.

"Seriously, you cry one tear, and I'm hanging up."

"Right. You're alive, and that's what matters, but your face is nasty."

"Thanks, you're so sweet. Listen, I need to ask you something." I held up a photo, "Do you know these two guys?"

The team didn't seem to be paying attention to me until I held the photo up.

"The bodyguards. Are they the ones who took you?" He asked.

I nodded.

"What do you mean bodyguards?" Cole asked Gabe.

"Chance and I talked about them because at the after-party, they weren't having any fun, never had a drink, and just kept looking around. We thought they were someone's bodyguards."

"Did you see if they were with anyone else?" Cole asked.

"No. They were either separate or together; I never saw them with anyone else."

I held up the picture again, "What about the suits?"

Without hesitation, Gabe replied, "They're Adolfo Casaretti's."

"Can you make a list of where you could get one?"

"Don't need to; you can only get them in one place in New York. Each one is handmade. They're fantastic suits."

"Expensive?" I asked.

Gabe smiled, "What do you consider expensive?"

I rolled my eyes, "How much?"

"Five thousand minimum."

"Five thousand for a suit? Is it lined with gold or something?"

"Hardy-har-har. No, smartass."

"You need psychiatric help if you're paying five grand for a suit."

"This coming from the girl who lives in forty-dollar jeans. You are disgracefully fashion deficient. If I let you pick out your girl clothes, you'd look Amish, so your opinion means nothing, and I said five thousand *minimum*."

"Seriously, get help. Maybe medication."

"Fuck off." There was no heat or malice in Gabe's words.

"You fuck off," I shot back, smiling.

"God, it's good to have you back. I seriously thought I lost you."

Gabe suddenly rolled out of view of the camera, and Chance's face appeared on the screen, "Hi sweetie, so good to see you."

"Hey Chance, it's good to *be* seen."

Chance looked around the room, "Hi guys, thank you for bringing her home. Mal, I'm going to New York tomorrow, you want me to take a photo to Adolfo and ask about these guys?"

"Can you pick me up on your way?" Uncle Mal asked.

"Of course."

"Good. We can talk to this Casaretti and see if he can give us anything on these assholes. Can you send me flight details?"

"On it." Chance blew me a kiss, "Love you, sweetie, see you soon."

"Love you too."

Chance waved and disappeared from the screen, and Gabe rolled back into view, "I'm hitching a ride, just FYI."

Looking around, Gabe switched to Italian and smiled at me, "So, which one is the man who *finally* got your attention and made you all gooey?"

I responded in Italian, "I'm *not* gooey."

"You could not be gooier. You're a gooey smitten kitten. He's the smoldering one on your left, isn't he?"

"Yes. And the one on my right can understand you."

Gabe looked at Smoke, "Hello, handsome one that can understand me. This is a big day for her, so I trust you'll refrain from telling your friend what we say?"

Smoke smiled at him and gave him a thumbs up.

"As I was saying, he's built like a fucking mountain and honey, you should climb that mountain. Look at him; he's gorgeous."

Smoke was smiling, looking like he was enjoying himself.

"He is, isn't he."

Gabe shrieked, "Look at you claiming a man. He likes you."

"No, he doesn't. I was just a job; he confirmed that when Uncle Doug showed up."

"Sweetie, he can't take his eyes off you."

"Because we're speaking another language."

"No, he's watching you with something else on his mind." Gabe sat forward, staring at me, "Here's the plan, just barge in his room and jump on the incredible hunk. You know you want to. For once, take a risk.

"Dust the cobwebs off your vagina and put your girly bugs on him. I'm one hundred percent sure you will not be disappointed."

I was beet red; I could feel it, and Smoke was coughing to try and hide his laughter.

"Did I mention shut up? We're done talking about this."

"Fine, we'll pick it up later, but seriously, jump him. You want to, he wants you to. I have no doubt he'd be great to jump on. Listen, this is really easy; girl likes boy, boy likes girl, bing, bam, boom...sex."

Gabe put his hands together, "I'm *begging you* to go for it."

I slapped a hand over my face shaking my head, but I was laughing. "You're a pervert with a one-track mind. Oh, and by the way, I so totally hate you right now."

"Hey, I'm just trying to get you laid. Getting laid is awesome. Orgasms are super awesome, especially when someone who knows what they're doing is giving them to you."

My face was crimson, but Smoke was looking at Gabe, smiling and nodding his head.

"See, Cutie McDimples agrees."

Smoke barked out a laugh.

"Shut up," I muttered.

"We need to finish this debrief, so wrap it up, kids," Uncle Mal called from across the room.

Switching to English, I whined, "Ah, c'mon Uncle Mal, just five more minutes."

"Pleaseee," Gabe begged.

Uncle Mal shook his head, but he was smiling, and Gabe and I laughed.

"I love you, Gabe, and I promise you I'm okay."

"I love you too. I'll see you tomorrow." He switched back to Italian, "Seriously gorgeous, jump on that man. Ride him till you can't walk."

I shook my head and flipped him off, "Goodbye, Gabe."

"Bye, gorgeous, see you soon."

The screen went black.

Cole leaned over and whispered in my ear, "What did he say that made you react like that?"

My face went scarlet again, but I didn't answer.

Smoke turned to me and spoke in Italian, "Your friend is right, he *would* let you jump on him."

"You shut up too," I responded in English, getting up and heading for the bar, Smoke's laughter following me.

I wanted nothing more than to follow Gabe's advice, but Cole had made it clear I was only a job to him.

Chapter 29

Cole

"What was that about?" I asked Smoke after Alex walked away.

Smoke smiled a smile that almost split his face, "I've been sworn to secrecy, but her friend was just trying to help her make a decision."

Smoke and I got up and joined everyone else at the table. "Alex, we've decided you should stay at Doug's place until this is resolved. Doug can take some time off to watch over you," the Commander told her.

"No," she responded, opening a bottle of sparkling water and taking a drink.

"Whoever this is could just show up at the ranch; Doug's place is safer," the Commander argued.

"Nothing would please me more than this psycho coming on my ranch. I'll leave the damn gate open."

Alex looked at the Commander, "Remember when that weirdo super fan showed up? After that, we put the security at the front gate and set up cameras outside and motion detectors in the most vulnerable areas.

"No one is getting on this property without someone knowing about it. I'm not hiding, and I'm not going to let this asshole dictate what I can and can't do."

"Alex...."

"No. I'm ready for the jerk this time. If he wants me, he can come and try and get me before I put a bullet in him."

Her anger was obvious as she turned and started walking for the door.

"Where are you going?" the Commander asked.

"I'm going to my happy place. I have my phone if you feel the need to check on me."

"Do you mind if I put a tracking app on your phone? I'd also like to tap into your security system if that's okay with you, and it probably wouldn't be a bad idea to put a tracker on you," Midas told her.

I was surprised when Alex walked back and handed her phone to him without argument.

"I'll show you the security system later if that's okay, and I'll gladly wear a tracker."

Midas nodded and pulled out his phone, clicked buttons on both phones, then handed her phone back. She turned around and left without another word.

The Commander let out a heavy sigh once the door closed behind her.

"Where is she going?" Jax asked.

"To the barn," both the Commander and the Rear Admiral responded in unison.

Boomer turned and looked at the Commander, "I'll stay here and keep an eye on her for a little while."

"Yeah, me too," Bruiser said, surprising all of us.

I wanted to say I'd stay, but I didn't. I also didn't want to explore how it made me feel knowing Boomer and Bruiser would be staying, and I wouldn't.

*****

After the biggest dinner I've ever seen and eating the best steak any of us had ever eaten, which Alex confirmed was from one of her cows, Alex, Smoke, and I headed back to Alex's house, each of us carrying leftovers Maggie had insisted we take.

When we got there, Alex put away the food, said good night, and we all went to our rooms. It wasn't long before I heard her crying.

This time I wasn't going to leave her to suffer on her own. I didn't bother to get dressed, heading to her room in nothing but my boxer briefs.

Her door was open, and the lights were off, but there was a nightlight near the bathroom door providing enough light to see where I was going.

I didn't knock, just walked through the door, closed it behind me and climbed in bed behind her. I pulled her into me, holding her tight, whispering in her ear, "I got you. You're safe now."

She wiggled until her body fit perfectly against mine and cried.

I heard her sniffling and reached over and got a tissue from the nightstand, "Blow," I ordered.

Alex blew her nose and tossed the tissue into the trash can on her side of the bed.

"Better?"

"No. I'm crying like a giiirl," she complained as another wave of tears came.

She sounded so insulted that she was crying, which amused me, but her tears almost gutted me.

I let her cry herself out, holding her tight, brushing her hair off her face. When her tears dried up, she rolled over and faced me.

I held her face in my hands, wiping away the stray tears on her cheeks, "For the record, you're not a girl, you're all woman, and I, for one, am extremely happy about that. I'll always come for you, angel. No one is going to take you away from me."

For the life of me, I couldn't figure out why I said that. She was a job; nothing was supposed to happen between us, and yet here I was next to her in bed, holding her tight against me and telling her no one was going to take her away from me.

But hearing her sobs earlier and seeing her tears now was like a switch being flipped inside me. I was ready to kill anyone who upset her, anyone who dared hurt her.

The thought of her being hurt or killed was abhorrent. There was something about her that made me want to keep any danger from touching her. I wanted to slay all her dragons and keep her safe.

“Are you in pain?”

“I’m still a little throbby, but it’s really not that bad. I’ve felt worse.”

“So, Spanish and Italian, do you speak any other languages?”

“Do *you* speak any other languages?”

I shook my head, “No.”

Alex looked at me, tears still clinging to her long eyelashes and started speaking French, her voice soft and sultry. She said something and put her palm on my cheek, staring at me, her eyes glittering with desire.

"That sounded sexy as hell. What did you say?"

She immediately averted her eyes from me.

"You smell good," she told me.

"I don't think that's what you said, and you smell good too."

"You just got used to me being stinky."

I started nuzzling her neck and kissing a path along her throat. "No, you smell amazing. Do you smell like this all over?" Her head tilted to the side, inviting me to continue.

My hands were moving with a mind of their own, running along the curve of her waist, over her hips. She wiggled and moaned, and I couldn't hold back my own groan in response.

I knew I should stop, but I didn't want to. What is it about this woman that obliterated my control? I wanted her more than I'd wanted a woman in a long time. Hell, maybe more than *any* woman.

She laid her arm across my chest, and I put my arm around her, my hand wandering down her back to her ass and up under her spaghetti strap camisole, caressing her soft skin. In response, her hand started lazily roaming my chest.

"Molest crying women often?"

"Not very often."

Actually never.

Alex unexpectedly flipped herself on top of me and looked down at me, "Cole Montgomery, did you just make a joke?"

Her hair was like a curtain around me; she was disheveled, her face was a battered mess, and she was still so fucking sexy. My hands were gripping her hips, while she let her hand roam over my chest, shoulder, and bicep. Her eyes staring into mine.

I couldn't resist the gorgeous, funny, sexy woman on top of me. I wanted inside her, wanted to taste her, watch her come apart for me. I knew I was making a huge mistake, but I just couldn't stop myself.

"I don't do relationships. I don't have what it takes for that. But every woman should have at least one one-night stand in her life, let me be yours. I know you want me. Take what you want, Alex, let me show you what you've been missing," I brushed her hair away from her face, "But before you decide, you need to understand, I *will* walk away."

"Why don't you have what it takes?" She asked, curious.

"SEALs have to keep a lot of secrets. We can't say where we're going or how long we'll be there, how long we'll be gone."

"That makes things hard, but not impossible. So, what's the real reason?"

I debated on whether or not I should tell her the truth before answering, "There's a lot of darkness in me."

Her brows drew together, "Are you abusive?"

"No!"

I could tell she was trying not to grin at the harshness of my response. "Well, news flash, there's darkness in everyone. What you do is necessary. It's not like the people you come up against are trying to give you flowers or create world peace. You run into places other people are running out of. You go places no one wants to go. You make the world a better place. You save lives. You saved *me*."

"Alex," I whispered.

"I know it's not PC, but some people deserve killing."

She palmed my face and kissed me lightly. Her expression changed, there was a fierceness in her eyes, but her voice was soft and steady, "You're not just a good man, Cole, you're a hero. You hear me? A fucking hero."

She stared at me for a moment as if she was looking for something in my expression before she spoke again, "So, does the one-night end when the sun rises?"

I was still reeling from what she'd said, and the abrupt change in topic was unexpected, but I answered as best I could, "It ends when we both leave this room."

"That doesn't seem like a lot of time. Are there other rules?"

"Other rules?"

"Yeah, like I'm not allowed to talk to you after, or you pretend I don't exist tomorrow?"

"No. No other rules, and I won't pretend you don't exist."

She climbed off me and out of bed. I hadn't expected her to consider my offer or agree but wasn't expecting the disappointment that washed over me when she got off me, and I waited for her to tell me to get out.

But instead, she walked across the room to the dresser and turned on a small lamp that bathed the room with a soft glow before she turned back and faced me. I was watching her closely, wondering what she was going to do.

With only a moment of hesitation, she reached down, grabbed the hem of her camisole, and whipped it over her head, exposing her breasts to me. The sight caused a sharp intake of my breath.

Putting her thumbs in the waistband of her matching sleep shorts, she teased them down until they dropped to the floor, and she kicked them away. It was the sexiest striptease I'd ever witnessed, and she wasn't even trying.

She stood there, gloriously naked in front of me, not moving, not trying to hide. She was letting me take my fill of the sight of her, and it was Hot. As. Fuck.

She tossed her hair over her shoulder, which had fallen forward over her breasts when she'd bent to take off her sleep shorts. She was hiding nothing from me.

Looking at me with vulnerability and anticipation, she told me, "I accept your terms."

This was not what I had expected. I could see she was nervous even while boldly standing in front of me, staring at me with those piercing green eyes. Her trust slammed into me, and that turned me on even more. She made me feel like a king.

Even with the bruising, her skin was creamy. My eyes raked hungrily over every square inch of her naked flesh, her glorious tits, her nipples standing at attention, begging for my touch. The curve of her waist, the flare of her hips, her long shapely legs, her beautiful pussy.

My eyes never left hers as I got out of bed and stalked toward her. My hands immediately caressed the curve of her waist and hips, back up to the swell of her breasts.

"Fuck, angel, you're so beautiful."

Her skin felt like silk under my hands. Smiling, my fingers traced along her 'Fight Like A Girl' tattoo.

When she spoke, it was a breathy whisper, "You're overdressed."

I took her face in my hands and looked down at her, "Are you sure?"

I didn't know what I was going to do if she suddenly told me she'd changed her mind.

She rested her hands on my chest before telling me, "I admit, I'm a little nervous, but I've never been more sure of anything in my life."

I leaned down and kissed her, deeply, meaningfully, as if I were claiming her.

Picking her up, I carried her to the bed and gently set her down. The feel of her skin against mine was sensual and electric. Stripping off my boxers, I climbed into bed next to her.

She seemed to want to touch me everywhere at once, gripping me, feeling me. Her hands on my waist, my ass, my back, in my hair, digging her fingers into my biceps. The feel of her hands on me sparked my senses awake. It felt like she was trying to absorb me through her hands.

I kissed her, my hands tangled in her hair, angling her mouth, taking the kiss deeper. It was a kiss of absolute possession. She rocked her hips against me, clutching at me. I ended the kiss and began kissing down her neck, my hand moving to her breast.

She threw her head back and gasped in response. I cupped her breast, rubbing my thumb over her peaked nipple, rolling it between my finger and thumb. She arched her back, thrusting her breast into my hand. I'd never wanted a woman so fiercely.

"I love how you respond to me."

Breathless, she replied, "You feel so good."

"I've been thinking about doing this for days," I told her as my mouth latched onto one of her nipples, and I groaned. Her back bowed off the bed in response.

I licked and sucked and nipped, swirling my tongue around and around, alternating one then the other. My mouth on one breast, my hand kneading and teasing the other, while she writhed and moaned.

I looked up at her. She was watching me, her mouth slightly open, her breathing quick.

"I knew you'd have great tits, but the reality is so much better than my imagination," I told her as I squeezed them, gently twisting her peaked nipples. She dug her fingers into my biceps and cried out my name.

My hand slid down her stomach, her muscles fluttering at my touch, her leg moving restlessly against mine. My fingers moving between her legs, she gasped and let out a moan of pleasure when I touched her core, and she opened her legs for me.

I kissed a trail up her neck, "You're so wet. Is this for me?" I whispered in her ear as I ran my fingers through her slippery folds. Her desire felt like it was branding me.

"Because of you," she sighed, rocking her hips.

I slipped my finger inside her, "Christ, baby, you're so tight; you're going to strangle my cock."

I pulled my finger out and slipped a second finger inside her, and when she whispered my name, it sounded like a plea.

I could smell her arousal. My fingers continued to work in and out of her while I took my time kissing down her body.

"Tell me what you want."

She raised herself onto her elbows, her hair puddling on the bed, and looked at me, her eyes hazy with passion.

"I don't know." Gasp....

"So far, it's all pretty fucking good." Whimper....

"I trust you. Use your best judgment, Cole."

She gave me a lustful look before she fell back onto the bed with a moan.

When I dropped my mouth to the core of her, she was exposed and wet. Her hands went to my hair, her fingers digging into my scalp, her hips thrusting.

I inhaled her scent and rumbled from somewhere deep inside, "You smell unbelievable; I could stay here all night."

I ran my tongue through her slit and lapped at her clit; she gasped and bowed her back, softly calling out my name. And I wanted to hear it again.

If ecstasy had a taste, it would be Alex. The taste of her was my new favorite thing. I felt her trembling for more, and it was driving me wild.

I went down on her like a man possessed. She bucked and squirmed, and I used my free hand to easily hold her where I wanted her while my tongue kept up the onslaught, swirling over and around her clit, my fingers easily sliding in and out of her.

She was mumbling incoherently, her hips rocking in time with my fingers and mouth, her hands fisting the sheets, her head rolling from side to side. I wasn't sure I'd ever been this hard.

“Don’t stop, Cole. Please don’t stop,” she begged breathlessly.

My mouth on her clit, I curled my fingers inside her, and she began to tremble and shudder until I felt her exploding, calling out my name.

I was caressing her stomach, her waist, nipping the inside of her thighs, then kissing the sting away, my fingers still moving inside her.

She rose up on her elbows and grinned at me. She looked disheveled and satisfied, "What did you just do to me?"

She reached down and rubbed her thumb over my mouth. “Your mouth is pure magic.”

She was smiling, and I couldn’t help smiling back. I sucked her thumb into my mouth and circled my tongue around it. Her eyes closed, and her internal muscles pulsed around my fingers in reaction.

“That was the first orgasm I ever had with a man,” she admitted shyly.

Knowing I was the first was a huge turn-on. “It will not be your last,” I told her confidently, smirking at her. "Please tell me you have a condom?"

"Nightstand," she pointed and collapsed back on the bed with a groan.

I opened the box, took out a condom it and rolled it on. I entered her gently, slowly, holding back because of her inexperience. My jaw was clenched tight. I pushed into her inch by slow inch, stretching her and letting her adjust, but it was taking all my control not to push all the way into her tight, hot sheath, and I groaned in agony from the effort.

She grabbed my ass, pulling me toward her, "Cole, it's okay, let go, I won't break."

"I don't want to hurt you."

"It probably can't be avoided. You'll make it better. Just do it."

Her trust in me felt like my heart was being squeezed. She pulled away from me and, before I could stop her, shoved back against me, pulling me by the ass, forcing me inside her. She gasped, her eyes wide, staring at me as I bottomed out.

I held still, giving her a chance to adjust, but every muscle was tight from the effort. Her internal muscles were clenching around me. I leaned down to kiss her. When I deepened the kiss, I felt her relax around me until she was rolling her hips against me and moaning into my mouth.

I ended the kiss and sighed her name in her ear, soft and desperate, "You're so tight. You feel so fucking good."

I pulled back and slid in and out of her with long, slow strokes. I didn't fuck her. I made love to her, which wasn't like me.

When she wrapped her strong legs around me, squeezing tight, it felt incredible and demolished any ability I had to go slow.

Her wet, tight heat surrounding my cock; I could barely hold back. The feeling pulled the groan out of me, and she made the most delectable sounds of pleasure in response.

My voice was hoarse and sounded unfamiliar, "Alex. Sweet, perfect Alex."

"Cole," she sighed and flexed her hips, staring at me.

Her green eyes were looking straight into me, holding me captive, making my insides go soft, reaching places no one had ever touched.

She held me with her gaze, and my mask disappeared. I felt aware in a way I never had before. She looked at me as if nothing else existed, and I felt a connection I'd never felt, and it alarmed me because the feeling was new, intimate, and felt extremely dangerous, but I couldn't look away from her.

Our bodies rocked together in perfect rhythm. I shifted my weight so I could reach between us to stroke her clit. She was bucking under me, her tits bouncing with every thrust, calling my name, and I felt the moment she went over the edge again, her legs shaking, her internal muscles pulsing around my cock like a vise, triggering my own release that felt never-ending.

Chapter 30

Alex

After I recovered and Cole took care of the condom, I laid on top of him, absently rubbing his chest, “Is it always like that?” I asked in a soft voice.

His big hand stroked my back, “No.”

I lifted myself up and kissed him, "Thank you for being really good at the sex."

He took my face in his hands and looked into my eyes, "I have news for you; you're really good at it too."

“Shut up.”

He smiled at me, “You shut up.”

I couldn’t help laughing, “You hide behind your gruff exterior, but you’re just a big ole goofball, aren’t you?”

Smiling, he rolled, taking me with him until he was laying over me, pinning my legs with one of his and started tickling me, “Who you calling goofball?”

I shrieked and bucked against him, trying to get away, “Cole! No! Ahh, stop!” My voice a high-pitched squeal.

“Who’s a goofball?”

I was laughing and squirming wildly, trying to get away, but he had no trouble holding me in place, “You are! Ahh, stop it! Goofball! Stop! Cole! Ahh, okay, I give, I give, you're not a goofball."

He immediately stopped. I was panting, smiling up at him, and he leaned down and kissed me, turning my insides into a gooey ball of mush.

When his lips left mine, I looked up at him and asked, "Now that Mr. Happy is relaxed, can I explore you?"

His eyebrows darted up, and he sounded almost insulted, "Mr. Happy?"

I giggled, "Well, it does seem to be pretty happy around me." I hugged him and laughed. "So, can I?"

Cole rolled us until I was straddling him and rested against the pillows, putting his arms behind his head like he was relaxing on a beach, "I'm all yours."

More than anything, I wished he meant that in a different way.

I stroked his face, running my fingers through his beard.

"The first time I saw you, I wondered if your beard was soft...it is."

I moved my hands to the side of his head, running his soft hair through my fingers. Leaning my head down, I kissed my way up his neck and licked around his ear, my hair falling around him, and I heard him inhale deeply.

I nipped his earlobe and sucked it into my mouth. Cole turned his head slightly, giving me easy access, and he rumbled a little, his hands moving into my hair.

I whispered in his ear, "You like that."

I moved to his other ear and showed it the same attention, loving that I could affect him. His hands slid along my waist, gripping my hips.

I let my hands travel down his shoulders to his biceps, and I ran my fingers over his tattoos.

I ran my palms over his chest, gently fingering his dog tags, “I love your chest hair. I like the way it feels under my hands, the way it feels going through my fingers. It's so masculine. Everything about you is so masculine.”

I ran my palms over his abs, tracing my fingers over his anchor tattoo, “I like that you're hard where I'm soft,” I told him. “The muscles, the tats, that face, you’re gorgeous.”

Chapter 31

Cole

I was captivated watching her, listening to her. She was a contradiction, innocent but bold, vulnerable but self-confident, shy but uninhibited, and she was knocking me off balance.

No woman had ever explored me this way. I wouldn’t allow it, wouldn't give up that sort of control, or share this kind of intimacy. It was foolish and reckless to allow Alex to do it, but I was enjoying it, maybe *too* much and was anticipating what she’d do next as she moved lower down my body. It didn't help that she was sitting wide open practically in front of my face and either didn’t notice or didn’t care.

She ran her fingers over my scars almost reverently, then leaned down and kissed each one. Lowering her head to my nipple, she ran her tongue around it, then sucked it into her mouth, nipping at it. I gripped her hips harder and groaned.

She picked her head up and looked at me, smiling, "Yeah, I liked it when you did that to me too."

Lowering her head, she licked and sucked my other nipple.

She sat up, lifting my hands in hers, measuring the size of my hands against hers, kissing each palm. Looking me in the eye, she sucked my right index finger into her mouth, swirling her tongue around it, and slowly pulled it out of her mouth.

"I can taste myself on you."

I sighed her name. Fuck, she was killing me. My hands start roaming her waist, her hips moving up to her breasts.

She grabbed my wrists, tossing my hands aside, "Hands to yourself, cowboy, it's my turn."

I smiled and stilled my hands but kept them on her hips. She carefully slid down me, kissing down my belly, her palms running over my chest and down my waist, sliding her hands along my stomach.

She slid down farther and sat between my open thighs with her legs over mine, again, wide open to me. Not surprisingly, I was half-hard by the time she got there.

Staring at my cock, she tilted her head a little to one side, her face questioning, a look of bewilderment. My dick twitched in response to her staring, and she looked up at me, surprised.

“Like what you see?” I asked.

Her face flushed, and she nodded, and it turned me on more.

She picked up my balls as if she were feeling the weight of them, rolling them in her hand, and I sucked in a breath and sighed her name.

She experimented, gently squeezing them, fondling them in her hand. Tentative at first, then bolder with my reactions. I was watching her, but she was concentrating on what she was doing to me.

She reached out her hand, gently touching my dick as if she might break it. My cock jerked the second she touched me.

Running her fingers along the throbbing veins and the tip, “It feels like velvet.”

I had to remember she was extremely inexperienced and may not have had the opportunity to explore a man’s body before.

She was driving me crazy, "Alex," I whispered.

She stopped and looked at me, a look of wonder but still touching me. I was getting harder by the second, my cock jerking and twitching.

She took me in her hand, and like my balls, she was experimenting. I was leaking precum, and she rubbed it with her thumb, circling it around the tip.

She looked down at her finger, drew her brows together, and then stuck her thumb in her mouth, tasting me.

"Fuck," I growled out.

She looked up at me and slowly pulled her finger out of her mouth, her eyes on me the whole time.

Trying my balls in one hand, my cock in the other, she was using her palm to spread the precum. I was getting more and more turned on, making more and more noise, my hips thrusting. When she started sliding her hand up and down my cock, the leaking was almost constant.

In a swift move, I unexpectedly pulled her against me. She squeaked as I rolled, so I was over her and was reaching for a condom.

“Hey, it’s my turn,” she grouched.

I rolled the condom on and then rolled us again, so she was straddling me. I put my hands back behind my head, grinning, waiting to see what she would do.

She smiled the most beautiful smile at me and climbed off me, getting out of bed.

My brows drew together, confused, "Alex?"

She didn't answer, just walked across the room, and all thoughts of what she was doing were forgotten, mesmerized by that beautiful backside. She grabbed a beige straw cowboy hat and popped it on her head before strolling back and climbing on top of me again.

I smiled at her, "Oh hell yeah."

Alex was unsure, I could see that, but she still fisted my cock, notched it with her opening, and slowly lowered herself onto me, her legs next to my body. We both moaned.

Once I was fully seated inside her, she started moving tentatively, rolling her hips back and forth. Then she raised herself up and down. I grabbed her hips and started moving her.

"Hang on a second, bossy. I'm trying to figure out which way feels best."

I smiled at her and stilled my hands but didn't remove them from her hips; she responded by moving her hips in a circular motion. She rose up and did it again, not losing the rhythm; she looked at me and smiled, looking proud of herself.

She looked lost in sensation; her eyes locked on mine. She ran her hands up her thighs, over my hands across her hips, spanned them over her belly, sliding them up her ribcage. She arched her back and cupped her breasts, squeezing them and pushing them together, never losing her rhythm or taking her eyes from mine, making delicious sounds of pleasure.

She rode me, slow and shallow then, deep and fast, circling her hips, rocking forward, driving me wild. I growled, taking her in, riding me, tits bouncing, her hair spilling out from underneath the hat on her head.

I snaked my hand between us to her clit, my other hand on her ass, and she widened her stance and sank deeper, and we both groaned. She reached her right hand behind her and grasped my balls, rolling them in her hand. I bucked against her, calling her name, but she didn't lose her balance or break her rhythm.

Calling my name, her orgasm was like an explosion, ripping through her like lightning. Holding the hat on her head, she threw her head back, and her hair pooled on my balls and thighs. It was one of the sexiest things I had ever seen or felt.

Still riding her orgasm, her internal muscles clenching against me, I had her by the hips, taking control. Alex didn't let go of my balls, applying gentle pressure staring at me, not breaking eye contact.

When my orgasm hit, I slammed her down on my cock as I thrust up and held her there as I came; my head driven into the pillow, calling out her name, pulsing and twitching deep inside her.

When I relaxed, she let go of my balls and put her hands on her thighs. Both of us panting, a slight sheen of sweat on us both, Alex sat straight and tall, looking at me in amazement, and I stared back at her. She smiled wide and laughed a little, her internal muscles spasming around my dick, and we both moaned.

Smiling at me, she tossed the hat, sending it sailing across the room, "Yeehaw, cowboy!"

I laughed, pulling her against my chest, still inside her. "Fuck yeah, angel."

I kissed her and rolled us over, and she laughed, causing me to slip out of her. We both groaned at the loss while I kissed her hard and passionately.

I was having fun with her. I couldn't remember smiling or laughing this much before, after or during sex.

Chapter 32

Alex

He went into the bathroom, I assumed to take care of the condom, and I heard the water come on in the tub.

When he came back out, he held his hand out to me, "Come with me."

I didn't know what was going on, but I put my hand in his and followed him into the bathroom.

"What's this?" I asked.

"You're probably sore, a hot bath will help."

"How sweet are you? Wow, that's a lot of bubbles."

"It's not like I have experience with girly shit. I might have put too much in there."

"Girly shit?" I asked, smiling. "Uh-huh, sure. Just go ahead and admit it, you secretly love bubble baths."

"Nope, this is my first one."

"Bubble bath virgin. Well, hang on, cowboy, I'm gonna make you a believer."

I checked the water temperature with my wrist and made it a little warmer. Then I lit the candles on the tub surround.

Smiling, I told him, "We'll be lucky if the bubbles don't overtake the whole bathroom. We might have to bail some of them out."

I put my hair up on top of my head and held it in place with a big clip.

"Now we get in," I told him as I stepped into the tub and sat down.

"Slide forward."

"Nope, it's your first time; you sit in front in case I have to save you." His mouth twitched, and I was surprised when he got in and sat in front of me. "Lay back and relax."

I wrapped my arms around him, stroking my hands up and down his wide chest. He relaxed against my left shoulder, giving me some of his weight, his hands roaming over my legs, distracting me.

After a while, I slid my hands down his stomach and along the inside of his thighs and between his legs, feeling his half-hard cock. I fisted him, and he placed his hand over mine, guiding me, teaching me what he liked.

His cock grew long and thick in my hand, and his breathing became erratic. His hips start thrusting, his movement causing little waves in the tub that spilled over the sides, my body sliding against his, slippery with soapy bubbles. He was whispering my name. He groaned long and low when he came, and it made me feel powerful that I could affect him this way.

Still gripping him and smiling, I rested my chin on his shoulder, "I think I'm getting the hang of this sex thing."

"You're a natural, baby."

I wrapped my arms around his shoulders and hugged him, kissing his neck.

We sat in comfortable silence for a little while, pressed together, our hands lazily roaming when Cole's stomach growled.

"What's the rule on food?" I asked him.

"What do you mean?"

"I could totally snarf down a snack, and your stomach is growling, but you said the night ends when we both leave the room. So, does that mean one of us goes to the kitchen while the other one waits? Or shall we be rebels and break the rules and both go? Or are you done here?"

He smiled at me, turning his head to kiss me, "I'm not done with you yet."

I couldn't help the smile that spread across my face, "Good. Then maybe we should go have some food so we can keep our strength up."

We got out of the tub, and he insisted on drying me off before he kissed me deeply, making my toes curl. He pulled on his boxers, and I put on an oversized t-shirt, and we walked through the house to the kitchen.

We made a buffet of the leftovers Maggie had sent home with us and ate and talked and laughed. When we finished, and I was loading our dishes into the dishwasher, Cole came up behind me, put his arms around me and started nuzzling my neck. Pushing back into him, I could feel his erection.

I turned around in his arms and looked up at him, "For an old guy, your stamina is off the charts," I told him, laughing.

"Old guy? You did not just call me old. I'll show you old," he grumbled as he bent down and plopped me over his shoulder and headed for the bedroom.

I wiggled and squirmed, and he shoved my t-shirt out of the way and smacked me on my bare ass in response. I screeched and laughed, shoving my hands down his boxers, grabbing his perfect butt.

He responded with a purely masculine sound that could only be called a growl and smacked my bare ass again and picked up his pace.

Chapter 33

Cole

The room smelled of sex and bubble bath, and I inhaled it, loving our combined scent. I found it intoxicating. I tossed her on the bed none too gently, and she squealed and laughed when she landed with a bounce. I crawled up the bed on my hands and knees like a predator until I was over her, looking down at her smiling face.

Tomorrow this would be over, but tonight, she was mine. I'd fucked women, I got off, she got off, and I left. But with Alex, I felt connected, not just physically but emotionally. She somehow silenced my demons.

I took her hard and fast, thrusting powerfully in and out of her. When we were both spent and boneless, she laid on top of me, seeming to like using me as a bed, which I didn't mind at all. If I was honest, it felt like she belonged there; the weight and feel of her were pleasing. Her head was against my chest, my hands wandering over her hair, down the small of her back to her ass.

Tonight, I'd done things I'd never done before, the eye contact, letting her explore me, the bubble bath. Things I'd never done with a woman because it was too intimate, and I didn't want anyone getting the wrong idea.

What was it about Alex that opened me up? There was a peace with her, a peace I'd never felt before and didn't realize I needed. She made me feel whole in a way I've never felt before. She made me hope for a normal life, and that made her dangerous.

I held her close and knew the moment she fell asleep. I didn't remember falling asleep, but when I woke up later, it was nearing dawn, and Alex was no longer in my arms. I briefly wondered if that's what woke me.

She was on her back, one arm over her head, one resting on her stomach. Her right leg bent, her hair spread out over the pillow, her beautiful body on full display. Even bruised and battered, she looked like a work of art.

I couldn't help myself; my hands wandered along her stomach and the curve of her waist. Alex shifted and sighed in her sleep. Before I was thinking, my hand was moving toward the swell of her breast, her nipple peaked under my touch, and I lightly rolled it between my fingers.

Even in her sleep, she was so responsive to my touch. I gently sucked one of her nipples in my mouth, and her back arched slightly, and her head lolled to the side.

I could smell her and lowered myself between her legs. Softly, my tongue swirled around her clit. Her legs shifted, and she sighed, a sound of pure pleasure. I tried to go slow to keep her from waking up, but her sighs and moans made it impossible.

My tongue moved faster, and she jerked and let out a little squeak, obviously awake because she lifted her hips, her hands fisting in my hair, trying to pull me closer to her. It wasn't long before she was coming, calling out my name.

I rolled on a condom and made love to her slowly, deliberately, with a tenderness I'd never shown, never breaking eye contact with her.

The power of it made me emotional, and that was unexpected. I knew this was the last time we'd be together, and I wanted it to last...forever.

Chapter 34

Alex

I wanted to say stay, don't go, I want to see you again, but I couldn't. I agreed to one night and one night only. The thought of this never happening again, of never waking up with him again, made me feel like I was being flayed open.

I knew he was about to walk out of my bedroom and never return. I wanted to lighten the overwhelming and depressing feelings I had about that. I didn't want his last memory of me to be crying and begging.

"So, do I get a t-shirt?" I asked, putting on my best fake smile.

He frowned at me, "A t-shirt?"

"Yeah, you know when you go somewhere special or do something fun, you get a t-shirt to commemorate the occasion."

He smiled, shaking his head, "I'll see what I can do."

But I knew he was kidding.

Cole was standing at my bedroom door, our one night over. I looked up at him, my palms resting on his chest one last time, the steady thump of his heart under my hands.

“I just want to tell you, the way you looked at me last night made me feel beautiful. The way you touched me, the way your body reacted to mine, it made me feel bold and confident, sexy.

You made me feel like a woman for the first time in my life. Plus, it was *a lot* of fun. Thank you seems inadequate for the most amazing night of my life.”

He kissed me long and deep. It was the last kiss we’d ever share, and I kissed him back with all the passion and emotion I was feeling. I wanted to memorize the feel of him, the taste of him, the scent of him.

This was the last time he’d hold me in his arms, and I wanted to find a reason to hold on to him longer. But when the kiss ended, he looked down at me, rubbed his thumb across my cheek and turned and walked away.

I made a mistake; I couldn’t have known he'd ruin me for anyone else, and I knew he had as sure as I knew my own name. No one would ever compare to him, how he made me feel, how completely he owned my body. His attention to detail was impressive, there wasn't a millimeter of my body his mouth and hands hadn't explored and set on fire.

Good or bad, this would change me forever. From now on, my life would be divided in two, before Cole and after Cole. He'd branded me in a way that was no different than a scar I could never get rid of.

He was a drug, an addictive drug I could never have again. He made me no promises, and I’d gotten exactly what I agreed to. He warned me he’d leave, but when he turned and walked away, I felt like he'd torn a hole in me, one I was sure would never heal.

I couldn't blame him, couldn't be mad at him; I'd done this to myself. But despite my feelings, I still couldn't find it in me to regret the night I spent with him.

I knew he still had to get dressed, so I threw on my clothes and hurried out of the house, pulling on my boots while I stood on the front porch, then I headed for the barn.

I needed the distance between us, and I had work to do. I didn't care that I was tired and sore; I've worked that way a million times before. I saddled my horse, Zeus and headed out with Zoey following me.

About an hour later, I saw a horse and rider coming my way and immediately recognized it was Gabe. When he got close, I jumped off Zeus, and he jumped off Clementine, and we ran for each other like some cheesy movie scene.

Both of us crying, he hugged me, picking me up and spinning me around, setting me on my feet before palming my face and hugging me tight again.

Once we had the tears out of our systems, we got back on our horses. Gabe knows me better than anyone else. Well enough to know I didn't want to talk about the kidnapping yet.

My goal for the day was to move cows to new pastures. It took all morning, but once they were in the new pasture, we took a break.

We sat shoulder to shoulder under a tree, our legs out in front of us, "So did you take my advice and jump on him?"

I had a feeling he thought this was safe ground to joke about, and if it had been any other day, it would have been.

I answered without looking at him, "As a matter of fact, I did."

"What?!" he practically screamed, jerking his head my way.

“Don't get excited, he has a one-night rule, so it was a one-night stand.”

He stared at me in shock, “What?! I want details.”

“It’s not that I don’t want to, but it feels private and special. I agreed to it, and it ended up being the best and worst night of my life. The best because of everything that happened and the worst because I’ll never be the same, and it’ll never happen again.”

“Oh, honey.”

I put my head on his shoulder, and he put his arm around me. I couldn’t help it, I started to cry, “It was one stupid night. How could one stupid night hurt like this?”

“Because sometimes all it takes is one night to fall in love.”

I lifted my head and looked at him, “What? I don’t love him.”

Gabe wiped the tears off my face, “You sure about that?”

After a moment of thought, I laid my head back on his chest and whispered, “No. What do I do?”

“You go on with your life. A man like that has a lot of armor up, and you just came busting through that armor. I’d wager he's scared of you, scared of how you make him feel.

“If the man has any brains, he’ll realize what he gave up and come crawling back. But if not, you can’t just wallow. There is someone out there who’s perfect for you.”

"But I don't want someone else," I complained.

We talked a little while longer before he stood up, pulling me up by my hands, and we walked to our horses.

He swung up into the saddle of his horse, "C'mon, I'll race you home."

I laughed at him, "You'll lose."

Chapter 35

Cole

The team was sitting behind the bunkhouse. There were three picnic tables side by side, creating one long table, and we were all sitting on the tables with our feet on the benches.

Midas was flying a drone, mapping the ranch. The drone's camera was streaming to Midas' computer and our phones, so all of us could see any problem areas.

Midas had just flown into the pasture about half a mile away, where Alex and Gabe were. They were sitting under a tree, having what looked like an intense conversation, and I wondered if they were talking about what had happened to her while she was in Peru.

When they got up and got on their horses, they went through the gate and stopped, their horses standing side by side. All of a sudden, the horses jumped forward and started running. They were obviously racing home. It didn't take long before Gabe was losing badly.

When they came off the road, between the house and the bunkhouse, Alex yelled over her shoulder, "C'mon, slowpoke."

"I'm rusty, and I think I broke my ass," Gabe yelled back, and I could hear Alex laughing.

They rode into the barn and disappeared. It took a while before they came out again and headed for the house, talking and laughing about something.

I turned, watching her as if my eyes couldn't stay away from her. She was wearing jeans with chaps and a t-shirt that said 'USN Ship Happens', with cowboy boots and a well-worn cowboy hat.

How was it possible that the sight of a hat could make me hard? And fuck, those chaps were sexy as hell, highlighting her perfect ass and I was imagining fucking her while she wore those chaps, her hat and nothing else.

I watched her walk away on those long legs, ogling her ass. *Yeah, yeah, you like how she looks, it gets you hard, move on.* When they reached the main house, they stopped and hugged. Gabe went inside, and Alex headed toward her house. After a while, when she didn't come back, I went to check on her.

She wasn't in the kitchen or living room, so I headed down the hallway toward her room. The door was open, and I saw her lying on the bed, sound asleep, her legs hanging over the side, her feet on the floor. It looked like she just sat down and fell asleep.

I always kept my U.S. Naval Academy t-shirt in my pack, almost like a talisman, and after she bolted from the house this morning, I pulled it out and left it on her bed. She was lying there with my t-shirt clutched against her chest, a hint of a smile on her face.

I stood smiling down at her. She looked so sweet laying there, and something about her hugging my shirt and smiling did something to me.

I wanted nothing more than to crawl in bed with her, haul her against me and never let her go. There was something close to an ache in my chest when I forced myself to leave her room to go pack.

*****

Boomer and Bruiser would be staying at the ranch for a little while to keep an eye on things. Midas had found a couple of problem areas with the drone and would be staying until he installed a few new cameras. I wanted to stay, but I couldn't. If I did, I knew I'd end up back in Alex's bed.

Bruiser was going to drive the rest of us home before coming back. He looked at Alex like a kid on Christmas morning when she tossed him the keys to the Camaro and told him to try and keep it under a hundred.

She told us not to be strangers, that her door was always open and gave us the gate code. Then one by one, she hugged each of us.

It was time for me to say goodbye to this amazing woman. I stared down at her, wanting to memorize everything about her. She hugged me tight, and I held her against me.

I could feel her ragged breathing, and she took a deep, shaky breath before she looked up at me with those beautiful green eyes. "I think I'll miss you most of all, cowboy."

I kissed her quickly, knowing if I kissed her the way I wanted to, I wouldn't be able to stop.

"Stay safe and be happy, angel."

"You stay safe too. Thank you for...everything. I'll never forget you, Cole."

Her voice cracked when she said my name and when I heard it, that ache in my chest reappeared.

I leaned down and kissed her forehead, letting my lips linger for a long moment. I wanted to pull her into me and never let go, and that thought alone had me dropping my hands from her as if she was suddenly electrically charged.

I wished I could stay, wanted to stay, even as I was getting in the car and being driven away.

I had to force myself not to look back. I wasn't sure if it would be worse to see her standing there or know that she'd walked away.

Chapter 36

Cole

Two weeks after we returned from Peru with Alex, the team had been sent back to get information from Edwardo Del Norte and take down his sex trafficking operation.

The op made me feel better; we'd been able to put a sex trafficker out of business and rescue his victims. Having the chance to kill some of the men who wanted to hurt Alex was a bonus.

We were currently on the plane on our way back from that mission. My teammates knew something was going on with me and Smoke was sure my bad mood had something to do with Alex and had been trying, with no luck, to get me to talk about it for the last couple of weeks. So, I wasn't surprised when he sat next to me and tried yet again.

"We know something happened between you and Alex, and not talking about it isn't helping you or the team. You've been angry since then, snapping at everyone, and that's not like you."

"I'm not talking about this, Smoke."

"You slept with her, didn't you? And you haven't been with a woman since, have you?"

"I'm *not* talking about this, Dr. Phil."

Smoke ignored me, "Was she shitty in bed? Is that it? You built it up in your head, and she turned out to be bad in bed?"

"Shut the fuck up, Smoke. Don't talk about her like that. She was...perfect."

Guess he finally got his way, getting me to say it out loud.

"So, you did sleep with her. If she was perfect, what's the problem?"

I looked at him, "You know the problem. We're SEALs; that's who we are. Our lives don't mix with relationships. I could be hurt or killed. If I was hurt, I couldn't give her any details. I wouldn't be able to tell her where I was going or what I did there or how long I'd be gone. Women don't do well with the secrecy and absence of our jobs."

Smoke shook his head, "Of all the women on the planet, Alex understands our lives; she pretty much knows everything we do. Her dad, her brother, and almost everyone she knows is a SEAL.

"She's strong enough to handle it. She grew up with it, she's lived with that secrecy and danger, and she still chooses you; she still wants you.

"You do realize Alex will find someone else to spend her life with. She'll get married and have kids with him, and with her life, it'll probably be a SEAL. So, your theory that you can't be with her because *you're* a SEAL is bullshit.

“You’re afraid. If you can stand the thought of her with another man, let her go and walk away. But if you can't, go fight for her, take the fucking risk. If you don't, I guarantee you'll regret it."

The thought of her with another man made me angry, and I felt almost panicked by it.

It was abhorrent.

Intolerable.

Painful.

I wanted to kill the man, and he didn't even exist yet.

I turned and looked at him, "I haven't heard from her since we left her house."

"Have you called or texted her?"

I shook my head.

"One night only, that's your rule. Did she agree?”

“Yes.”

“Is it possible you haven’t heard from her because she’s respecting *your* rules? We all saw the way she looked at you. I'd bet my trident she wanted more than one night, and if you’d be honest with yourself, you want that too. We haven’t seen you at the ranch, so I’m assuming you haven’t gone to see her either?”

I turned and looked at him, “What do you mean you haven’t seen me at the ranch?”

“We’ve been going there a lot.” He chuckled, “She’s teaching all of us yoga. She says it will improve our balance and flexibility. We’ve met a couple of SEALs from her brother’s old team and some others that we really like.

“There’s something about that place, about being surrounded by other SEALs, and Maggie never stops feeding us. That place is SEAL nirvana. We just figured you weren't coming by because of whatever happened between the two of you."

"Why didn't you guys tell me?"

"Jax has been talking about how great it's been to hang out with Falcon again. Boomer was going on and on the other day about how much fun he had herding cows. Midas can't shut up about how he's going to find a way to beat Carl in that first-person shooter game they've been playing. We were all talking about what a workout stacking hay bales is and how much harder yoga is than it looks."

It was a moment before he spoke again, "Bruiser is still staying with her."

"I looked at him, shocked, "He is?"

Smoke nodded, "I think she's gotten under his skin and has taught him that not every woman is a 'psycho'. They get in the ring and spar almost every day.

"You just haven't been paying attention because you've been cranky and stuck in your head. You haven't wanted to hang out with us; you've said no every time we've asked."

I sat stunned, staring at him; how could I have missed that?

He waited a long moment before speaking again, "Tell me this, what *don't* you like about Alex?"

"What?"

"You heard me."

I thought about Smoke's question for a minute and answered honestly, "Nothing. I like everything about her. She's open and honest, down to earth, she doesn't play games. She doesn't bitch about stuff. She's kind and easygoing, she's fun, and she makes me laugh. She makes me feel whole and human."

"You're a fucking idiot, you know that don't you?"

"Thanks. Why don't you tell me what you really think?"

"If I ever found a woman who looks at me like Alex looks at you, who treats me like she treats you, who made me feel the way she makes you feel, a woman who not only accepted what we do for a living but embraced it, I'd grab hold of her and never let go. I'd do everything in my power to keep her."

I was surprised by Smoke's words. I had no idea he felt that way, "You and one woman?"

"Yeah. You think I don't want that? You think the other guys don't want that? But the odds of finding a woman I care about who can deal with what we do are slim. You think the risk is loving her; it's not. The risk is losing her."

I ran my hands through my hair, "I've never done the relationship thing; I don't know how to do that. What if I fucked it up?"

He chuckled, "You're a guy, of course, you'll fuck up. But I get the feeling she's never done the relationship thing either. You two can figure it out together, but first, you have to be brave enough to take what you want. You gotta talk to her, you know, have a conversation. You know how to do that, don't you? You just open your mouth and make words come out."

"Yes, asshole, I know how to have a fucking conversation."

"Good. You should do that," he said, smiling and walking away, leaving me sitting here with his words and my thoughts spinning in my brain.

Once I knew they were safe, I never thought about the women we rescued. But I hadn't been able to get Alex out of my head. I kept recalling memories of her. I couldn't count the number of times I'd jerked off thinking about her, looking at the picture of her against the bricks I'd stolen. Or thinking about her riding me with her cowboy hat on, or how she felt in my arms.

I had visions of pounding into her in her bed, my bed, against the wall, on the kitchen counter, in the shower, on the floor, anywhere and everywhere. It was like I was fifteen again, and my dick had a one-track mind.

For the first time, I was regretting my one-night rule. Alex had made me realize the emotionless encounters with women had gotten old. Something in me changed that night with her, something was different about Alex, how I felt about her, and it wasn't just the incredible sex.

The sex was part of it. When Alex told me it was the most amazing night of her life, I wanted to tell her I felt the same way. I'd never had trouble leaving a woman before, but I had to force myself to leave her that morning.

She'd fucked the hell out of me during our night together, had wrung me out. She made me come more times in one night than I ever had before, and I could have kept going.

But more than that, I missed her. Missed talking to her, missed the sound of her laugh, missed just spending time with her, and that was confusing because I'd never missed a woman before.

I wanted nothing more than to sink into her again, watch her come apart for me, fall asleep with her next to me, inhale her scent. I wanted to see that megawatt smile and those sparkling green eyes. I wanted to spar with her sassy personality.

It was like a vortex had opened up and sucked me in. What was it about her that had me so twisted up in knots? And when had I lost complete control of my body?

I didn't know what was happening to me. Her magical pussy must have put some sort of a spell on me. What I needed was to get her back in bed and fuck her out of my system.

Chapter 37

Alex

Out of sight, out of mind is bullshit.

Cole had been out of my sight for nineteen long days, but he was never out of my mind. Every day without him had felt like an eternity. Somehow, I was still alive, even though it didn't really feel like it anymore.

I was on the Navy base, headed to an update about my kidnapping, and Cole was going to be there, and I'd have to see him, interact with him. I wasn't sure I could do it. But I wasn't a coward, despite all evidence to the contrary considering how strongly I wanted to turn around and run away.

I guess this is the Friend Zone. I never realized how dreadful the friend zone was until right this second. Thing is, we aren't really friends, so this must be some other zone, a worse zone. For the millionth time, I internally smacked myself for being irrational since I'd only spent one night with him.

I was being escorted down the hall by a young sailor, and I followed him until he stopped and pointed at a door. The door had an electronic keypad, and I didn't know the code, so I knocked and waited. It wasn't long before Smoke opened the door.

I walked into the room, and when they saw me, the team hugged me one by one. All except Cole, who was across the room, not coincidentally, as far away as he could get, and that made my crushed heart ache more. *Yep, the whatever zone I'm stuck in sucks, big time.*

When my eyes met Cole's, it felt like my heart had been pierced; it physically hurt to see him. I gave him a small smile and a little wave that was really just a raise of my hand. He smiled back and gave me a chin lift.

A chin lift. Something I'd seen a million times, but when Cole did it, it was somehow one of the sexiest things I'd ever seen. Looking into his eyes was like a knife to the heart, my body reacting to the memory of his touch, an instant throbbing between my legs.

I tore my eyes away from his; I couldn't look at him another second, or I'd run and throw myself into his arms and want to kill myself when he told me to get away from him.

I looked around to avoid looking at Cole and noticed a bulletin board at the front of the room with photos on it. There was one picture at the top and at least twenty photos below it. I walked up to the board and looked at the pictures.

Cole came and stood next to me. I felt him before I saw him. Like I was tuned to his frequency. My body reacted, that familiar jolt, like a shooting star rocketing through my veins, the thumping between my legs.

My breath was uneven, and my heart was pounding...or breaking; I didn't know which, but it hurt.

But I was here for a reason, and I didn't want him to see how much he affected me.

"Those are the people we found at the compound where you were held," he said from beside me.

The sound of his voice flooded me with memories, and I squeezed my eyes and thighs shut as if that could block them out.

When I felt like I wouldn't start sobbing, I cleared my throat, my voice soft, "You went back to Peru?"

"Yes."

I pointed to one of the pictures, "This is the one I bit." I continued to look at the photos, pointing at a second picture, "This is the one I kicked." Then I took a deep breath and pointed to a third picture, "This is the one who hit me and cut me."

Cole's hand moved to the small of my back, and I leaned against him before I realized what I was doing and straightened with a shake of my head and a stuttering breath.

"The bodyguards?" I asked, seeing their pictures.

"Mercenary brothers out of Mexico. Hired muscle."

I tapped the picture at the top with my finger, "This is the boss from the barn."

"Edwardo Del Norte."

I looked at him for the first time since he came and stood next to me and lowered my voice, "Del Norte? The one who offered the bonuses?"

Cole nodded.

"Did you catch him? Did he say who hired him?"

"We did catch him; he won't be hurting anyone else. None of these men will be hurting anyone else."

"Because you guys killed them," it was a statement, not a question.

"Yes."

"Good."

"He said the person who hired him was Mr. Protector, but we're pretty sure that's an alias, or miscommunication, something lost in the translation," Uncle Mal said from behind me.

I spun around and looked at him, "What did you say?"

"Mr. Protector," Uncle Mal repeated.

"Does that mean something to you?" Cole asked me.

I staggered to one of the chairs and fell into it. I stared into space, looking at nothing. I felt like the floor had dropped out from under me, like the ground was shifting under my feet.

Cole sat in one of the chairs next to me, and Uncle Mal sat on the other side, the rest of the team taking seats around the table. They knew something was wrong and were all staring at me.

Cole took my hand, rhythmically rubbing his thumb over the top of it, "Alex?"

When he picked up my hand, it distracted me from my thoughts. I looked down, watching him gently rub his thumb across my skin, causing my heart to flutter in my chest. Wishing he was doing it because he wanted to touch me and not because he wanted me to share information. It felt electric, so much so I expected to be able to see the current arcing between us.

As I watched his thumb gently caressing my skin, the only thing I could think about was how I would never be with him again, never kiss him, never feel his arms around me.

I was dangerously close to losing it. I hadn't expected it to be this hard to see him again, and I wanted to run away and cry. He was too close. Close enough to smell, close enough to touch, close enough that if I just leaned forward....

"Alex?" He repeated gently.

I looked up at him, my eyes filled with sadness and unshed tears. After taking a deep breath and focusing on the information they needed and not how I felt because Cole held my hand in his, I told them, "In high school, I got the nickname the Protector."

"Why?" Cole asked me.

I didn't look at him, "It's such a long story, but bottom line, I stood between the bullies and the kids they picked on. I fought for them because those kids couldn't or wouldn't. The bullies and mean kids called me the Protector of the Misfits."

"Fight like a girl," Cole said absently.

“Like when you broke Brooks Kennedy’s nose on the first day of school?” Uncle Mal asked.

I looked at him, “That was the day it started.”

“But that wasn’t the only time?”

“No. It went on all through high school.”

Uncle Mal ran his hands through his hair, "Why didn't you tell us?"

"If I had, you and dad and the guys would have done something. Something outside the lines that could have ended your careers, maybe put you in jail. Telling dad or you guys any of it would have been like throwing gas on a flame."

Uncle Mal looked at me and shook his head, “It breaks my heart that you had to go through that alone. It doesn’t make it any easier, but I understand why you didn’t tell us; we would have killed them.”

I stared off, talking to no one in particular, "Mr. Protector isn't a coincidence. A stranger didn't do this to me. It's someone who knows me, someone I probably know. But it could be anyone; the whole school knew me that way.

“The mean kids called me the Protector in a derogatory way. The kids being bullied called me the Protector as a good thing. All through high school, only four people called me Alex."

"Alex, you need to cancel your performance at the benefit," Uncle Mal said.

I looked at him, "No. I told you, I'm not going to have my life dictated by a psycho. I made a commitment, and I intend on keeping it. I'll be surrounded by people backstage, no one's going to snatch me off the stage, and most of the people who will be at my table are SEALs.

"Besides, the benefit seems like a good place for my stalker to show up. If everyone acts natural and it doesn't look like I'm being watched, maybe this psycho will pop his head out of his hole, and we can end this once and for all. Or at least get some clues."

"What benefit?" Cole asked.

"It's an annual event for all the local non-profits,” I told him absently.

I looked at Uncle Mal, "It seems to me the only thing I have to worry about is going to the bathroom alone, and you better believe I won't be doing that again."

By the time the meeting was done, I was mentally drained. I'd given them as many names as I could remember, but mainly I was wrecked from being in the same room as Cole and dealing with all the feelings swirling around inside me.

I felt raw.

Ripped open.

I just wanted to go home, crawl into bed and maybe never climb out. I was proud of myself that I hadn't broken down and cried, but I was on edge. A breakdown *was* coming, and I wanted to be far away and alone when it happened.

As I was walking out the door, someone touched me on the shoulder, and I was surprised when I turned around, and Cole was standing there, "Alex, are you okay?"

I looked at him and nodded, "I'm okay. How are you?"

"I meant, are you okay after all this?"

"I'm fine. Good." I nodded my head, "Yeah, I'm great."

He narrowed his eyes at me, "You don't look fine, good, great. Talk to me."

He looked concerned. Okay, so maybe I'm not as good an actress as I thought.

"I don't know what to tell you; it's all good."

It was obvious I was lying, but at least he didn't call me out on it, or maybe it really didn't matter to him.

"Your bruises are gone."

All I wanted was to turn around and run away from him.

"Yeah, all healed up. I have to go now. It was really good to see you. You look good, cowboy."

My voice cracked, and my hand involuntarily covered my heart before I got control of my feelings.

"You look good too, angel." His brows pulled together, “Are you sure you're okay?"

"Yeah. I'm just tired."

I felt the sting of tears behind my eyes and blinked to keep them from falling; my vision was blurring. I needed to go, and I needed to go fast.

Chapter 38

Cole

She stared at me, holding me with that emerald gaze, and I watched her eyes fill with tears again, and my heart constricted in my chest.

I was about to gather her in my arms and hold her close when she took a step back, turned and quickly walked away, her surprised escort scurrying to catch up.

She was wearing jeans, her 'Talk To Me Goose' t-shirt showed off her perfect breasts, she had cowboy boots on her feet, and that gorgeous hair was down and flowing around her.

This was the first time I'd seen her in person without bruises on her face. She wasn't wearing any makeup and was so stunning she took my breath away.

When she leaned into me as she was looking at the pictures, I was disappointed she hadn't stayed against my side, but Smoke was right, I created the situation, she was just abiding by my rules.

She'd been close enough I'd been able to smell her. That familiar, unique scent and I'd inhaled it, wanted to drown in it.

Smoke walked up and stood next to me while I watched her walk away.

"She's trying to put on a brave face, but she's afraid."

Frowning, I told him, "Yes, she is. But there's something else, something bigger. She seems sad."

"The rest of the team is going to that benefit. It starts about five-thirty, so I'll pick you up at five on Friday?"

“Something else I missed everyone talking about?” I asked him.

He smiled at me, “Yep.”

I stared at Smoke for a moment, then turned back to watch Alex disappearing down the hall. I wanted to see her again. I wanted to put the smile back on her face, and since I’d forced myself not to look her up online or listen to her music or watch her videos, I actually wanted to see her perform.

I turned back and smiled at him, "Yeah, that sounds about right."

Smoke smiled wide and clapped me on the shoulder before we walked back into the room.

During the meeting, Alex had made it clear her next-door neighbor, Brooks Kennedy was the ringleader of the bullies she dealt with in high school.

He was now my top suspect as her kidnapper. When Smoke and I went back into the room, I told the Commander, “We should talk to Gabe and find out what information he has about this Brooks asshole.”

“I was thinking along those lines too. I’ll call Gabe and set it up.”

*****

The Commander managed to set up the interview with Gabe the day after we talked to Alex. When he came in, he said hello to everyone, and the Commander got us down to business.

"We need to talk about Brooks Kennedy," the Commander told Gabe.

"You think he's behind Alex's kidnapping?" Gabe asked.

"Do you think he's capable?" I asked him.

"He's had a thing for Alex since high school but kidnapping her would risk everything he's got, and that's a lot. He comes from serious money. I don't know if he's crazy enough to risk his entire life for her, and I may not be the best person to ask since I hate that fucker."

"Tell us the history," the Commander said.

"Brooks was the school bully for as long as I can remember. The school year started about a week before Alex moved here. On Alex's first day of school, Brooks knocked my books out of my hands then shoved me so hard; I fell on my butt and slid on the floor a little. Not an uncommon event.

"Alex was walking by, headed for the office and saw what happened. She stopped and knelt down, started picking up my books and asked if I was okay."

It didn't surprise me that even as a young girl, Alex would stop and help a stranger; that was just the kind of person she was, the kind of person she'd always been.

"That's how I met her, and I swear I fell in love with her right there for helping me. From behind her, Brooks told her I had to take a beating because she interfered. He said, "unless you want to stand in for him."

"He told her those were the rules to teach people not to interfere with his business. Alex picked up my books and helped me up. She turned around, looked Brooks in the eye and told him she would stand in for me.

"Brooks was a couple years older than we were, he was sixteen at the time, and we were fourteen. He was about six feet, one-eighty, one ninety, a football player. Alex had reached her full height, but she was a beanpole. He had her by a few inches and seventy-five, eighty pounds."

As I sat listening, my hands fisted, and I was struggling to control my anger.

"There was a crowd watching, other kids, Brooks' friends. No one had ever volunteered to stand in for someone before or stood up to him, and there was an audible gasp from the crowd when she told him she'd stand in for me.

"Brooks smiled his creepy smile, pulled back, and threw a punch at her, but she dodged it, and he missed. He immediately pulled back again and caught her on the side of the face."

I wanted to kill Brooks Kennedy. My entire body went rigid, and the team reacted at the same time I did.

"Son of a bitch."

"Fucker."

"What the hell."

"Motherfucker."

"Asshole."

"She stared at him for a few seconds, and he grinned at her, then she pulled back and popped him in the face." Gabe smiled at the memory, "It was a thing of beauty. He fell on his ass, his nose was bleeding, and everyone, including his buddies, started laughing. Later we found out that Alex had broken his nose.

“Alex and I became friends that day. I introduced her to Josie, Jen, and Wes. The five of us started hanging out, and Brooks and his friends started calling us the Misfits.

“Alex told us she didn't care if Brooks was bullying one of us or someone else, to film it, that when there was enough, someone would have to do something about him. But Brooks knew what we were doing and changed tactics.

"So they wouldn't get caught on film, you'd be walking, and suddenly you'd be surrounded by Brooks and five to ten other guys. We called that *The Circle*.

“Whatever was filmed from the outside was just their backs, you couldn't get film inside the circle, so there was no proof of what they were doing.

“Once you were inside the circle, someone would put their hand over your mouth and then there were hands all over you. Josie was a favorite target because she was curvy even back then.”

“This guy needs to go in the ground,” I hissed, and the rest of the team reacted as well.

“I hate this guy.”

“We need to kick the shit out of him.”

“Motherfucker.”

“Son of a bitch.”

“If Alex would see it, she’d walk up and kick one in the balls from behind or the back of the knees or his back. Whatever it took so they'd go down, making a hole so she could snatch the kid inside the circle out. That's when Brooks started calling her the Protector of the

Misfits. She was the queen of the outcasts. Persona non grata."

"And what about Alex?" I asked.

"What about her?"

"Was she in this circle?"

Gabe nodded, "Yeah."

"What happened to her?"

"The same thing, just more...aggressive."

"Aggressive how?" I demanded.

"Where the rest of us would be squirmy and just try and survive it, Alex would fight back. She'd swing or kick in every direction at anyone she could get at.

"They were bigger, stronger, and she couldn't stop that many hands, but she made sure she wasn't the only one being assaulted. She did some damage of her own. That made them more aggressive with her."

I was getting more and more agitated, angrier; I wasn't sure I was going to be able to stop myself from paying Brooks Kennedy a visit he wouldn't survive.

"Whatever Brooks pulled, Alex would try and figure a way to keep him from doing it. She just always seemed to screw up Brooks' plans. She was our warrior, not just the Misfits, but any kid, anytime, anywhere.

"She kept us safe, made it better for us, but it made it land on her because Brooks wasn't running the school like he had been. He lost a lot of his power and Alex was the reason why. He couldn't torture kids the way he had, so he concentrated on her.

"He wanted to find what would get her to accept defeat. Even after he graduated, his cronies kept it up and she had to put up with it at home since the Kennedy property butts up against the ranch. But no matter what they did, she never backed down, never gave up.

“The start of the next school year, Brooks decided he wanted to date her. Alex was always confused by that, but then Alex isn’t a normal girl.”

“What the hell does that mean?” I snapped.

Gabe looked directly at me when he spoke, “She didn’t have any female influence growing up. She was raised by a team of SEALs; they didn’t teach her how to be a girl, they taught her how to be one of them.

“She hates shopping, doesn’t care about her hair or makeup or her clothes, but she knows how to run, how to fight, how to shoot. She never learned how to flirt or play games; she doesn’t bat her eyelashes.

“She’s not deceitful. If she gives her word, she keeps it, even when there are consequences for her. Are you going to sit there and tell me you haven’t noticed any of that?” He was angry and sat staring at me, waiting for my answer.

My response was contrite, “I noticed.”

“She doesn’t even think she’s pretty. She’s confused when men stare at her. In her mind, she’s still that gawky teenager, still a Misfit.”

I thought about some of the things she’d said, telling me she didn’t understand why men stare at her. That I should throw away pictures because they were ridiculous, and she looked like a clown. Telling me I made her feel like a woman for the first time in her life. When Gabe spoke again, it snapped me back to the conversation.

“But it was obvious that she wasn't going to grow up pretty; she was going to be seriously smokin' hot."

I growled, a low rumble from deep inside me.

"Easy big guy. My point is when she started filling out, Brooks noticed, but so did every other boy, grown men for that matter. I'm gay, and I noticed.

"Brooks saw how gorgeous she was going to be, and he wanted her. But he also knew she hated him, and he was never going to get her, that she'd never say yes to him.

"So yeah, he's a freakin' whacko, but he's also got a lot to lose. He likes being rich, he likes all his power, and it's been twelve years since he graduated high school; if it is him, why kidnap her now, why not years ago?"

Those were questions I couldn't answer yet, but kidnapper or not, Brooks Kennedy needed to go in the ground.

Chapter 39

Alex

On the night of the benefit, Gabe and the band, and I did a sound check. Gabe wasn't part of my band, but since he was performing at the benefit, he was going to play piano tonight while I performed.

After the sound check, we all went backstage to change. I had my hair and makeup done while Gabe's friend, Raffi, an up-and-coming dress designer, fussed over me after I changed into the dress he'd made for me for tonight.

Gabe got dressed in his bright blue suit, crisp white shirt, and silver tie. It all went well with his blonde hair and set off his sky-blue eyes, but Gabe didn't have to contend with a finicky designer or the whole hair and makeup thing, and I envied him for that.

I put on the boots I'd be wearing, and Raffi fussed over me more. I wanted to smack him and tell him to stop. Somehow, I didn't, but I really wanted to. I hated this part of things, but tonight I felt more on edge than usual.

Once we were in our dressed-up glory, Gabe and I stood side by side in front of the mirror.

Looking at myself, I couldn't help but comment for Gabe's ears only, "Well, if everything goes in the toilet, I have a serious future as a stripper."

Gabe shook his head at me, "You don't look like a stripper."

"Then you're blind."

Gabe rolled his eyes at me and walked away, shaking his head while I took one last look at myself.

We had our pictures taken by Oscar, one of the most famous photographers on the planet. The same photographer who had taken the photos of me before my last concert, the night I was kidnapped.

I've worked with him many times before, and while I like him, he can be obnoxious when he's working. I considered smacking him too.

All of it was jacking up my already out-of-control nerves. So it was a good thing when Chance made a bottle of tequila appear when Oscar started ordering me into different poses, and my mind was reeling about what happened after my last performance.

Raffi left, and Chance hugged me, then hugged Gabe, said good luck to all of us and left, going out to our table.

Finally, after what felt like three hundred hours, Gabe was introduced and went out on stage. He played for about ten minutes, and listening from backstage, I couldn't help but marvel at how insanely talented he is.

Gabe finished playing, I heard him say thank you, and the band members went out and took their places. I heard a few notes from the bass and guitar and a few beats of the drums as they tested sound levels, making sure their instruments were still tuned and the sound system still working.

I put in my ear monitors and stood by the stage curtain, where a mic was shoved into my hand, and I tried to calm myself down.

Waiting to be called on stage was the worst part for me. I knew once I hit the stage, I'd be okay, as long as I didn't trip and fall flat on my face, but as usual, I felt on the verge of a monster panic attack.

A hush fell over the audience, and I heard Gabe's voice, "Ladies and gentlemen, please welcome Alex Walker to the stage."

I heard the applause, and someone pulled the curtain back. I took a deep breath and walked out onto the stage between the drummer and Gabe's piano, looking at Gabe as I walked past him, which helped calm my nerves.

Once I was standing front center stage, the crowd exploded with applause, catcalls, and whistling. I was actually embarrassed and glared at Gabe, my face telegraphing, 'I told you so' before looking out at the audience again. Into the microphone, I said, "Thank you," but the crowd didn't settle down.

I looked over at our table and smiled. I saw Cole's entire team was here, and just as I was about to look away, I saw Cole and my heart skipped a beat.

He was sitting away from the team, at the end of the table next to Chance. Their chairs were turned around, giving them an unobstructed view of the stage. Cole was sitting forward in his seat, and I briefly made eye contact with him before looking away.

Chapter 40

Cole

When Alex walked out from behind the curtain, and I saw her, it felt like time slowed, as if she were walking in slow motion.

When she reached the front of the stage, and I could really see her, I felt as if all the air left my lungs, as if my heart stopped completely and then restarted triple time a few seconds later.

Photographs couldn't do her justice; they didn't compare to what I was seeing. She was wearing a sleeveless, cobalt blue dress that had a pattern stitched with silver beads that sparkled under the lights when she moved.

The dress molded to her body, and while the scoop neckline wasn't overly deep, she still had serious cleavage showing. The dress was shorter in length but had a three-inch silver beaded fringe all the way around the hem, making it appear longer.

On her feet were over the knee blue suede boots with a chunky heel leaving only about four inches of leg showing between the bottom of the beaded hem and the top of her boots. With the heels, I estimated she was standing almost six feet tall. She was a beautiful, giant vision in blue.

Her makeup was a smoky cat-eye with a dramatic black wing, her luscious lips were pink. Her hair was loose and softly curled, and it flowed all around her. Whatever was done to it, it appeared there was more of it than usual, like a magnificent lion's mane around her head.

I couldn't get the image of bending her over and fisting that sexy hair while I pounded into her with those fuck me boots on. If my dick got any harder, it might rip a seam on my pants; I couldn't drag my eyes away from her if my life depended on it.

I wanted to stalk up and pluck her right off the stage caveman style.

"Fuck," I muttered, running my hands through my hair.

Chance was smiling but didn't look at me, "Yeah, she cleans up nice."

Nice? Holy hell, she's perfection.

"How's everyone doin'?" Alex asked from the stage, snapping me out of my fantasy.

There was a huge cheer from the crowd and more catcalls and whistling. There were photographers around the room, and almost everyone had their phone out snapping pictures or taking video. I was too stunned to do anything; I barely felt able to breathe.

She was smiling, and the audience finally started settling down. "Thank you for coming; it's great to see so many people here tonight. As you've just heard, Mr. Carmichael is an extraordinary pianist. But he's also a gifted songwriter. We're going to do a few of his songs tonight; this one's called Live Free."

The music began, and Alex started singing, and I was stunned at the power of her voice.

I soaked up every detail. While only a few inches of her legs were showing, every step caused a little bit of thigh to peek-a-boo out from behind the beaded fringe at the bottom of her dress, which was somehow sexier than if she was showing her entire leg.

When she swayed or moved, the beaded fringe swayed and moved against her thighs. Her legs looked a mile long in those boots. She was sex on legs, really, really long legs.

When she finished the song to applause, I felt like I still didn't have my bearings. My heart was pounding in my chest, and I'd had no luck controlling my raging libido.

From the stage, Alex said, "If you like to line dance, get out on the dance floor because this is your song."

Three-quarters of the room, including Boomer, jumped out of their seats, cheering.

"This one's called Gorgeous."

I'd heard Gabe call her gorgeous more than once, obviously his nickname for her. The song had a snappy country-rock feel to it, and the lyrics, which were amusing, made it clear it was a song about Alex if you knew anything about her.

When the song ended, she looked out at the audience, "We're debuting this one tonight. You guys are the first to hear it live."

The audience cheered.

"It's called I Wish You Could Stay."

The melody was brutally beautiful, the lyrics haunting, the combination almost painful to hear.

Alex sang with a ragged edge of pain in her voice, and it felt like a knife to my heart, realizing it was about one amazing night and longing to be with someone there was no hope of being with. A song about heartache and loss. When the song ended, the crowd erupted, and I noticed more than one person wiping away tears.

"She's amazing," I breathed out more to myself than anyone else.

She next sang a bluesy song called Mercy Road and then another called Calamity, and I realized that not only was Alex a phenomenal singer, but Gabe was also an excellent songwriter. Some of the songs had catchy music and fun lyrics. The others felt emotional, as if they were reaching into you.

Alex had the voice of an angel one minute and a siren the next. Clear and clean, sassy, and raunchy. She didn't just sing; it was as if she felt the music and lyrics inside her, her attitude shifting with the lyrics, smiling, serious, lusty, sexy.

My cock had turned to steel, there was a real risk of exploding in my pants, and I was sure I wasn't the only man in the room with that particular issue, which made me angry for some reason.

Alex marched back and forth across the stage on those long legs, in time with the beat of the music, belting out songs. From her outfit to her voice to her dance moves, she commanded attention; she was assertive. Confident. She owned the stage, and it was impossible to take my eyes off her. Alex wasn’t a good singer; she was a fucking rock star with the most beautiful voice I've ever heard.

For the most part, it was as if she knew the audience was there; she just didn't see them.

But every now and then, her eyes would lock onto mine while she was singing. The lyrics she sang while looking at me had to do with sex or kissing and every time, my dick twitched in response.

I couldn't help but smile; I'd never been this turned on in my entire life, and she wasn't anywhere near me. When Alex sang to me from the stage, I knew she was delivering me a message, and I was receiving that message loud and clear.

"Some of you may have heard our next song, it was in a movie and won a few awards; it's called Treasure You."

The crowd exploded, cheering and whistling and couples immediately paired up on the dance floor.

The song was made for her voice. I was mesmerized; I couldn't believe that huge voice was coming out of her. The song had several long notes, and I wondered how anyone could hold a note that long with that kind of power in their voice.

The crowd went insane when Treasure You ended, and the entire room gave her a standing ovation. I was standing and clapping along with everyone else, completely and utterly enthralled.

Our table and the rest of the team on the dance floor were making an extreme amount of noise. Alex said thank you and did a cute little curtsey.

After the applause died down, Alex stood front, center stage, "Our final song tonight is called Fatal Love."

I was surprised by the crowd's reaction; I'd never heard of this song, but it was obvious a lot of the crowd had because they enthusiastically rushed to the dance floor.

The song had a quick, thumping bassline and a strong drumbeat. Not one that was traditional for dancing, but it made you want to move, almost forcing you to move.

It had a fast lyric about having sex that was so fantastically intense it might be fatal, but you'd go out happy and smiling and be glad that's how you were pronounced dead.

More than once, Alex's attention landed on me, singing those erotic lyrics right to me, and when she did, it was like we were the only two people in the room.

The dance floor was packed, the crowd was jumping up and down with their arms in the air. Boomer was near the stage, singing along with her, staring up at her.

Alex had the crowd lit up, and she knew it; energy radiated off her like flames. She saw Smoke, Boomer, and Jax on the dance floor with their phones aimed at her, looked right at them, and pointed at them as she marched across the stage. They went crazy, and I smiled at their reaction.

She strode across the stage with that long stride, her hair billowing out behind her and without slowing down, held the mic toward the crowd, and as a group, they sang-shouted the next line of the song, "Gimme that fatal love!" She smiled before putting the mic back to her mouth, and the crowd went wild. She had the entire building electrified.

As the song ended, Alex was standing facing the crowd, her feet slightly apart, the microphone in her right hand. She sang the last word and when the last drumbeat of the song hit, she dropped her head back and threw her right arm straight up over her head at the same time.

The entire room was on their feet applauding, the whistles almost deafening. Her chest was moving up and down with her labored breaths. She stood frozen for four or five seconds before she lowered her arm, lifted her head, and smiled one of the most dazzling smiles I'd ever seen.

Alex put the mic to her mouth and said thank you, and Gabe and the rest of the band moved and stood on either side of her. Gabe took her hand, and they all bowed to the crowd, smiling.

Gabe whispered something in Alex's ear, and she smiled broadly and bumped her shoulder into him before looking back out at the audience, her eyes catching mine briefly; she smiled at me while I stood with everyone else in the room, clapping and whistling. Then they all turned and headed backstage.

Chance turned toward me, "We've got interview obligations to do now. Probably half an hour, forty-five minutes, then, other than schmoozing, she should be mostly free to enjoy the rest of the night."

Chance smacked me on the shoulder and walked away, and I sat down again.

Alex had done something to me. My brain was scheming against me, bombarding me with memories, the taste of her, her mouth on mine, her tight, responsive body, her hair spilling around us, how she felt in my arms.

The way she looked when she called out my name when she came under me, over me, when I was inside her, the look of lust and mischief in her unique eyes.

Damn, if I could get her out of my head, and the way she looked and sounded on stage in that dress, those boots, that voice, singing those erotic fucking lyrics at me, that sexy body swaying and dancing to the music was seared into my brain.

Alex was reaching inside of me, unlocking the places I'd kept hidden. Fueling desires, I'd kept locked down tight because since I'd met her, I'd most definitely been feeling something, and I realized I didn't want it to stop.

Alex was the first woman I was attracted to as much by her personality as her body. For the first time in my life, I felt a connection to a woman, and it scared the shit out of me, but at the moment, I could hardly care. I had to have her again, I wanted her more than I wanted my next breath, and right here, right now, all I could think was...Alex. Is. Mine.

When I saw her come out from backstage with Gabe and Chance, they were laughing, and I saw them take selfies. Then Gabe and Chance went one way, and Alex headed to the bar, ordering a shot and downing it, nodding her head at the bartender who poured her another one.

Men gravitated to her, followed her, surrounded her, wanting pictures, trying to get their hands on her.

Alex was talking to the men surrounding her, shaking hands, nodding politely but absently, signing autographs, and taking pictures with them, but she looked uncomfortable and overwhelmed. She looked cornered, trapped, and any one of them could be her kidnapper.

Jax and Bruiser stood nearby, not interfering but watching her and the crowd, blending in, ready in case anything suspicious happened. But I noticed they were both frowning, watching her.

I was moving before I could even think about it. I'd be damned if I stood by while assholes put their filthy paws on what was mine. Just the thought of it caused a jolt of possessiveness that made my hands fist.

I was single-minded in getting to her, stalking toward her, and when the men surrounding her noticed me approaching, they wisely moved out of my way.

When Alex's eyes met mine, she looked surprised and almost desperate. When I was close enough, I reached my hand out to her, "Dance with me."

Alex smiled at me, tossed back her shot, and put her hand in mine. "Hi."

I smiled back at her, "Hi."

When we cleared the crowd of men, I let go of her hand and put my hand on the small of her back as we walked to the dance floor.

"Thank you."

"For what?"

"For saving me. I was feeling like a three-legged antelope surrounded by a pack of lions."

Chapter 41

Alex

I thought Cole looked delicious in his dark blue suit, white shirt, and light blue tie. I wasn't surprised when my girly parts went on high alert, screaming, oh yes, please.

I'd spent so much time with him in his work gear; I still wasn't used to him in civilian clothes and in these particular civilian clothes, he was hot enough to set the place on fire.

I hadn't been expecting Cole to be here tonight or to save me from the handsy creepers that were surrounding me and definitely hadn't expected him to ask me to dance.

I would take it. I wanted more of him, more of what we'd shared during our one night, but Cole was the one with the one-night rule; he had to be the one to break it.

But I had the feeling Cole did feel something for me. At least I hoped he did, and it wasn't just that I was out of my alcohol-infused mind with lust for him. But even if he didn't break his one-night rule, I'd still get this dance, and I wasn't going to give that up. *No way. No how.*

Cole stopped when we reached the middle of the dance floor, other couples all around us. I rested my right hand on his chest and snaked my left hand up to the nape of his neck and started running my fingers through his hair and along the back of his neck and sighed.

Cole's hands rested low on my hips, holding me, pressing my curves against him. It felt right, familiar, like coming home. I hoped I didn't look like an idiot because I couldn't seem to wipe the goofy smile off my face.

"You were amazing up there. I've never seen anything like that; you owned this place. You really are a rock star."

I smiled up at him, "Thank you. It actually looked like you were having a good time."

"And this dress, those boots, the whole package is so fucking sexy, and...you're very tall tonight."

His words took me off guard, and I couldn't help but smile, "So you have a little stripper fantasy, huh? Too bad I didn't know that before."

Cole cocked a dark brow at me, "Alex, how much have you had to drink?"

"You know, I just don't know. Being in this outfit, with all this crap on my face, being on display is nerve-wracking, and I had to have my picture taken by a cranky photographer who apparently doesn't like my attitude, *and* I had to do interviews, which I hate. Plus, my stalker is probably here.

"Luckily, Chance brought a bottle of tequila backstage. *But* I didn't want to wait for him to find glasses, so I drank it out of the bottle like a proper lady, and that's where I lost count."

I couldn't help the giggle that escaped me, "And I had a couple of shots before we started dancing."

I gave it some thought before I shrugged, "I think that's all."

"Are you drunk?"

"No, but I feel *really* good."

My right hand started roaming his chest, and I looked up at him; "Did I ever tell you that when I drink right to my limit, I lose the filter between my brain and my mouth?"

His eyebrows shot up, and he grinned at me.

"Yep, whatever I'm thinking just pops out."

"Such as?"

"Such as...have I told you how yummy you look tonight? Because you do. You look fucking fantastic in this suit."

Cole smiled at me, "I look yummy?"

"Oh yeah, so yummy, and you always smell so good."

I put my face in the crook of his neck and inhaled deeply, "Mmm. You smell like you."

"What else?" Cole asked in a husky voice.

I looked into his eyes, "I really want to kiss you again. Because you're a really good kisser." I nodded, "I mean really, really good, I could kiss you all day long. And even though you're so yummy in these clothes, I liked you naked."

Cole's grip tightened on my hips, his voice a growly purr, "I like you naked too."

"Yeah?"

"You naked is one of my favorite things."

Hearing those words made me smile wide, and my insides started dancing.

“You can't imagine what I want to do to you in this dress.”

I looked at him, serious, curious, “What do you want to do?”

Cole leaned his head down until his mouth was next to my ear, his voice deep and throaty, “I want to bend you over, pull this dress over your beautiful ass, and fuck you so hard you don't know where I end, and you begin.”

I gasped, and when Cole pulled back and looked at me, my lips were parted, my eyes were wide, and I felt the blush on my cheeks. My heart was hammering in my chest, and my lady parts were doing the cancan while screaming yes, yes, yes.

I smiled a slow wide smile at him, “Okay.”

“Okay?”

“It means yes. And can I just say you’re the maestro of dirty talk?”

He smiled at me, and I smiled back.

I grabbed Cole’s tie and pulled him a little closer to my face, “You haven't steered me wrong yet, cowboy. If you think that would be fun, then that's what we're gonna do because you're excellent at the sex.”

Cole smiled, his big hands spanning my back, right above my ass and growled at me, “Vixen.”

I looked up at him smiling, “Stripper vixen.”

I palmed the side of his beautiful face, my voice soft and sensual, “Your stripper vixen if you want.”

“Fuck angel, my cock is so hard it's painful.”

My stomach flipped over like an Olympic gymnast when he called me angel and spoke those dirty words to me.

I smoothed his tie and looked up at him, a playful smile on my face, “That's bad, huh?”

“Have some pity, woman.”

“You're such a delicate little flower, Cole Montgomery.”

“Let me take you out of here, and I'll show you how delicate I am,” he said, with a sexy smirk.

“I really want you to do that. You have *no idea* how much I want that, but I'm stuck at this shindig for a little while longer.”

The song ended, but Cole didn't let go of me, "Gabe is headed this way."

He’d never taken his eyes off me, so I didn’t know how he’d seen Gabe.

I dropped my forehead on his chest, “Ugh, twenty bucks says he's coming to be a buzzkill.”

“Hi, kids,” Gabe said as he reached us.

I shifted and tucked myself into Cole's side, one hand on his back, one hand on his chest, his arm around me, his hand on my hip like a brand.

“We were in the middle of something really good, so congratulations on winning the bad timing award, Gabe.”

Gabe laughed; Cole smiled, and his big hand squeezed my hip.

“I've come to tell you some of the press got here late, and we need you over there, and you two need some cold water thrown on you.”

“Why?” I asked.

"Because the two of you dancing is practically porn."

I smiled up at Cole, "Did you hear that? We're practically porn!"

Cole leaned down and whispered in my ear, "We *will* be porn later."

His words went from my ears straight between my legs. I leaned into him and giggled, Cole squeezing my hip at the sound.

Gabe looked at Cole, "Did you get her drunk?"

"No, you got her drunk."

"Boys, don't fight because I'm not drunk. Told you he came to be a buzzkill; you owe me twenty."

Gabe smiled, "Lost your filter?"

I snuggled closer against Cole, "Yep."

"She really has to do these interviews, and it might be a good idea to separate you two for a couple of minutes. Sorry."

It didn't seem like Cole wanted to let me go, but he nodded at Gabe. Gabe grabbed my hand and started fast walking, dragging me behind him before I could protest. I almost had to jog to keep up. Watching us go, Cole put his hands in his pockets.

With Gabe dragging me by the hand, I turned around smiling, looked at Cole, and waved enthusiastically at him. He smiled back at me and gave me a chin lift.

Then he looked at Midas and Boomer, who were across the room and jerked his head toward me. They both nodded and started moving to shadow me.

After Gabe, Chance and I talked to the press; we walked away from them with me in between them.

Gabe told Chance, "We need to get her some water."

“Pfft, you guys are such worry warts. You need to loosen up. Have a frickin’ drink; it's a party, man. Hey Gabe?”

“Yeah, gorgeous?”

“Did you see Cole? He looks so delicious. And you were right about this dress.”

Chance looked at me, “You mean the dress you bitched about for two months?”

“Shut up. I have a really good feeling Cole is going to break his one-night rule, and I’m excited about that. You think dancing was porn?”

Chance shot a look at Gabe, questioning.

“What Cole said he wants to do to me, now *that’s* porn. And it's gonna be good porn. Because he's so good at the sex.”

I dropped my head back, “*So good.* I just wanna jump him all the time. If I could, I’d keep him locked up and naked. He called me vixen.” I looked at Gabe, “Vixen. Viiix-en, that's such a good word, don't you think?”

Gabe and Chance started laughing.

The three of us stopped at the bar, and Gabe ordered me a club soda with lime and drinks for themselves.

Gabe handed me the glass, “Drink this.”

I put the straw in my mouth and started drinking while we walked back to our table, people stopping to talk and take photos along the way.

We’d just finished taking a few photos with people when Brooks Kennedy was suddenly in front of us. I was instantly stiff, my hand fisted, my posture defensive.

“Well, well, well, if it isn’t the most famous of the Misfits. Get a new member of your little club?” Brooks bit out, looking at Chance.

He turned his attention to leer at me, looking me up and down, "And perfect Alex, don't you look absolutely scrumptious tonight. Let's go out to the parking lot and have some fun."

"Ew, gross."

Brooks reached for me, and I slapped his hand away, "You're exceptionally stupid, Brooks. Go away, or you're going to need a testicle retrieval operation."

Brooks smiled at me, "Ooh, foreplay. I like it."

I didn't even see Cole walking across the floor toward us, but suddenly he was there standing next to me. He put his arm around me possessively, pulling me into his side, glaring at Brooks as I slipped my arm around his waist.

"You keep showing up where you're not wanted, Kennedy."

Cole's voice was calm, and he looked relaxed enough, but I could feel how rigid he was; his entire body was humming with tension and hostility.

"I won't say it twice, never come near her again," Cole told Brooks, his voice hard, laced with venom and danger.

I had a feeling if I could see Cole's face, I'd be seeing the Reaper for the first time.

Brooks glared at Cole, then smiled a sinister smile and held his hands up in capitulation, "No need to get touchy, just offering my congratulations."

Brooks focused his attention on me, "I will catch *you* later, lovely Alex."

Then he turned and walked away.

Cole watched him go for a moment before turning to face me. "You alright?" He asked, looking down at me, one of his hands palming my face.

I smiled, "Yeah. He's just a grade-A asshole. Nothing new there."

Cole led me to our table, with Gabe and Chance following us, and I set my glass down and said hi to everyone. Everyone had comments about my performance and my outfit. There were hugs and more pictures.

"I'm going to get food. I'll be back. Cole is gonna escort me; there's a lot of pervs here tonight for some reason."

Smoke grinned, "I'm sure it has nothing to do with that outfit."

Cole glared at him, but Smoke just chuckled and shrugged.

I needed to go to the bathroom before we hit the buffet. I was pretty sure Cole was on board with breaking his one-night rule, but I wasn't taking any chances that he'd pull out his iron control and change his mind. All bets were off; this was guerrilla warfare. *Or girl-rilla warfare as the case may be.*

So, while I was in the bathroom, I took off my fancy panties, folded them, and tucked them in my right boot. When I stood up, I made sure they weren't visible.

When I came out of the bathroom, Cole was waiting for me. I asked him if he'd take a selfie of us and was a little surprised when he did.

I didn't know that while I was in the bathroom, Cole talked to Smoke and Bruiser about the conversation with Brooks, telling them to make sure the rest of the team knew about it and had eyes on Brooks until I left the party.

We hit the buffet and arrived back at our table and sat down. Gabe was on the other side of Cole, Smoke on the other side of me.

After we'd eaten, Raffi, the dress designer, called my name from across the room, and when I looked that way, Raffi waved me over. Oscar, the photographer, and another man were with him. I held up a finger to them, the universal sign for wait a minute.

I reached into my boot and took out my panties, turned toward Cole and put them in his hand under the table.

I leaned over and whispered in his ear, "I thought you should have some incentive."

Cole looked down and saw what I'd placed in his hand just as I was closing his fingers around them.

I stood up, leaned over, and whispered in his ear, "But be careful, they're wet."

Gabe saw what I had done and started choking. While Cole quickly shoved my underwear in his pants pocket, I stepped behind him, smacking Gabe on the back with my right hand, my left hand resting between Cole's shoulders.

"You okay there, buddy?" I asked Gabe, laughing.

I leaned over and whispered in Cole's ear, "And now I'm going commando."

I looked around the table, smiling, "duty calls," I said as I spun and walked away, the fingers of my right hand trailing along Cole's shoulders as I went.

Chapter 42

Cole

I dropped my head back and closed my eyes. As much as I wanted to chase her down, toss her over my shoulder and carry her out of here, at the moment, it was not physically possible for me to get up.

I could not remember ever being this hard for a woman, and I wasn't lying when I'd told her I was in pain. I watched Alex walk away, knowing she didn't have panties on and could swear the little wench was purposely sashaying that sweet ass just a little more.

After giving my dick several minutes to calm down, I was crossing the floor toward her, my long sure strides eating up the distance between us. Alex saw me coming and grinned.

When I reached her, I put my arm around her, looked at the men, and told them, "Gentlemen, Ms. Walker has to go now."

Without another word, I turned her and started walking toward the door.

"Took you long enough," she complained as we started walking out, and she tossed a wave over her shoulder at our table.

Once we were outside, I walked her to her car without a word.

“I can't stand it anymore, Cole, kiss me.”

“I can't.”

She nodded and tried not to look disappointed, to look like my rejection didn’t bother her, but I saw that it did, “After what you've put me through tonight, I'm barely holding on here; if I kiss you, I'll lose it. When I come, it’s going to be inside you.”

Using the keys that Gabe gave me, I opened the car door. She got in, and when she was settled, I closed the door and headed around the car to the driver’s side.

Once we were on our way, Alex looked over at me. My jaw was clenched, and my hands were opening and closing on the steering wheel, and she may have noticed we weren’t going the right direction to her house.

“Cole?”

“Not a word Alex. I'm serious; I need you to sit there and be quiet right now.”

She smiled at me and pretended to zip her lips.

When we reached our destination, I went around and got Alex out of the car and walked her to the door. As soon as I had the front door opened, I threw her over my shoulder, kicking the door closed behind me.

Alex squealed in surprise, balancing herself with her hands on my ass. I marched through the house to the bedroom, turning on the light before I set her on her feet at the foot of the bed. I went to the nightstand and retrieved a condom, stripping off my jacket and tie dropping them on the floor.

“Turn around,” I ordered.

Alex immediately complied, and gently, I pushed her down so her upper body was against the mattress. I nudged her legs apart and shoved her dress up over her ass. She was exposed and vulnerable with her perfect backside in the air.

I shoved my pants and boxers down, tore open the condom and rolled it over my rock-hard cock, leaning down and kissing the small of her back. She shivered in response. We both groaned as I dug my fingers into her bare ass.

I wasn't gentle, couldn't be gentle; her sounds of pleasure were raw and intense. She was crying out my name, pushing back into me, letting me know I wasn't hurting her.

Sliding my hands up her thighs, my fingers moved between her legs, feeling how slippery she was.

"Fuck, you're so wet for me, angel," I growled, slipping my fingers inside her, working them in and out until she was pushing back, fucking my hand. When I skimmed my fingers over her throbbing clit, she arched her back and called out my name.

I rubbed her clit faster and harder, while she squirmed and bucked against me. I knew she was close, and it wasn't long before her body tensed and spasmed uncontrollably as she came around my fingers.

While she was still in the middle of her intense orgasm, I thrust balls deep into her with a primal sound. Her internal muscles were still spasming, gripping me tight. I had my hands on her hips, my fingers digging into her, controlling her, driving deep, my hips pistoning with every stroke.

She caught my rhythm immediately and pushed back into me with the same intensity, writhing, demanding more as I hammered into her. The sounds of our bodies coming together, loud in the room.

I dominated her, one hand fisting her hair, pulling her head back, the other on her hip controlling her movement. Alex bowed her back, moaning like a porn star as I thrust in and out of her.

I took her hard and fast.

It was frenzied.

Carnal.

Animalistic.

I was taking what I needed from her, my hands gripping her, manhandling her. I let go of her hair and moved my hand around her, fingering her clit.

Alex dropped her forehead against the mattress, fisting the comforter in her hands, every part of her shaking, crying out my name like a chant. When I slapped her ass, she gasped and jerked back into me hard and shattered into a million pieces, yelling my name.

Her orgasm triggered mine. I came with a roar, an overwhelming explosion. The orgasm reverberated through my whole body like shockwaves after an explosion, drowning all my senses.

Joined together, both of us panting, I stroked my hands up Alex's exposed back and down to her ass until I recovered some of my senses.

Her ass was pink where my fingers had dug into her, my handprint from where I had slapped her; I leaned down and kissed the marks causing shivers and clenching of her internal muscles around me.

When I slowly pulled out of her, she spasmed against me as if her body were trying to keep me inside her, and we both groaned when I slipped out of her.

I went into the bathroom to deal with the condom, and Alex collapsed against the bed, her legs hanging off, her breathing ragged.

I'd never come like that. I'd pounded into her, taking what I needed from her without thought or control, and it was the most intense sexual experience I'd ever had. But now that my head was clearing, I was afraid in that loss of control, I'd hurt her, and if I had, I'd never forgive myself.

"Alex?" I called from the bathroom, concern in my voice.

She flopped over; her arms flung across the bed, but she didn't answer me. Her hair was covering her face, in disarray all around her head and spread out over the mattress, but she made no move to brush it away.

Her dress was bunched around her waist; her legs were bent over the edge of the bed, her feet on the floor, her legs slightly spread apart.

I knelt on the bed next to her and started moving her hair, "Where the hell are you?"

I finally got her hair moved so I could see her face. She hadn't moved, her eyes were closed, and her breathing was still erratic and uneven.

"Alex?"

She opened her eyes to slits and looked up at me.

"Tell me I didn't hurt you, baby."

Alex blinked and grinned at me, "Hurt me? No. Killed me, put me in an orgasmic coma, yes. That was not what

I expected; I may have blacked out for a minute. You're a freakin' sex god."

Fuck, she was perfect. I smiled down at her, rubbing my thumb across her cheekbone; my voice low and full of emotion, "Then you are my goddess."

Alex put her hand over mine, her voice soft, "Gah, Cole, that's the best thing anyone has ever said to me."

I took her face in my hands and kissed her gently, passionately, deeply.

When I pulled away, she was breathing hard, "Help me up. I want this crap off my face."

I climbed off the bed, took her outstretched hands, and pulled, but she wasn't helping at all, she was totally limp, her arms straight, but her body hanging.

She started laughing, "You've made me boneless."

I couldn't help but laugh with her. Alex got up and went into the bathroom and removed her makeup. When she reappeared, I was sitting on the foot of the bed waiting for her. She was beautiful with the makeup on but to me, she was even more beautiful without any makeup at all.

"There she is."

Alex grinned, walked up to me, and put her right foot on the bed next to me, "Unzip me."

I unzipped her boot and ran my hands up her thighs to her bare ass, "Bossy."

She switched places with her other foot, "Again," she ordered with a smile. Her hands on my shoulders as I happily complied.

I traded places with her and removed her boots, then stood her up and helped her out of her dress. During the evening, I'd heard just how expensive the one-of-a-kind dress was. Not wanting to drop it on the floor, I put it on a hanger and hung it in the closet.

"Where are my panties?" She asked me.

"You gave them to me. I'm keeping them."

She smiled, "I don't think they'll fit you."

I smirked at her, "That's not why I want them."

Alex laughed and unhooked her bra and tossed it to me with a smile on her face. "Then you might as well have this too since they're a matching set."

I was hard by the time she was undressed. Picking her up, I put her back in bed and made love to her tenderly, with slow, deliberate thrusts. Worshiping her, kissing her, looking deep into her eyes, and I felt whole again.

Then I pulled her into me and curled around her and slept deeply for the first time in a long time.

Chapter 43

Alex

I woke up and, for a minute, had no idea where I was. Then the memories of the night before filled my head, and I smiled. Stretching, I sat up and looked around.

I assumed I was at Cole's house but wasn't sure. The clock said it was six-thirty, and I was surprised I'd slept that late. Until the kidnapping, my internal clock woke me at five no matter what happened the night before.

I saw a picture on the nightstand I hadn't noticed last night and picked it up. It was one of the pictures Oscar had taken of me the night I was kidnapped. I was standing against a brick wall, looking up at the camera.

I realized Cole must have stolen this picture, and that made me smile. Looking around, I didn't see any other photographs in the room, and my heart swelled until I thought it might burst. I held the picture to my chest and stomped my feet, wiggling back and forth with a huge smile on my face. *He does like me.*

I put the picture back on the nightstand, stood up, and walked into the en suite bathroom. I used the toilet and brushed my teeth with the new toothbrush that was left on the bathroom counter.

Then I ran my fingers through my hair until it stopped looking like something was living in it. Without any clothes to wear, I put on Cole's shirt from the night before and rolled up the sleeves.

I quite literally hadn't been in a position to check out the house on my way in the night before, so I took the opportunity to look around. I saw a second bedroom and bathroom and a large room, like a den, set up like a mini gym.

The living room and kitchen were one large room separated by a work-space counter with stools. Off the kitchen was a screened porch, where there was a large round table with six chairs. Through the screened porch, there was a deck and what looked like a private pier leading straight to the beach.

My phone and wallet were on the kitchen counter. Gabe must have given them to Cole along with my car keys.

I didn't see Cole inside the house but I saw the coffee was made, so I poured myself a cup and went out on the deck.

Cole was sitting in a deckchair like a Greek god, wearing nothing but board shorts, that wide, perfect chest on display, those long muscular legs stretched out in front of him and crossed at the ankles.

I smiled at him, "Morning."

He smiled back at me, "Good morning."

"Is this your house?" I asked, standing at the railing, looking out at the ocean and sipping my coffee.

"Yeah."

"It's beautiful."

"You like it?"

I turned around and leaned against the railing, looking at him, "It's light and bright and open, it's at the beach, but not right on the beach, so it's private; you have your own private pier leading to the beach, the screened porch, this deck. What's not to like?"

"It's not that big."

"It's absolutely perfect just the way it is."

Chapter 44

Cole

It looked like she did like my house, and I liked that. Her ranch, the ranch house, her house were big. My house was small in comparison, but I loved it, and it made me feel good that she didn't snub her nose at it.

Watching her sipping her coffee, I let my eyes lazily wander over her. I took in her rosy cheeks; her long bare legs stretched out in front of her, her bare feet, her messy hair blowing in the breeze. Every time I saw her, she seemed more beautiful.

Alex watched my eyes roaming over her, "I have a bag in my car, but until I go get it, I borrowed your shirt; I hope you don't mind."

I picked my phone up off the table and pointed it at her.

She smiled at me, "What are you doing?"

"I'm taking a picture of you."

"You can take my picture if you take one of us together."

She smiled wide, set her coffee cup down and spread her hands on the railing. I snapped a couple of pictures of her and held my hand out for her. Still smiling, she picked up her coffee and walked toward me.

"I like you in my shirt; it's a good look for you."

I took her coffee cup and set it on the table next to my chair, then slipped my arm around her waist and pulled her into my lap and kissed her hard and deep.

"Good morning," I said as my hands roamed under her shirt. "Jesus, you're naked under here."

"Someone stole my undergarments."

I was nuzzling her, my hands roaming her naked body, "I didn't *steal* them; you gave them to me."

“How are you feeling?” I asked her.

“Fanfuckingtastic. How are you feeling?”

I kept nuzzling her, kissing her neck, my hands under her shirt, squeezing her breasts and rubbing my thumbs over her nipples that had peaked to hard nubs, “Like I want to take you back to bed. I can't promise you forever, Alex. Hell, I can't even promise you next week, but if you want, I'm yours this weekend."

She moaned and dropped her head back in response to my wandering mouth and hands, her voice breathless, "Okay."

"Okay? Just like that?"

"Just like that."

"How about I take you out to dinner later then we'll go drink some beers and play some pool."

"Are you sure you want to do that?"

"Why wouldn't I?"

"I might kick your ass."

I smiled at her, "Not possible."

"Oh, them's fightin' words, cowboy. It's on like Donkey Kong now."

I chuckled, "You're such a little weirdo."

Smiling at me, she slipped her arms around my neck and put her face close to mine, "Yep. But it's not gonna stop me from kicking your ass tonight. Now kiss me again."

That was just one more thing I liked about her, I could tease her, and she didn't get mad or sulk or pout.

When I finally dragged my mouth from hers, I asked, "Do you want to go for a run with me this morning?"

"Sure, but I need a piece of toast or something first. I don't like to run completely empty."

"I'll get your bag out of the car, we'll have something light to eat and then we'll go. Unless you need to wake up more."

I was nuzzling her neck again, and she tilted her head, exposing her long, beautiful throat to me, running her fingers through my hair.

"That sounds good, but you're going to have to stop that, or I won't let you get up."

Reluctantly, I went and retrieved her bag, and Alex went into the house to see what there was to eat. I brought her bag in and saw her bent over, leaning into the freezer, my shirt barely covering her delectable backside.

I dropped her bag off in my room, grabbed a condom, and came back into the kitchen. I wasn't going to be able to keep my hands off her.

I came up behind her, wrapping my arms around her, engulfing her, my right hand on her left hip, my left hand on her right hip. Alex leaned back into me, giving me her weight, turning her head to kiss me.

"Why do you have such a big bag in your car?" I asked absently.

"Sometimes my life overwhelms me, and I run away, so I stay ready," she told me casually.

I was nuzzling her neck and rubbing my cheek against hers, my beard on her skin making her squirm. She leaned back into me and moaned as a result of my roaming hands. Reaching her left arm up behind her and around my neck, she palmed my stiff cock with her right hand.

"Alex," I growled in her ear, sending shivers through her body.

I wondered if this was what addicts felt like, needing another hit because I couldn't get enough of her.

"You want toast or fruit? I can make you eggs," she said distractedly over her shoulder.

I whispered in her ear, "I have everything I want right here."

Alex giggled, and as usual, the sound went straight to my dick.

As good as she looked in my shirt, I turned her around and ripped it open. The buttons popped and flew, scattering across the floor, exposing her beautiful body to me, "I need you naked."

She chuckled, "Yeah, I'm getting that. I can practically hear your dirty thoughts."

Smiling wide, she slipped the shirt off her shoulders, letting it drop to the floor. I loved how willing and uninhibited she was.

I stripped off my shorts and ripped the condom open with my teeth, and quickly smoothed it down my rock-hard shaft.

I held my arms out, "Hop up."

Smiling, Alex jumped up and wrapped her strong legs tightly around my waist, holding onto my biceps, my hands holding her by the ass, and I kissed her long and leisurely.

I didn't need to hold on to her, she was strong, she wouldn't let herself fall, leaving my hands free. I leaned over and sucked one of her nipples in my mouth, one hand squeezing her other breast, the other going between her legs.

Her hands were tangled in my hair, and she sighed my name.

"You like that, angel?"

She rocked against me, "Mmm, you know I do." She was moaning my name and fucking my hand, "Stop teasing."

I smirked and moved us, so her back was against the wall, "Am I teasing you?"

"Let's see how you like it," Alex said as she grabbed my cock and started stroking me.

I dropped my head back and groaned, fisting my hands in her hair, "Put me inside you."

Alex rubbed my dick against her, positioning me at her entrance, then sliding my cock back through her slippery folds.

"Alex," I said in a deep, raspy voice.

"Not so funny now, huh, cowboy?" Her voice sexy and sensual. I brushed her hand aside, taking my cock in my hand.

We moaned each other's name as I pushed into her. Sliding in and out of her with long, deep strokes, her tits bouncing with every thrust.

"You feel so fucking good. I think you might be a witch. I can't keep my hands off you; the more I have you, the more I want. What have you done to me, Alex?"

I was filled with unfamiliar emotions. She was changing who I was, opening me to who I didn't know I wanted to be.

Sighing my name, Alex whispered, "I feel the same way."

She gripped the back of my head, running her tongue over my ear and sunk her teeth into my earlobe before sucking it into her mouth, and I was shocked how erotic it was. Bracing one hand on the wall, I started thrusting faster.

"Touch yourself. Make yourself come."

Without hesitation, Alex reached between us to stroke her clit. We both looked down and watched as I slid in and out of her in the most intimate way two people could be connected while she stroked herself. Our pubic hair meshing, mine black, hers auburn, both of us moaning a guttural sound at the erotic and sensual sight.

Alex started speaking French. I recognized my name but had no idea what else she was saying. Her voice was sultry, and it turned me way the hell on, especially with the way she was writhing and bucking against me, her legs tight around my waist, her feet locked behind my back.

When she came, she cried out my name and let her head fall back against the wall with a thud. Her arms were around my neck, her fingers tangled in my hair. She squeezed her internal muscles around me tight.

"That feels amazing, do it again."

She did, and for the next few strokes, each time I entered her, she squeezed me tight until I exploded. I kissed her as if my life depended on it and if someone asked me right that second, I would have said it did.

When I was finally able to pull myself away from her, we got dressed, and Alex settled on toast for breakfast.

She wore shorts and a tank top, with tennis shoes, her hair in a ponytail. I put one of my SEAL ballcaps on her head to protect her from the sun. Grabbing a couple of towels, we walked down the pier to the beach holding hands, and it felt like the most natural thing in the world.

"I'm about to Linda Ronstadt your ass," Alex said when we reached the sand.

"I have no idea what that means," I replied as I set our towels down.

"Blue Bayou."

I started laughing, and Alex took off running while I was distracted, but I caught up quickly. I liked running with her, she took it seriously, and I didn't have to alter my pace or distance for her, and several times, she sped up, making me work to keep up with her. She was a good running partner, and I spent some time wondering how we could do this more often.

When we came back, I lifted her in my arms and kissed her hard before walking toward the house holding her hand.

Walking up the pier, I was surprised to see Smoke sitting on the deck.

Alex smiled at him, "Hey, Smoke!"

"Hi, Alex. Good to see you; you were great last night."

"Thanks. Did you have fun?"

"Yeah, I did." He grinned at her, "Did *you*?"

“Smoke,” I warned.

Alex smiled back at him, not looking embarrassed at all, "I had an unbelievable night and a pretty good morning. I know it's still early, but we’re going to have a sandwich; you want one?"

"You don't have to make our friends or me a sandwich," I told her.

It didn't escape me that I said 'our' friends. Based on the look on his face, it didn’t get by Smoke either.

Alex smiled at me, "It's sandwiches, not a five-course dinner for ten. I think I can handle it all by my lonesome. Stay and relax with Smoke."

Before I could throw him out, Smoke told Alex, "I'd love a sandwich."

Alex smiled, and I watched her disappear into the house before sitting in a chair next to Smoke. He was staring at me, a smirk on his face.

"What?"

"You willingly have a woman in your house."

"So?"

"You brought her *here* last night, and she's still *here*."

"I'm aware, Smoke. What's your point?"

His smile got wider, "Just making an observation. If it means anything, we like her, and I think she's really good for you."

I was surprised by that comment and quirked an eyebrow at him.

"Watching you down there with her, you looked...happy."

I wasn’t ready to admit I *felt* happy with her.

“Brother, you’re in a shit-ton of trouble with that one, but damn, are you one lucky bastard. Hey, if you don’t want her, can I have her?”

“Don’t make me hurt you, Smoke.”

Smoke held his hands up in surrender and laughed. "She's making sandwiches."

"Did you hit your head? What the fuck is wrong with you today?"

"I'm just soaking in the fact that for the first time since I've known you, you invited a woman to your house, let her stay the night, played with her on the beach, and now she's in your kitchen making sandwiches, and you seem just fine with that."

I smiled, "I *am* fine with that."

"Seriously, you're a moron if you let her go."

While we were eating, Alex told Smoke, we were going out later, and she was going to kick my ass playing pool.

*****

After a day of watching movies, making love, and talking, we got dressed to go out. I was wearing jeans and a black t-shirt; Alex wore a pink and white checkered long-sleeved shirt that was tucked into skinny jeans, pink cowboy boots with her hair down. Smiling, I stood staring at her.

She looked down at herself, then up at me, “What?”

“You look great,” I told her, pulling her into me by the waist and kissing her. When I pulled back, she was panting for air.

“Are you okay going on my bike?”

"You have a motorcycle?" I could hear the excitement in her voice, and she grinned at me, "Can I tell you a secret?"

"You can tell me all your secrets."

"Damn, Cole, what are you trying to do to me saying shit like that all serious and sexy?"

I grinned at her, "What's your secret, angel?"

"I've never been on a motorcycle."

I couldn't keep the shock out of my voice, "Never?"

She shook her head. "I can totally see you on a motorcycle. I'm really excited," she told me, bouncing a little on the balls of her feet.

I took her face in my hands and kissed her again because I just couldn't help myself.

We went out to my bike, and she smiled wide, seeing it, "And it's a Harley."

I handed her a helmet, and she pulled it on after twisting her hair on the top of her head.

"Check me out; I'm a biker chick."

I laughed, shaking my head and buckling the strap, noticing the helmet was a little big on her. She smiled at me the whole time, excitement shining in her green eyes.

I put on my own helmet and got on, and she straddled the bike behind me, her hands on my hips.

Taking her hands in mine, I wrapped them around my waist. That was all the encouragement she needed, she wiggled up against me and plastered her chest against my back, her head next to mine, holding me tight, and I swear I felt her smiling.

The team's favorite bar was on a boardwalk, about two miles from my house; being close to the base, it was known as a bar a lot of SEALs frequented. It was called Harry B's after Harry Beal, the first Navy SEAL.

The boardwalk had shops and restaurants, a pizza place, a diner, a coffee shop, a bakery, fancier Italian and seafood restaurants, as well as other businesses and shops.

I parked and turned off the engine. Alex got off the bike, and I did the same.

She was beaming, "That was so fun. Can we do that again? Maybe for a longer ride?"

I couldn't help smiling back at her, "Absolutely."

Alex pulled off her helmet, shook out her hair and looked around, "This is fantastic, and it's so close to your house."

"Where would you like to eat?"

"Which places are good? Are there any you don't like?"

I liked that she didn't tell me I could choose, that she didn't say she didn't care where we ate.

"Actually, they're all pretty good, so you can choose any of them," I told her, taking the helmet from her.

Her response was immediate, "Then I choose the diner."

"Really?"

"If you'd rather go somewhere else, I'm okay with that."

"No. I'm just a little surprised that's what you picked."

She smiled at me, "I love a good diner."

She was always surprising me. For someone famous with money, she was the least pretentious person I knew.

We went into the diner, and while it was obvious she was recognized, no one approached her. We ate, talked, and laughed, and I forced myself not to think about how easy it was to be with her and how much I liked spending time with her.

After we left the diner, we walked across the street to Harry B's with our arms around each other, Alex's hand resting in my back pocket.

From the moment we walked in, the attention of the bar shifted to her. She didn't seem aware of the eyes on her or had become adept at ignoring the attention.

I wasn't sure if the way everyone in the room stopped to look at her was because they recognized her or because she had a presence about her, a presence she wasn't aware of. I had a feeling even if she weren't famous, people would stop what they were doing just to stare at her.

I ordered drinks, a beer for myself, and a margarita on the rocks for Alex, and we headed to the back of the bar to the pool tables.

We were about halfway through our second game when the rest of the team unexpectedly showed up. Smoke obviously told them we'd be here. From their broad smiles, I knew they were fucking with me, wanting to see for themselves I really *was* out with Alex. She seemed happy to see them and hugged each one of them hello.

When she got to Smoke, he bent her over his arm, and I snatched her away from him, putting a possessive arm around her, glaring at him, and he laughed at me.

With everyone here, we split up into teams, and after a few games, I took her out to the dance floor. While we were dancing, a woman approached us and asked me to leave with her. I didn't remember her, but she made it clear we'd previously spent a night together.

She was heavily made up, wearing a short skirt that barely covered her ass, high spike heels, her large breasts straining against her extremely low-cut shirt.

The type of woman who would normally get my attention, but compared to Alex, I realized how artificial and obvious she was and wondered how I could ever have been with someone like her.

"I don't know what makes you think it's okay to hit on me when I'm obviously here with someone, but it's rude and obnoxious," I told her in a dismissive tone.

I was angry and annoyed. Worried how this was making Alex feel. For the first time, I felt ashamed of my sexual past.

The woman didn't go away, instead she arched her back, her hands on her hips, "C'mon lover, I'll make you feel good, just like last time."

Alex looked at the woman and calmly told her, "You're just being sad and pathetic now; you should go before I have to kick your ass."

It surprised me how much I liked Alex being possessive of me and even better, she wasn't throwing a fit or sulking out the door knowing I'd slept with this woman.

The woman glared at Alex, "Butt out; the grownups are talking. Besides, he's way too much man for you, little girl."

I felt Alex tense before she turned around; facing the woman, and I wrapped my arms around her.

"Back off. If he wanted a bitch, he'd get a dog," Alex snapped back.

I smiled at the stunned look on the woman's face, and I heard laughing from the tables closest to us.

The woman screeched loudly in response, "Do you have any idea who I am?"

Alex looked around the room and called out, "Does anyone know this chick? Apparently, she doesn't know who she is."

I couldn't help but laugh along with everyone else who was watching and listening attentively. I'd seen Alex riled up before, but never like this.

The woman looked like she was close to screaming and snarled, "Shut up, you ginger hillbilly."

Alex stiffened, "Ginger hillbilly? Oh, *hell* no. That's it, you and me, outside *right* now." Alex wiggled against my arm, "Lemme go, I'm gonna rip that bad dye job hair right out of her head."

I could hear comments from behind us, "I got twenty on the redhead."

"Let her go!"

"Yeah, let her go!" That comment came from Bruiser.

The woman held out her hands and wiggled her fingers as if saying, 'bring it on'. I tightened my hold on Alex and lifted her off her feet as she leapt for the woman.

My head next to hers, I whispered, "Easy, wildcat."

I felt her relax a little but didn't set her on her feet.

"You need to leave now, or I'm going to let her go, and she *will* hurt you," I told the woman, and I knew I wasn't lying.

I don't know if it was the look on Alex's face or mine, but fortunately, the woman chose to listen and stomped away. After she'd gone a safe distance, I set Alex on her feet but didn't let go of her. She was still looking at the woman, giving her the stink eye.

"Alex, look at me."

She slowly turned in my arms until she was looking up at me, her hands on my chest, "Why didn't you let me kick her ass?"

I was grinning at her, "I didn't want to spend the rest of our night bailing you out of jail."

"You would have bailed me out of jail?"

"Absolutely."

She smiled that megawatt smile at me, "That's so sweet."

I palmed her face and rubbed my thumb across her cheek, "I'm sorry about that."

"It's not your fault; you didn't encourage her. I'm aware you have a past, and it wasn't as a monk." She grinned at me, "It's really not my business anyway, although I'm a little concerned about your taste in women."

Damn, this woman was perfect.

"I think I like you being possessive of me."

"I wasn't being possessive of you," Alex argued.

"You are the worst liar in the world." I put my forehead against hers, "And I like that too." I bent and kissed her, "C'mon, wildcat, let's go back to our game, then I'm going to take you home and fuck you senseless."

"Are you just trying to distract me again so you can win?"

I grinned at her, "Is it working?"

Alex smiled up at me, sliding her arms around my neck, "Well, that really wasn't your best work; you'll have to do better if you want to distract me."

I pulled her into me and kissed her deeply, feeling the softness of her tongue against mine, not giving a shit that we were standing in the middle of a crowded bar.

When I pulled away, I smiled down at her, "Alex and margarita, delicious." I rubbed her bottom lip with my thumb, "Better?"

She looked dazed, "I don't know, my brain stopped functioning."

I threw my head back and laughed, steering her toward the bar. I ordered her another drink, and we went back to the pool tables.

The team was grinning at us when we got back. Smoke had a beer in his hand. Looking at me and smiling, he raised it in a silent toast. I rolled my eyes and shook my head at him.

"You could have taken her," Jax told Alex.

Bruiser held his hand out as we walked by him, and Alex slapped it. I had a feeling that wasn't the first time they'd done that.

"That was awesome," Midas told her.

Boomer smiled at her, "You annihilated her."

Smoke took hold of her hand, "*Please* marry me."

Alex shook her head at him, "Sorry, it's still a no."

I wrapped my arm around her waist and sat down, pulling her into my lap, my arms around her.

She was smiling at me, "Thank you for bringing me here. I don't know the last time I had this much fun."

I cocked an eyebrow at her.

She lowered her voice, "I can hear your dirty thoughts again, so let me rephrase. I don't know the last time I had this much fun where we weren't naked. Or partially naked. Crap, now I'm having dirty thoughts." She hid her face in my neck and giggled.

I squeezed her, "I swear, you're going to be the death of me, woman."

It wasn't long before I told the team we were heading out. Taking her hand, I led her out of the bar, "Are you familiar with the reverse cowgirl?" I asked her, smiling.

Alex giggled and leaned into me as we walked, "Ask me again in a couple of hours."

I'd never had a woman in my space before. Never lived with a woman, not that a weekend was living with a woman, but it was the closest I'd ever come. I thought it would be stifling, but it was easy and fun being with her and I was surprised on Sunday when I didn't want her to leave.

Since Alex left my house, I hadn't been able to get her out of my head. More than that, I had an uncontrollable need to see her.

I was falling for my tantalizing redheaded minx, who was rocking my world one minute at a time.

Chapter 45

Alex

The following Wednesday, I'd been home about five minutes when I heard a knock on the door and answered it. I was surprised to see Cole standing there wearing his work uniform. I was barefoot, wearing jeans and a light blue t-shirt that said, 'Been Doing Cowboy Shit All Day'.

He looked like something bad had happened. His hair was a mess like he'd been running his hands through it.

"Are you okay?"

"No," he said solemnly.

Worried, I opened the door wider, "Come in. What's wrong?" I asked, closing the door behind us.

"I couldn't...I can't...Fuck," he ran his hand through his hair, messing it up even more, letting out a long sigh.

I was seriously concerned because I'd never seen him like this, "Cole, what is it?"

He hugged me tight against him as if I were his salvation, his voice gruff, "You're in my head. You've crawled under my skin. I can't stay away from you."

Swoon.

I looked up at him, "So, you're saying you like me, and that upsets you?"

"Yes...No." He let out another heavy sigh, "Fuck, Alex, what are you doing to me?"

"I could ask what you're doing to me, but it doesn't seem smart for both of us to freak out at the same time."

"I'm not freaking out. I don't *get* freaked out." He sounded insulted.

I stood and simply stared at him.

"Fine. I'm freaking out a little."

I took a step away from him, "I'm going to say something that might end up being a mistake, but I'm going to say it anyway."

I took a deep breath, "You scare the shit out of me because I know that any day I spend with you could be the day you walk away.

"But even if the day comes when you walk away, I won't be sorry for the time I spent with you. I won't regret it because of how you make me feel when I'm with you. I'd rather feel this, experience it for a little while and get hurt than not ever feel it at all. Even if you walk away, even if it hurts, it's still worth it."

He looked at me as if I'd slapped him, his voice soft, "I don't want to hurt you, Alex. The *last* thing I want to do is hurt you."

I knew that and nodded, "There's something between us. If there wasn't, you wouldn't have broken all your rules. You wouldn't be here right now.

"I'm not good at this stuff, but I think you're scared of how you feel. If it makes a difference, I'm scared too. But if you need to, if you have to, you can walk away. I don't want to be with you if it's not what you want too."

He reached for me, but I took several steps away from him, putting distance between us, and he looked hurt and confused.

"I just got home. It looks like you just got off work too. I haven't had a chance to shower yet," I told him, pulling my shirt over my head and quickly stripping off my jeans and underwear.

I walked away, unclasping my bra, letting it hang from my finger before dropping it to the floor, "You'll feel better after a shower," I called over my shoulder.

I could hear him behind me, his boots clunking as they hit the floor, the sound of his clothes coming off.

Once I was in the bathroom, I turned on the water and started unbraiding my hair, but he stopped me and did it himself. When my hair was down, I took him by the hand and walked him to the middle of the shower and stood in front of him.

The water flowed over his back from the shower head behind him, hitting me in the back from the shower head on the opposite wall behind me.

I put a dollop of shampoo in my hand and washed his hair, my fingers rubbing his scalp before rinsing out the suds, the lather flowing down his bare back and over the curve of his perfect ass, then I massaged conditioner in his hair. He repeated the process on me, taking his time washing and conditioning my hair.

I could see his walls were down, his eyes filled with raw emotion and a hunger I'd never seen before. We didn't communicate with words, but we were having the most honest and intimate conversation we'd ever had. The simple act of washing each other was more sensuous and erotic than I could have ever imagined.

Soaping up my hands, I washed his chest, neck, and arms, moving down to his hands and washing between his fingers, then he took the soap and mimicked my every move.

I turned him to face the wall, and he leaned forward and braced his hands against it and bowed his head. I washed his back and his ass and the backs of his legs. We changed places, and he did the same to me.

I maneuvered him to the tile bench, and he sat. I went down on my knees in front of him, his hard shaft twitching in response.

I rested his foot on my thigh, slowly washing his thigh, his calf, his foot, running my fingers between his toes. Lifting his other leg, washing it the same way.

I kept my eyes on his while I soaped up my hands and washed his cock, his head dropping back against the tile, his groan low and loud.

After rinsing off the soap, I looked up at him, my hand around the base of his cock, lowered my head and took him in my mouth. His hips thrust, his deep rumble reverberating off the tile walls.

I sucked harder, taking him deep, swirling my tongue around his shaft on the way up and around the tip before sliding down him again. Releasing him from my mouth but still pumping him with my hand, I sucked one of his balls into my mouth.

His hips jerked, and his hands tightly gripped my wet hair, "Fuck Alex!"

Surprising me, he stood up with me in his arms as if I were made of air. I reached over and turned on the rain shower above us and wrapped my legs around his waist, hooking my feet on his ass. His cock was straining for me as if it knew exactly where it wanted to go.

Our mouths connected; the kiss was sensual.

Frantic.

Greedy.

Consuming.

His kiss left me dizzy and panting. Before I could catch my breath, he was kissing me again. The sensations he was causing were driving me wild. Still devouring each other, he thrust into me, or we thrust into each other; it was hard to tell which.

It was uncontrollable.

Unstoppable.

Emotional.

It was powerful and overwhelming.

We surrendered to each other. He took me up against the shower wall, his thrusts long and deep as if he needed to become part of me, to own me, and I responded with the same intensity.

Steam fogging the air, the only sounds, the water and our gasps and moans, our bodies coming together, the whispering of each other's names. When he buried his head in the crook of my neck, I felt him suck my skin, marking me.

We were in perfect sync. It was as if we could both feel what the other felt as if we were breathing each other, as if our hearts were beating as one.

It felt different.

Intimate.

Sacred.

I've never felt this alive or this afraid. He was either telling me he loved me or saying goodbye. Tears slipped out of my eyes and rolled down my face, and he kissed them away.

Our release hit at the same time, both of us calling the others name, both trembling, riding the shockwave.

Cole sat on the bench, and we clung to each other, panting and weak, his body buried deep inside mine, while mine continued to sporadically convulse around him.

The way he held me against him, the way he caressed me, it felt as if he'd decided something. I just didn't know what it was. I didn't know if it was the thing that would set me free and let me fly or the thing that would destroy me.

Chapter 46

Cole

"I'd rather feel this, experience it for a little while and get hurt than not ever feel it at all. Even if you walk away, even if it hurts, it's still worth it."

Something about those words resonated in me. I didn't want to hurt her. The last thing I wanted to do was hurt her. I also didn't want to let her go.

I've done things. I've killed people. And I'll do it again because it's part of my job, a job I love. But Alex didn't care about the things I've done or the things I'll do in the future. By some miracle, she didn't see *any* darkness in me and being with Alex quieted the demons inside me. Something I would have never thought possible.

She was right; I was afraid of how she made me feel, simply *because* she made me feel. But I hadn't realized that like her, I'd rather feel whatever this is than never experience it.

When she took me to the shower, I felt like my soul bonded to hers, and when her tears fell, I knew she felt it too.

I wasn't walking away now, couldn't walk away now, she was mine, and I was hers. Whatever speeding train we were on, it was too late to get off, and all I could do was hope it didn't derail and kill us both.

It had been a month since that day in the shower, and since then, we talked on the phone or texted almost every day. I went to her house at least twice a week, and she spent the weekends at my house.

We spent our time talking, making love, eating, relaxing, watching movies, swimming, running, going for rides on my bike and hanging out with the team. She was even teaching me how to ride a horse. It was getting harder to deny I'd never been happier.

Today, I showed up at her house without warning in the middle of the day, which I'd never done before. I found her in the arena working one of the horses.

When she saw me, she looked concerned, "What's wrong?"

"We're being spun up."

"When?"

"Tomorrow. Early."

"Come on." She took my hand and led me into the house, and we spent the day together talking, eating, and making love.

I woke her up about two in the morning to kiss her goodbye. I told her to go back to sleep, but she got up and put on her bathrobe and walked me out to my car, hugging me tight, "All of you be safe and come back whole."

It didn't surprise me she was concerned for the whole team.

"You be safe. Don't go anywhere alone, don't take any unnecessary risks," I told her.

"I think that's my line. Is there anything I can do while you're gone?" she asked me.

"Just be safe; that fucking stalker is out there somewhere."

She smiled at me, "I meant is there anything I can do for *you* while you're gone?"

"No." I kissed her long, deep, and passionately.

"Is it okay if I say I'll miss you?"

I palmed her face, kissing her again, "I'll miss you too, baby."

There were no tears, no questions, no drama. I appreciated it more than she could know, but then I shouldn't be surprised, she'd been doing this her whole life, and even if she hadn't, my guess is she would have handled it with the same strength and grace.

After I got in my car, she told me, "Keep your head on straight and go kick bad guy ass. Safe in. Safe out."

She smiled and waved, watching me drive away.

Chapter 47

Alex

It had been eight days since Cole and the team had left on their latest mission. I was surprised by how much I missed him and how much I worried.

Gabe had been keeping me busy in the studio. He'd written two new songs; I'll Keep the Boots On and Vixen. It wasn't hard to figure out where he got the ideas. I really needed to stop telling him things when I've been drinking.

It was about nine in the morning, and I was in the arena next to the barn working a horse when I could swear I felt the air around me change. As if our hearts were intertwined, I knew it was him. I spun around to see Cole walking toward the arena smiling.

I smiled a huge smile, climbed over the arena fence, and took off running straight for him, and I wasn't slowing down; I couldn't slow down. Cole stopped, putting his right foot back to keep his balance as I jumped into his arms, hitting his chest with an oof, wrapping my legs around his waist.

His arms went around me, holding me by the ass, my arms around his neck, and we stood kissing intensely, a kiss of longing and absolute ownership. Our mouths hot and demanding, I moaned into his mouth, and he responded by holding me tighter against him.

When he pulled away, we were grinning and gasping for breath.

"Welcome home. I missed you," I told him, still panting.

"I missed you too."

"How was it? Everyone whole?"

He smiled, "It was good, and everyone is fine."

"Put me down and let's go home; we've got eight days to make up for."

He set me on my feet, and we headed for home, our arms around each other. He flashed me a wicked smile, "I've never had welcome home sex."

I smiled back at him, "Me either. Take a picture of us to commemorate the occasion."

Still smiling, Cole pulled out his phone. He was getting much better about taking pictures of us.

We put our faces close together, "Say welcome home sex!" I said and started laughing.

He clicked the picture and pocketed his phone.

"C'mon, let's go pop our welcome home sex cherries," I told him, and Cole laughed.

He kicked the door closed behind us. We didn't make it past the living room before we were stripping off our clothes and coming together in a hard and fast frenzy.

Once we had recovered and were breathing normally, we headed to the bedroom for round two.

Then he slept like the dead. I left him in bed sleeping and went back to work. He had to be exhausted; I'd never been able to slip out of bed without him waking up before.

I didn't come back until just before dinnertime, and when I checked on him, he was still asleep. Figuring he'd be hungry when he woke up, I prepped some food and went to take a shower.

I'd just finished slathering conditioner in my hair when I saw Cole standing naked outside the shower, "Hey, sleepyhead."

Spreading his feet and putting his fisted hands on his hips, doing his best superhero pose, he smiled at me, "I'm not sleeping anymore."

I could see how hard he was, and he already had a condom on. At the sight of him, I started laughing and couldn't stop.

It took a minute before I could speak, but I was still laughing, "I can see that. Looks like you brought me a present and it's a big one too. Get in here, Superstud, and impress me with your superpowers."

And not surprisingly, he did.

Chapter 48

Cole

It was late afternoon, three days later, when I received an alarming call from Falcon; he told me Alex had been kidnapped again.

The news nearly stopped my heart.

"Tell me exactly what happened," I ordered impatiently once I could think again.

"We went to the Bailey farm to pick up produce. We left the farm and were almost home when we saw a truck that had lost its load of hay and was blocking half the road.

"We've seen that before, so it wasn't as if there was anything about it to put us on high alert. I was shot with a tranquilizer dart. Never saw it coming.

"When I woke up, I was here in the truck about two miles from where we'd been, and Alex was gone. I drove back to where we saw the truck, but there's nothing there."

I ran my hand through my hair, feeling frantic.

"When did this happen?" I demanded.

"I'm not sure; I don't know how long I was out. I'd guess at least one or two hours ago. I'm so sorry, Reaper."

Alex had been kidnapped again, and I wasn't there to prevent it. I was sure Brooks Kennedy was responsible, but we had no proof.

Since we'd received the call from Falcon, we'd been trying to locate Brooks, but he wasn't at his house, and no one seemed to know where he was, which convinced me, even more, it was him.

After Peru, Alex started wearing a tracker, and it was working until it wasn't. Midas was trying to figure out why it was no longer sending a signal but had only been able to come up with her tracker was being 'glitchy,' or something was blocking the signal.

We couldn't track her phone, leading us to believe the battery had been removed, so we couldn't track her that way either.

None of this information helped my mood or eased my panic. Both the tracker and her phone showed her last known location at a marina about an hour from the ranch.

We headed to the marina, but there was nothing out of the ordinary here. There were too many boats and warehouses, buildings, and businesses to search, but if we didn't find something soon, quantity wasn't going to stop me.

I told Boomer and Bruiser to watch the area and tasked Midas with looking for any business surveillance, ATM, or traffic camera footage and to look for any properties or boats in the area that were connected to Brooks Kennedy.

“The rest of us are going to search that fucker’s house,” I told the team.

“We can’t just go in there. We need authorization,” Jax responded, knowing exactly which fucker I was talking about.

I pulled out my phone and made a short phone call, “We’re authorized.”

“Did you just call the President?” Smoke asked me.

“We needed authorization; I got us authorization. Let’s go.”

When we arrived at Brooks’ house, we made quick work of the locks. Above the fireplace in the living room was a giant portrait of Alex. Every fiber of my being wanted to kill Brooks Kennedy.

"I knew this was the fucking guy,” I snapped. Unfortunately, being right wasn’t going to help us find Alex.

“You two take upstairs; I’ll check down here.”

Jax and Smoke nodded and headed up the stairs.

I’d finished searching downstairs, not surprised I didn’t find anything. I was on my way upstairs when Smoke and Jax came out of one of the bedrooms and closed the door behind them when they saw me.

“All clear up here,” Jax called out.

But I knew something was up from the looks on their faces and the way they were blocking the hallway and the door to that bedroom.

I took the stairs two at a time, Smoke and Jax trying to keep me from going in the bedroom, pushing against my chest, which just made me more determined.

"You're not going in there," Jax told me.

I shoved past them, opening the door so hard it slammed against the wall. I could only stand there staring; my jaw clenched tight, my hands fisted, fury coursing through me at what I was seeing.

All four walls were covered floor to ceiling with photos of Alex. The only furniture in the room was a recliner that could spin in any direction and a small table with a box of tissues, a bottle of lube and a trash can. I felt sick and disgusted.

“Motherfucking fucker. I am going to kill this fucking psycho!" I shouted.

Smoke nodded, "I really hate this guy."

As I looked around, some of the pictures caught my eye.

Alex sitting next to a boy. They were up a tree, their legs dangling. The boy had to be Gabe.

"These pictures go back years. She's maybe fourteen or fifteen in this one."

Five kids walking, two girls on Alex's right, laughing at each other. Gabe and another boy on her left, caught in a conversation. Alex standing straight and tall, towering over them, in the middle of a stride, staring straight ahead. They were obviously at school. The so-called Misfits, I guessed. There was a tag on the photo that said, ‘The Protector’.

"She's probably only sixteen in this one."

Alex circled by boys, rage on her face. Hands all over her, the photo caught right when she was connecting an elbow to one of their faces, his head snapping backward. One leg kicking out toward another boy. Brooks standing across from her, smiling.

Smoke came and stood next to me, "Jesus, is this that fucking circle?"

“That would be my guess, too,” I responded.

Alex piggyback on the back of a young man, Gabe on the back of another man. Alex and Gabe were looking at each other, laughing.

"I’d bet that's her dad and her brother."

Jax pointed to one of the pictures, "Who's this kid? He's in a lot of these photos."

"It’s Gabe," I responded, not able to tear my eyes away from the walls.

There was a newspaper article with a headline that read, ‘Decorated Navy SEAL Charles Walker dies’.

Underneath was a photo of Alex standing alone, hugging herself, a look of anguish on her face watching a body bag being loaded into a van. Looking at the picture, it felt like my heart was being crushed.

“He had to be on her property to get this picture.”

Near the headline about her dad, there was an article from the school paper; ‘Senior Alex Walker wins state cross country title with record-setting time, third year in a row.’ Below the article were photos of Alex during the race and crossing the finish line.

A close up of Alex on Zeus, it looked like she was coming right at the camera. She was leaning forward, her hat on her head, waving a coiled lasso in one hand, the other holding the reins.

Alex and I dancing at the benefit, a picture of Brooks' face was glued over mine. I ripped the picture off the wall, turned around and stormed out of the room, bellowing, "Where the fuck is she!"

I called Bruiser as I jogged down the stairs and out of this hellhole, "Anything?"

"No, all clear here. Did you find anything at the house?"

I didn't answer the question, telling him, "We're headed back to the base; meet us there."

Once we were back at the base, I sat staring at nothing. I felt powerless, a feeling I'd never felt before. I couldn't stop thinking about those pictures.

Her life hadn't been all rainbows and flowers. The photo of her surrounded by boys at school was haunting me. Hearing it was one thing, seeing it, another. What had she suffered at their hands? How many times did she have to endure that? I wanted to track down each and every one of those bastards and dispense a little payback.

And now she was missing, and that freak had her.

Hang on, Alex. Just hang on, baby, I'll find you. If it's the last thing I do, I'll find you.

Chapter 49

Alex

I woke up on the floor and didn't know where I was, but I knew it wasn't anywhere good since I was chained by my right ankle and my shoes were gone. *Fuck me sideways, not again.*

I stood up, trying to remember what happened, but I had no idea how I ended up here. I was dizzy, and my head was foggy. *Where am I this time, and who the hell is doing this?*

Clarity hit me like a tsunami when the door opened, and Brooks Kennedy walked in, "You're finally awake." He smiled an evil smile at me, "I have waited a very long time for this. I finally got what's mine."

I should have been scared shitless, but instead, my first reaction was anger. Scratch that; what I was feeling was rage.

"Unfortunately, your boyfriend and his pals are making things difficult, and I have to take care of him first."

"He's not my boyfriend. He's got nothing to do with this; just leave him alone," I snapped.

"I've been watching; he's had his hands all over you. He touched what's mine; he has to pay for that."

It made my skin crawl when he said he'd been watching us, and I wondered how long he'd been doing that.

"What is your malfunction? I'm not yours, you crazy fruit loop. You'll never get close to him; he'll kill you first, the same way he killed Del Norte and all his men. You remember Del Norte, don't you? The scumbag you hired to kidnap me."

Brooks walked and stood in front of me, "Still the Protector, huh? Well, you aren't protecting anyone anymore. I own you now."

He grabbed me, his fingers biting into my shoulders and licked up the side of my face from my jaw line to my ear. It was gross, and I jerked my head away, feeling like I might throw up.

"I'm finally gonna have soooo much fun with this sweet little body. By the time I'm done with you, there won't be any fight left in you. You'll do what I say when I say it.

"We're going to have the most beautiful babies. Of course, you won't have anything to do with them; I wouldn't want them to pick up any bad habits from you."

That statement got my attention and turned my stomach. But I knew him, knew if I showed him fear, I was done for.

He started pacing the room, looking unhinged, "I'm gonna kill your G.I Joe. I'm gonna do it real slow, and you're gonna watch the whole thing. Think the Protector can save him?"

"He's Navy, genius."

Brooks turned and looked at me, "What?"

"You're dumber than stupid. He's a *Navy* SEAL. G.I. Joe is Army, you fucking idiot."

I couldn't stand the thought of him hurting Cole. I knew I wouldn't survive watching Brooks kill him, and at that moment, I knew without a doubt Brooks would do it if he got his hands on Cole.

He walked up to me until his face was only inches away from mine, "You know what I love most about you? You're just so damn spunky. You were the only one, Alex. The only one who never just took it, the only one who fought back. That's what makes you so special. The question is how much can you take, Pro-tec-tor?"

"You're a crazy psycho and use a toothbrush or at least eat a breath mint; your breath is atrocious."

"You've always been such a smartass. But you never did know when to keep your pretty mouth shut. Well, now I'm going make this smartass mouth do anything I want, whenever I want.

"But first, I need to run a few errands for our trip, and I have to collect your G.I Joe. Be my obedient, good girl and stay put." He laughed, but it was a deranged sound.

"He's Navy, you stupid fucking twit!" I yelled as he left, closing and locking the door behind him.

"FUCK!" I screamed.

In a frenzy, I started tugging, pulling, jerking on the chain and ankle cuff, trying to get free of it. But after ten minutes, the only thing I accomplished was tearing the skin off my ankle and making it bleed.

Where am I? How long have I been gone? Why hasn't Cole come to get me? Okay, now I'm officially scared.

Many hours later, when Brooks came back, he opened the door and pointed a gun at me.

The last thing I saw was Brooks Kennedy shooting me.

Chapter 50

Cole

Alex had been missing for twenty-four hours, and I felt like I was going out of my mind. I hadn't been able to sleep, and any time I tried to eat anything, I felt sick. The Commander looked exactly like I felt, and the team didn't look much better.

Bruiser stood next to me. He didn't say anything for several minutes before putting his hand on my shoulder, "She knows we're looking for her; she knows we'll come for her."

"We're going to find her," Smoke said.

"She won't give up," came from Jax.

"She's one of us; we won't stop until we find her," Boomer murmured.

I knew they were trying to make me feel better, and I appreciated it, but it wasn't helping. She had to be wondering where I was. Wondering why I hadn't come for her.

I couldn't help but think about what Brooks was doing to her. Was he beating her? Cutting her? Sexually assaulting her? I was deathly afraid I'd never see her again, and if I did, she wouldn't be the same.

I couldn't imagine not seeing her again. Never hearing her laugh, never feeling her hand in mine, never holding her against me. I couldn't lose the best thing that ever happened to me.

I couldn't stop blaming myself. I should have protected her better. I knew she had a stalker, and while precautions had been taken, I couldn't help but think I should have done more to keep her safe.

I was anxious, in a panic, and those were new feelings for me. I took a deep breath; these thoughts wouldn't help her, and they weren't helping me either. I needed to keep it together so I could find her.

I wanted to give her a happy ending. But I wasn't in a position to do that...was I? It was selfish of me to be with her at all, but I couldn't help myself.

Every cell in my being wanted to give her a life without any more pain, any more heartache. I wanted to see her smiling and happy every day for the rest of her life.

I sat with my elbows on my knees, my head in my hands. What I'd been ignoring for weeks clicked into place. There was no denying it any longer, no pushing it aside, no pretending. Like being hit by a freight train, I finally realized I was in love with her.

If I was honest with myself, I'd loved her since the first time I kissed her, and it only made my heart ache more that I might never be able to tell her.

I couldn't imagine a world where she didn't exist or one where I couldn't see her or be with her. The thought of not finding her was terrifying.

I couldn't think this way, wouldn't allow myself to think she was dead. She had to be alive; the alternative was unacceptable. Whatever she was going through, we'd deal with, but she couldn't die after I just found her.

Several hours later, Midas started yelling excitedly, "Her tracker is back!"

I stood up so fast my chair toppled over with a crash. I stood looking over Midas' shoulder, "Where the fuck is she?"

"She's on the water and traveling at a good clip."

"She's on a boat. Let's go."

I didn't wait for a response, just stormed out of the room to go find the woman I loved.

Chapter 51

Alex

I was a little shocked when I woke up. I surmised Brooks shot me with a tranquilizer dart because I wasn't dead, but I did feel sick. I could feel I was on a boat, and from the look of the room I was in, a very fancy, expensive boat.

My wrists and ankles were tied with rope this time. It took some doing, with my arms tied behind my back, but I finally managed to get the ropes untied and snuck out of the room. I didn't see anyone but I assumed Brooks was here somewhere, and I definitely didn't want to run into him.

It appeared I was on a yacht, and we were in the middle of the ocean. Hiding wasn't going to help since, duh, it was a boat; eventually, I'd be found. I couldn't run anywhere because there wasn't anywhere *to* run.

Moving slowly and carefully toward the back of the boat, I was hoping there was a dinghy I could steal. But when I got there, I didn't see anything except endless ocean. What I did see was a large box that said 'Life Preservers' on it.

Frequently looking behind me, I opened the box and stole a life preserver that had an emergency strobe light attached to it. Sneaking to where I was better hidden, I quickly put it on, then climbed over the side and hung from the railing.

This is a really bad idea, Alex. That was my last thought before I let go and dropped into the water. While I bobbed in the dark water, I watched the boat get farther and farther away until I couldn't see it anymore.

It didn't take long before I was shivering, my teeth were chattering, and my body ached. I was beyond cold. I waited what felt like a long time after the boat disappeared, and when Brooks didn't come back, I turned on the emergency strobe and started swimming to try and stay warm.

I don't know how much time went by before I started hallucinating, or maybe it was wishful thinking and my imagination. But Cole appeared. He kept telling me to hang on; he was coming for me. I. Will. Find. You. He kept saying, just like when we were in the jungle.

"Okay, cowboy, but hurry."

I knew it wasn't real when he was there one second and just disappeared the next, and I was alone again in the dark, cold water.

The next time imaginary Cole was there, Smoke was with him, and they both told me to hang on, that they were coming for me. I knew it wasn't real, but it was still comforting and kept me going.

I swam until I was too exhausted to keep going and was currently on my back, bobbing in the water, trying not to panic that I couldn't feel my body anymore.

Chapter 52

Cole

It seemed to take forever to get on a boat and start heading for her signal. We were traveling as fast as our boat would allow, but it still felt too slow.

Midas broke the silence, "Her tracker has gone offline again."

"Why?" I asked.

Midas didn't say anything.

"Why Midas?" I yelled.

"If I had to guess because she's in the water," he said quietly.

"Fuck."

"She's a good swimmer," Bruiser said.

"She's strong, in shape," Boomer chimed in.

"She's out here somewhere in the middle of the fucking ocean," I yelled, waving my arms at the water all around us.

It was almost two hours before we finally arrived at her last known location. *Where the fuck are you, angel?*

We were looking through binoculars and using high-power spotlights to search for her, which was like using a pen light in space to locate a dime.

The fear I felt made me feel like I was losing my mind. We'd been doing this for an hour with no luck when I thought I saw something in the distance and watched it. I wasn't sure I actually saw something or was imagining it.

"Turn the spotlights off," I called out.

The spotlights cut off, plunging us into darkness.

"There," I said, pointing, "Is that a strobe light?"

Bruiser was driving the boat, but the other four sets of binoculars aimed in the direction I was looking.

"Bruiser, ten o'clock!" I yelled.

The boat made a hard turn, and we hung on as we sped in that direction. As we got closer, we could clearly see the strobe light, and when we got closer still, we saw Alex floating in the water.

Without thought, I stripped off my shoes and pants and dove into the water. *Please let her be okay.*

I swam to her and wrapped my arm around her, swimming back toward the boat. Even with the bulk of the life preserver, she felt too fragile.

"I've got you, baby. You're safe now."

Her eyes popped open, and she looked at me, and I'd never been so relieved in my life.

Her speech was soft and slurred, "I know you're not r-really here, but I'm glad to s-see you again, c-cowboy."

"I'm glad to see you too, baby. I'm sorry it took me so long to find you."

"D-did you t-take the s-scenic route this t-time? I'm t-trying to hang on for him, but I d-don't know how much l-longer I'll last. I know he's l-looking for m-me."

"Who's looking for you?"

"You. The r-real you."

Her eyes closed just as I got back to the boat.

"She's delirious, maybe hallucinating," I said to no one in particular.

Boomer and Smoke carefully lifted her out of the water, and Jax helped me into the boat.

Smoke stripped the life preserver off her limp body and looked at me, “Her clothes need to come off.”

I stripped off her t-shirt and jeans while the rest of the team respectfully averted their eyes. Boomer and Midas spread out an emergency mylar blanket, and I gently laid Alex down on it, then I covered her with another emergency blanket, and Smoke got to work on her.

I immediately went to her side and took her hand. She felt too fucking cold. Her lips were blue, her face and body too pale. She looked so frail and defenseless, and I’d never seen her that way, and it struck a chord deep inside me.

Jax draped an emergency blanket around my shoulders while Smoke started an IV; not an easy thing to do on a speeding, bouncing boat, but it didn’t seem to faze him.

Once the IV was in place, he took her vitals, "Temp is below ninety-five. She’s hypothermic."

Someone handed me a pile of heavy blankets, and I covered her with them, hoping they’d help warm her up.

"Open your eyes, baby." She didn't move. "Alex! Look at me!" I said forcefully.

Her eyes slowly opened, her voice soft, "W-why are you y-yelling? L-look, S-smoke's here again t-too."

She started shivering, her teeth chattering.

Smoke smiled at her, "Hey, killer."

"Hey, f-fake S-Smoke."

She looked back at me, "It was B-Brooks. Fucker s-shot me with a t-tranquilizer dart. T-twice. I had t-to j-jump off his b-boat. I had t-to. H-he's n-nuts. W-wanted m-me to h-have his b-baby."

My blood ran cold, wondering if he violated her.

"You did good, angel."

"He's b-bat shit c-crazy. Can you t-tell the real C-Cole for m-me? B-Brooks wants to k-kill him; he went l-looking for him. He'll n-never s-stop."

"Baby, look at me." I waited until her eyes met mine, "I promise you I will find him and end him. You don't have to worry about him anymore."

"N-no. You'll g-get in t-trouble, I couldn't s-stand t-that."

I smiled down at her, "I won't get in trouble. You know people who know people. You'll have my back."

Alex nodded her head slightly, "A-always. I'll always h-have your b-back. I'm so t-tired. I'm s-supposed to b-be getting d-drunk r-right n-now."

"Why is that?" I asked her.

"It's m-my b-birthday. G-guess I h-have another r-reason n-not to c-celebrate. Another W-Walker d-dead on my b-birthday. H-how ironic."

"Did you know?" Smoke asked me.

"No."

"Someone died on her birthday? Do you know what she's talking about?" Jax questioned from behind me.

"I have no idea."

As if she didn't hear us, Alex started talking again, "I'm going t-to die t-today, and he'll n-never know what h-happened to m-me. I don't want to l-lose him."

Tears leaked out of her eyes and ran into her hair before she closed them.

She was fucking killing me. My voice was hard when I barked at her, "Alexandra Harlow Walker, look at me."

She opened her eyes, her voice too soft for my liking, "D-don't t-triple name m-me."

I smiled down at her, my voice softer, "I will when you deserve it. You are going to be fine. This is real. *I'm* real. You're out of the water. You will fight do you hear me? You're one of the strongest people I know. You will live."

I leaned over her and palmed her face, holding it between my hands, "You will not die, I forbid it. Do you hear me? I forbid it, Alex."

"You're b-bossier than he is. He's only b-bossy in b-bed."

Alex looked at me, smiling a weak smile, her voice low, "He's really g-good at the s-sex, s-so it's okay when he's b-bossy in b-bed. H-he's the S-Superstud," she said with a small laugh.

Smoke stared at her, then burst out laughing, and I could hear more laughing from behind me.

Smoke turned and looked over at me.

"Not a fucking word," I said, without taking my eyes from Alex, but I was smiling.

"Why is she like this?" Boomer asked.

"One of the symptoms of hyperthermia is an almost drunk-like state," Smoke replied.

Alex reached out and unexpectedly grabbed Smoke by the wrist, "D-don't let him f-feel guilty, w-when I d-don't come b-back. It w-wasn't his f-fault. P-promise you'll h-help him. P-promise."

Smoke looked down at her, “You’re going to be okay, Alex.”

“P-promise me, S-Smoke.”

“Okay, Alex, I promise.”

Alex looked at me, "I w-waited my whole l-life for you. The r-real you is g-going to be s-so mad at m-me."

"Why would I be mad at you?"

"I really t-tried not t-to, b-but I c-couldn't help it."

"What, baby? What couldn't you help?"

Her voice was barely audible, "I f-fell in love w-with you." Her eyes closed, and her body went completely limp as she lost consciousness.

I felt like my heart might explode. I leaned down, my cheek against hers and whispered in her ear, "I love you too, angel."

"Tell me you’re keeping her. She thinks she’s dying, and the only thing she cares about is making sure you’ll be okay," Smoke said from the other side of her.

I didn't take my eyes off her, “She’s mine; she’s not going anywhere."

Midas chuckled, “Superstud?”

“Yeah, we’re gonna need details on that,” Jax quipped.

"So, when's the wedding?" Boomer asked.

Chapter 53

Cole

Alex was still unconscious.

Once we got to the hospital, I refused to leave her. I was by her side when they photographed, cleaned, and bandaged her right ankle. It was obvious she'd tried hard to get out of whatever had been put around it; most of the skin was torn off with her efforts.

They forced me out while they performed a rape kit, and I was glad she wasn't awake for that but hated the reason it had to be done. I felt sick thinking about what Brooks had done to her, sicker still that he wanted her to have his baby. I couldn't help but worry he tried to accomplish that.

My emotions alternated between fear, concern, and pure rage. I was going to kill Brooks Kennedy with my bare hands.

Since Alex had been admitted, I'd been sitting holding her hand and watching her sleep. It was irrational, but I desperately wanted to crawl in bed with her and hold her to me to reassure myself she was alive, but I couldn't. Instead, I sat and watched her chest rise and fall rhythmically while she slept.

After a while, the doctor came into her room.

I stood up and looked at him, "How is she?"

"Your wife is young and in remarkable shape. I expect she'll make a full recovery."

I didn't correct his thinking that I was her husband because, with the doctor's words, I felt like I could breathe for the first time in days and knew he wouldn't tell me anything if I told him Alex and I weren't married.

The doctor looked down at Alex's chart before speaking again, "Her rape kit was negative; it doesn't look like she was sexually assaulted."

I barely had time to register my relief at that information before the doctor went on, "And miraculously, everything looks good with the baby."

What fucking baby? I stared at the doctor, my brows together. "Baby?"

"Your wife is about six weeks pregnant."

Stunned, I looked down at Alex sleeping. Six weeks. Six weeks pregnant meant it was my baby. Our baby.

"I take it the baby wasn't planned?"

"No."

I didn't have to think hard about when it happened. I'd known it was a possibility, but now it was a reality. Alex and I were going to have a baby. That news should have terrified me, should have sent me running, but strangely, it didn't. In fact, I was smiling down at her.

The doctor left, and after a little while, I laid my head on her bed, resting it on one forearm and needing the contact with her, I splayed my other hand on her stomach and slept. Much like when I was on a mission, I didn't sleep soundly.

Later, when I felt her move, I lifted my head, and I smiled at her, relieved to be looking into those beautiful green eyes.

"You're awake." I stood up and brushed her hair off her face. "How are you feeling?"

Her voice was raspy, "Tired. Thirsty. Hungry."

"That's to be expected," I told her as I raised her bed up, picked up the water and helped her take a drink before sitting on the bed next to her hip, taking her hand in mine.

"You had me worried, angel. I was scared I lost you. I never want to feel that way again."

"I didn't mean to?"

It came out as a question, and I laughed a short laugh before kissing her forehead, "I know you didn't."

"Um, did I hit my head?"

I was suddenly concerned, and it came out in my voice, "Why? Does your head hurt? Do you have a headache?"

"No."

"Then why do you think you hit your head?" I questioned, lacing our fingers together.

She looked down at our clasped hands, "I'm confused."

Now I was even more concerned, "About what?"

"You're holding my hand," she said.

I brought her hand up to my mouth and kissed the back of it.

"Why are you holding my hand?"

"I like holding your hand." I smiled at her, "I like kissing you more, though."

She laughed a short laugh, "Yeah, right."

"Don't believe me?" I said, lowering my head and kissing her gently.

She stared at me, "Am I in a coma?"

"No, baby, you're not in a coma. Alex, what's going on?"

"I'm not sure."

"Tell me."

"Why am I in the hospital?"

"Hypothermia. You were in the water a long time. It took us longer to find you than I'd hoped, and by the time we found you, your body temperature had dropped below ninety-five, but you're going to be fine."

She nodded, "Why was I in the water?"

"You don't remember?"

"No."

"Brooks kidnapped you again, and you jumped off his boat to escape."

"Brooks kidnapped me?"

"Yes."

"Again?"

"Yes."

"And you found me?"

"Yes." I smiled down at her, "I told you no one was going to take you from me."

She frowned at me, looking confused, and tilted her head, "Okay. Just one more question." There was a long pause while she stared at me before she asked, "Who *are* you?"

I huffed out a laugh, "That's not funny, angel." Alex didn't laugh and still had a confused look on her face. "Alex, you're kidding, right?"

She stared at me and slowly shook her head.

I stood up and ran my hand through my hair, "Fuck. What's the last thing you remember?"

"Gabe called me and said he wrote a song. He wanted me to go to L.A. and sing it for him."

"What was the name of the song?"

"Um, Treasure You, I think."

"Have you ever been to Peru?"

"Peru? No."

"How old are you?"

"Twenty-four. How old are you?"

This wasn't happening. I reached for her hand but stopped myself before I touched her.

"Who are you? What's your name?"

"I think I better go get the doctor."

I felt like I'd just been hit by an eighteen-wheeler. I stood up and stared down at her for a moment before I turned and walked toward the door.

"Wait," she called out to me.

I turned around and looked at her.

"Will I see you again?"

"You can count on it."

She sounded hopeful, "Promise?"

"Yeah, angel, I promise," I answered as I walked out of the room.

"Fuck, fuck, *fuck*," I muttered as I stepped out into the hallway. The Commander, the team, and Gabe were heading down the hall toward me.

"No one goes in there until the doctor sees her," I told them.

"Reaper, what's going on?" The Commander asked.

Jax looked at me, "What happened? Is she okay?"

"I'm not sure. I need to find the fucking doctor. Just make sure no one goes in there until the doctor sees her."

"Cole, what is it?" Gabe demanded.

"She can't remember the last two and a half fucking years," I told them, walking away down the hall.

*****

It was some time before the doctor came out of her room, taking me aside and speaking to me privately. He obviously still believed Alex and I were married, or he wouldn't be telling me anything.

When the doctor was finished explaining, I went back to where the Commander, Gabe and the team were waiting. I couldn't believe what I was about to tell them.

"She has retrograde amnesia. A result of the hypothermia or maybe the trauma. They're not sure."

"Amnesia?" Bruiser asked, unbelieving.

I looked at Gabe, "The last thing she remembers is you calling her and telling her you wrote Treasure You and wanting her to sing it. She has no memory of being a singer or of either kidnapping."

The Commander shook his head and ran his hand over his face, "Will she get her memory back?"

"They don't know. There's a chance she'll never remember. There's a chance she'll remember everything. But we have to be very careful about what we tell her. The doctor said suddenly finding out about the missing parts of her life could be detrimental, so we can't tell her anything about it."

"Does that mean we can't see her?" Boomer asked.

"Not now, maybe later. As far as she knows, she's never met any of you."

Midas frowned, "So, she has no idea who *you* are?"

"No, she has no idea who I am."

"Jesus, Reaper," Smoke said.

What I didn't tell them was Alex was pregnant. She didn't know she was pregnant; I wasn't going to tell anyone else before she had that information.

Because the doctor still believed I was Alex's husband, he told me I could give her that information but told me I'd need to be patient since she wouldn't remember details. I didn't inform him that she didn't remember me at all.

The doctor thought finding out she was pregnant on top of everything else could cause a setback. He told me to wait a few days and see how she was handling the memory loss before I told her.

I couldn't keep *that* information from her for long but didn't want to give her the news when she was dealing with losing her memory, so I was hopeful her memory would come back in the next few days.

The doctor gave me prenatal vitamins for her and told me some of the things I could expect due to pregnancy hormones.

He said he told Alex she couldn't drink alcohol or ride her horse, that she needed to rest when she was tired, and she needed to eat. He made it sound as if those instructions were part of the recovery from the hypothermia.

Chapter 54

Alex

The gorgeous man came back into my room a little while after the doctor left. I was still reeling from the doctor telling me I had amnesia, which was about the funniest thing I'd ever heard. I thought he was kidding until he started running tests and never cracked a smile, but I was semi-convinced he was an actor hired to play a joke on me.

I was happy to see the gorgeous man again, but I didn't know why other than he was just so handsome, and he seemed to know and like me.

"You came back."

He sat on my bed next to my hip, "I told you I would."

"Please tell me who you are."

"My name is Cole Montgomery. I'm a Navy SEAL."

I nodded my head, "Did I meet you at the ranch?"

"No. You're...you're my girlfriend."

I had no idea how huge it was for him to call me his girlfriend, but hearing it, I started laughing and couldn't stop. When I finally got control of myself, the only thing that would come out was, "Yeah, sure. How is that possible?"

"What do you mean?"

"You look like that," I said, waving my hand in front of him, "and I'm just an awkward dork who plays with cows and horses. You could have any woman you want; why would you want me?"

I couldn't stop the amusement I felt from him saying I was his girlfriend.

"Do not do that." He sounded mad.

"Do what?"

"Put yourself down. You're not *just* anything. You're not a dork. You're smart and kind and funny, strong, and brave and the most beautiful woman I've ever seen. Any man would be lucky to have you. But no other man will have you because you're mine."

Wow, he was really intense, but his words slid over me like silk. No one had ever said anything like that to me before.

"Did the doctor explain what happened?"

I couldn't help laughing again, "You mean that I'm amnesia chick?"

He didn't look amused. I cleared my throat under his penetrating stare, feeling like I'd done something wrong, "Yes, the doctor told me. How do I know you are who you say you are?"

"The Commander and Gabe are outside; do you think they'd let me in here if I were a stranger?"

"They would if you're all playing a prank on me and you're an actor. You're pretty enough to be an actor. I don't know you, but I know them, and I wouldn't put it past them."

He smiled a lopsided grin, "You think I'm pretty?"

I felt my cheeks flush with color, "Yes. You're extremely handsome, but I'm sure you know that. Just because you're supposedly not a stranger doesn't mean you're my boyfriend."

I couldn't help it; I started laughing again. The thought of this man and I together was preposterous to me.

He didn't get mad this time but did pull out his phone. After clicking several buttons, he turned the phone to face me. I gasped at what I was seeing and took the phone from him.

There, plain as day, was a picture of this gorgeous man and me. We were both dressed up and looked happy together. But I was wearing makeup I'd never worn, and my hair looked completely different.

I looked at him, "Man, you had me going there for a minute."

"What do you mean?"

I waved his phone at him, "Obviously, this is photoshopped. I've never worn a dress like that, I've never done my hair like that and I've never worn makeup like that. I don't even know how to do that to my hair or my face. So, who are you, really? A friend of Gabe's? Are you one of Chance's models?"

"It's not photoshopped, and you didn't do your hair and makeup; someone else did."

I laughed again. "I let someone else do that to my hair and put that makeup on my face? I don't think so, but seriously, nice try."

"I promise you; that picture is real. Let me see the phone; I have other pictures."

I handed him the phone, and he brought up more photos and gave the phone back to me. I scrolled through them. There was the gorgeous man smiling, holding me off my feet while I was reaching for a blonde woman. It looked like we were in a bar. The two of us kissing in that same bar. A selfie of the two of us, our faces pressed together, he was smiling, and it looked like I was laughing.

There was a picture of me in a man's shirt and nothing else, the ocean behind me. The only word I could think of when I looked at it was...tousled. Me wearing the same shirt kissing him on the cheek, my arms around his neck, him looking at the camera with a sexy smirk on his face. It looked like I was sitting in his lap. In every picture, we looked incredibly happy.

Still looking at the pictures, I whispered, "What. The. Fuck." I looked at him, "No, really, what in the actual fuck?"

"I'm sure you have questions."

I looked at the phone again, "That's the understatement of the century."

"The doctor doesn't want anyone giving you much information. It could be damaging if you found out too much. I know that isn't what you want to hear, but it's the way it has to be for now."

He picked up my hand, "I'm going to go and let Gabe and the Commander visit with you. I'll be back later, and when you're discharged, I'll be here to take you home."

"Home to my house? Or do we live together?"

He smiled at me, "No, we don't live together and yes, home to your house. Can I bring you anything when I come back?"

"I could eat a burger; I'm starving. Will you make me a promise?"

He answered immediately, "If I can."

"Promise you won't lie to me."

He kissed my palm. I should be freaking out a stranger was touching me and kissing me. I didn't understand why, but I wasn't.

He stood up and looked down at me, "I would never lie to you, angel."

"Where did you come from?"

He smiled at me, "Originally, from Colorado." He leaned down and kissed my forehead, "Get some rest. Everything is going to be fine."

True to his word, he came back later with food and stayed with me, making sure I was eating and drinking enough, but like Gabe and Uncle Mal, he refused to tell me anything.

Chapter 55

Alex

The next day when I was released from the hospital, Cole drove me home. I didn't have much to say, I was busy looking out the window and trying to find anything different, but as far as I could see, everything looked the same.

I still wasn't a hundred percent convinced this wasn't all an elaborate prank, that I wasn't being punked. If I was honest with myself, I wanted it to be a prank instead of having a two-and-a-half-year hole in my memories especially since I couldn't remember anything about the man sitting next to me.

Shocking as it was, Gabe and uncle Mal confirmed that Cole and I were, in fact, an item, and Gabe showed me more pictures of us together. The idea was still comical to me; the man could have *any* woman he wanted. I wanted to know how it came about, but I wanted to hear it from Cole.

When we reached the gate, it was new, and a code was required to open it; Cole punched in the code, and the gate slid open.

When we got to the end of the driveway, we didn't turn left to the house but instead turned right and pulled up to a house I'd never seen before.

I looked over at him as he parked the car, "Where did this come from?"

"Where did what come from?"

"This house."

"This is your house."

After he shut off the engine, he came around and helped me out of the car, and I stood staring at the beautiful house in front of me for a minute. This house killed the idea of my amnesia being a prank; I was standing on my property in front of a house I'd never seen before; it wasn't just plopped here overnight as a joke.

"Are you just dropping me off, or can you show me around this house first?"

I thought that was probably the oddest thing I'd ever asked anyone, but the day was still young.

"I'm not going anywhere."

He really was extremely sweet.

We went inside, and I couldn't help my reaction, "This is my dream house, right down to the courtyard, the glass walls, that kitchen, the pool. I've dreamed about this house for years. I can't afford this house; how is this house here?"

"You built this house about a year and a half ago. I didn't know you then, and we never discussed how you paid for it. You've sold horses for a lot of money; maybe that's how you did it."

I nodded, but it didn't seem likely that's how I paid for it.

"What's missing off the walls? It's obvious there are pictures missing. Why were they taken down?"

"Gabe took down everything that happened in the last two and a half years."

"Promise me if there's something big I need to know, you'll tell me."

"How are you feeling?"

"I'm tired."

"How about a nap, and when you wake up, I'll feed you. Anything special you'd like to eat?"

I followed him to the bedroom, "I really want a chicken salad sandwich and some cauliflower with blue cheese. And I don't know why but I want garlic. A lot of garlic. Maybe some melon, and I wouldn't mind some potato salad. And that was pretty slick how you avoided answering me."

He put me in bed, kissing me on the forehead and even though I didn't think I would, I fell asleep. I don't know how long I slept, but after I woke up, I took a shower in my dream bathroom and went to see if Cole was still here. I found him in the kitchen.

He smiled when he saw me, "You're awake."

Damn, he was handsome, and when he smiled, he was more handsome if that was even possible.

"Do you feel better?"

"I'm still tired."

"That's probably going to last a little while. Are you hungry?"

I nodded. "I also think I need to put on a pot of tequila."

He smiled at me, "I understand the feeling, but the doctor said no alcohol. How about a smoothie instead?"

"Not really the same, but okay."

He pulled out a chair at the table for me, and I sat down. He brought me the smoothie, and I took a drink, "Mmm, is it pineapple?"

"Pineapple coconut."

"It's really good. Is there more of this?"

"Yes."

I watched him bring a bowl of mixed fruit, a bowl of cauliflower with blue cheese, a small bowl of roasted garlic, a container of potato salad and plates with chicken salad sandwiches before he sat down.

I popped a clove of roasted garlic in my mouth, "This looks great, thank you. I can't believe you made all this."

He grinned at me, "I got most of it from Maggie."

I laughed and nodded my head, "Nice to know you're honest too. You could have lied."

He handed me a pill, "I told you I wouldn't lie to you."

"What's this?"

"Vitamin. The doctor said you need to take one every day."

I nodded and swallowed it while he watched me.

I was a little shocked how much I ate. I guessed I missed a few meals. Although I did wonder why I hoovered the garlic like there was a vampire apocalypse. I liked garlic, but I'd never eaten a whole bowl of it before.

After we ate, he cleared the dishes and put them in the dishwasher, telling me he had it covered when I tried to help.

When he was finished, he took my hand, and he led me to the couch, giving me another glass of the yummy smoothie, and we sat down. He knew his way around this house better than I did, so I had to believe he'd been here before.

"I hate having this hole in my head."

"You're going to get your memory back, but you have to be patient. Let it come in its own time."

"You don't know that for sure; my memory could be lost forever. You said I was kidnapped by Brooks twice. Tell me about that."

"I'm not sure it's a good idea. Those aren't happy memories."

"Yeah, I got that from the being kidnapped twice thing, my shredded ankle and waking up in the hospital. Brooks always was a psycho. Where is he now? Did the police catch him? Was he arrested?"

"Not yet, but we're working on it, and when I find him, he won't be arrested."

From the dangerous look on Cole's face, I wouldn't want to be Brooks Kennedy.

"So, it's possible he could kidnap me a third time?"

"No," he said harshly. "We're going to find him. In the meantime, you'll be protected."

"Because you've been assigned to babysit me?"

"I have not been assigned to babysit you."

"Then why are you here?"

"I'm here because I like being with you. I like being near you. I like you. You're my...girlfriend; where else would I be?"

He kept stumbling on the word 'girlfriend' as if it were foreign, and he'd never said it before, which wasn't helping convince me he wasn't playing a part.

"If you won't tell me about Brooks, tell me how we met. How did you and I end up together?"

He groaned and looked at me like he was in pain, and I got up and started pacing.

"So, you won't tell me that either? Is it some big secret? Something bad? This is bullshit. I have the right to know about my life, and if you can't or won't even tell me how we met, what am I supposed to think about that?"

"Baby, please come and sit down."

It was the please that made me sit back down on the couch, but I was mad and frustrated, "I find it hard to believe I'd be with someone as bossy as you."

Although I had to admit, I did like the way it made me feel when he called me baby and angel.

He pulled me right up next to him and put his arm around me. I didn't feel nervous or scared; it felt familiar, so I didn't move away and laid my head on his chest.

"You *are* with me. I can't tell you everything, but I will tell you part of it. You were kidnapped, and my team and I were sent to rescue you. That's how we met."

"So, I was a job?"

He nodded, "It started that way."

He shifted and without any effort, lifted me into his lap. I rested my palms on his chest. The way he looked at me was powerful. Mesmerizing. It felt like there was an invisible tether between us.

"You know this couch is big enough for both of us to sit on."

He grinned at me, "I like you right where you are. Now, do you want to hear the story or not?"

I waved a hand at him, "By all means, please continue."

"The first time you saw me, you ate me up with your eyes. You were so flustered by my good looks and hot body you couldn't look away. You were so adorable."

I rolled my eyes and shook my head at him, "You're very conceited. It's shocking that your pretty head fits through the doorway."

But I was smiling, and he smiled back. He tucked a strand of hair behind my ear like he did it every day, but to me, it felt intimate.

"You were filthy and a mess, and I still thought you were the most beautiful woman I'd ever seen, and you were feisty as hell. You were so real, had such a great laugh, unique eyes like an exotic jungle cat, beautiful long hair, plus you have great tits and a luscious ass I can't keep my hands away from."

I couldn't help it; I let out a very unladylike snort, "Perv."

He smiled at me, "I told myself to stay away from you, but I couldn't because you're a force of nature, *and* you kept ogling me, which made it hard to ignore you. The more I got to know you, the more I realized how big your heart is, how special you are. We had a one-night stand when the op was over."

"What!? We did not. That doesn't sound like me at all. I wouldn't do that." I pulled back and searched his face as if that would tell me whether he was lying or not.

"I didn't think it was you either, but that's what happened and believe me when I tell you, it was one of the greatest nights of my life. You wrung me out."

"Shut up."

He grinned at me, "You shut up."

I jerked back from him, and pointed my finger at him, my voice serious, "Cole don't."

He looked confused, "Don't what?"

"You were going to tickle me."

His smile was huge and made my insides twist like the first big drop on a roller coaster.

He took hold of my finger and kissed it. "I wasn't. But you're remembering a time I did. See, the memories are in there, they're just not ready to come out yet."

"I agreed to a one-night stand? Was I drunk?"

"No, angel, you weren't drunk. I wouldn't have slept with you if you were drunk."

"So, you were drunk?"

He shook his head at me, "No one was drunk."

"How long after we met did this one-night stand happen?"

"About three days."

"Three days!" I dropped my head on his chest, "Ugh, I'm a slut. How many one-night stands have I had in the last two years?"

I felt his chest moving, heard the rumble in my ear; he was chuckling, "You're not a slut, and I was the only one."

I picked up my head and looked at him, "If it was a one-night stand, how come you're still here? Did this just happen?"

"No. It was a couple of months ago."

His big hands came up and palmed my face, his thumbs gently rubbing my cheekbones. I couldn't take my eyes off him. I was spellbound.

"The first time I was inside you was like heaven. I was a goner after that. Even though I tried to stay away from you, you owned me. I couldn't stop thinking about you. We saw each other a few weeks later, and I couldn't resist you; I had to have you again."

I could feel how hot my face was and knew I had to be beet red, and the throbbing between my legs was something I'd never experienced before.

"Oh my god. Do you talk like that all the time? No wonder I fell in bed with you and didn't care that you're bossy and conceited. So, if we've had sex, we've kissed?"

"Of course."

His words had given me the strongest desire to kiss him. I rested my palms flat on his chest, "Prove it."

He took my face in his hands, and his head lowered toward mine. My breath hitched, my lips parted in anticipation, but instead of kissing me on the mouth, he gently kissed my cheek. Then moved and kissed the other. My eyes closed at the gentleness of his lips on my skin.

He kissed me on the lips once. Twice. He stared at me, and his pupils dilated, and his eyes had turned a dark blue. Then his soft lips were on mine.

I opened to him without hesitation, and his tongue swept into my mouth and tangled with mine. His breath was my breath, his scent invading my senses.

I leaned my weight into him and moaned softly into his mouth. It was as if time stopped, and there was only the glorious sensation of his tongue melding and entwining with mine, soft at first then more demanding.

My hands were in his hair, pulling him closer, his arms around me, holding me tightly against him. When he pulled away, our breath was coming in ragged pants and gasps. We stared at each other, and he gently rubbed his thumb over my bottom lip.

It took a minute before I caught my breath and could speak again, "How could I have forgotten *that*? My brain doesn't remember you, but it feels like my body does. Although it could just be because you look like that and are a seriously good kisser."

I rested my head against his chest again, my face in the crook of his neck, his arms around me. I liked the solid feel of him under me, the way his hands felt on me. It made no sense, but I felt safe.

I could smell him and inhaled, "You smell really good. You smell like Déjà vu."

I could hear the smile in his voice, "You do like smelling me; somewhere in there, you remember that."

"I like *smelling* you? That's weird, isn't it?"

"No. I like smelling you too."

"We don't kiss like we're strangers."

"No, we don't. Even when we *were* strangers, we didn't kiss like strangers. The first time I kissed you, my whole world shifted."

"Damn, that's hot; you sure know what to say to a girl. Soooo, you've seen me naked?"

Still smiling, his hands were roaming over my back and hips, but he wasn't groping me, "I've seen every glorious inch of you, angel."

That statement made my cheeks heat up again.

"And I've seen you naked?"

He smirked at me, "You have."

"Have we had a lot of sex?"

His smile was huge, "Oh yeah. But don't ask me to prove that. As much as I want to, I don't think it's a good idea right now. In your head, I'm a stranger, and it would feel like taking advantage of you. I probably shouldn't have kissed you, but I have a hard time keeping my hands and mouth off you."

I felt sad and laid my head back on his chest. "What if I never remember the best sex with you? The only memories I have are the worst sex. I really want to remember being with you."

"You will. You just need time."

I raised my head and looked at him, "But what if I don't? It feels crappy that I can't remember, especially since you can. You said I was your girlfriend, which means you know you're my first boyfriend. How could I forget you?"

"You didn't forget me; your head just misplaced me for a little while. You'll remember, angel. You're not freaking out that I'm here. You're not running from me; you're not scared of me. You're in my lap and you're kissing me. Even if you don't ever remember, we'll make new memories."

"But you'll always have the old memories, and I won't."

He smiled a wicked smile and waggled his eyebrows at me, "We'll recreate them,"

I laughed, "My first boyfriend is a bossy, conceited pervert."

He smiled back at me and gripped my hips harder, "And you like me that way."

"I don't know you, but I do like you. Everyone else looks at me like I grew a second head, and no one wants to say anything to me. It's like everyone is keeping a giant secret.

"It's crazy because I only met you yesterday, but the only time I feel better or normal is when I'm with you."

"Because you trust me. Even if you can't remember me, in here," he said, touching my temple, "You remember me in here," he rested his hand over my heart. "You know you can trust me. You know I won't hurt you, that I'll protect you.

"I can't imagine how frustrating it is not to be able to remember. How scary it is. Or how hard it is to have to be patient. But I know you; you're too stubborn not to remember. It's going to happen. Now, how about we watch something, and you rest?"

"Okay."

He plugged in a movie and laid down on the couch, taking me with him. It wasn't long before I fell asleep on top of him.

Chapter 56

Cole

Four days after she'd gotten out of the hospital, there was still no change in her memory. Other than that, her only complaint was still being cold sometimes.

Even though the Commander had given me some time off, yesterday, Alex had insisted I still go to PT with the team. I hadn't wanted to leave her, afraid Brooks might show up and try to take her again, but she'd promised she wouldn't leave the house.

When I returned this morning, she was still sleeping. When she came out into the living room, she was adorable; her hair was messy, she looked sleepy, and she had a blanket wrapped around her shoulders.

"How was PT?" she asked, yawning.

I smiled at her, "It was good. How are you feeling today?"

"I'm hungry all the time, and I'm having the weirdest cravings, proven by the fact that I'm eating garlic like there's a vampire invasion. For some reason, I feel like I'm in an all-you-can-eat contest for every meal. Now, I'm no doctor," she looked at me, smirking, "Am I?"

I couldn't help but smile at her, glad she was joking about it.

"No, you're not a doctor."

"Okay then, is the hunger a side effect of the hypothermia? I'm eating so much I've gained weight, but I can't seem to stop. I'm going to have to go on a diet. Also, I'm still tired and take a nap every day, which isn't like me."

I noticed the tears gathering in her eyes.

"What's happening to me?"

I scooped her up and carried her to the couch and sat down with her in my lap. She curled into me and rested her head against my chest.

The doctor told me to expect her to be more tired and have food cravings. Also, I should expect mood swings and fatigue, I couldn't risk she would go on a diet, and while I was hoping her memory would come back, and I wouldn't have to pile this news on top of everything else, it was obvious I had to tell her.

"Alex, I need to tell you something. I don't think it can wait any longer. It might be a bit of a shock...It will be a shock."

Her voice was soft and muffled against my chest, "Is it something bad? I don't think I can take any more bad news."

"No, it's not bad. You're pregnant," I blurted.

She froze and huffed out a breath, lifting her head to look at me, "I'm sorry, I just hallucinated; I thought you said I was pregnant."

"I did. You're pregnant."

"I don't understand what you're saying to me. I'm pregnant? How could I be pregnant? I can't have a baby. And how would you know, and I don't?"

"We were...distracted in the shower one day and forgot the condom. The doctor thought we were married and told me when you were in the hospital."

The tears that been threatening disappeared, replaced by anger, "Distracted? Explain that. Explain how you were so distracted you forgot protection."

I smiled at her, "You stripped off your clothes and walked through the house naked, saying we needed a shower. Then you washed my hair and soaped me up, which was fucking hot, by the way, and when you put your mouth on my...."

She slapped her hand over my mouth, a flush of color creeping up her face, "This is your fault. I blame you."

I removed her hand from my mouth and kissed her palm, "Baby, if you want to blame me because you make me lose control, I'm okay with that."

"Don't be all sexy smug because your caveman side is proud you knocked me up. Why aren't you freaking out? Oh my god, I'm knocked up. Shit, is there something wrong because of the cold water?"

I had snaked my hand under the blanket and was rubbing her belly, "Not that they know of. The doctor said everything looked good, but we need to go to your doctor just to make sure. You'll make an appointment with your doctor; we'll have everything checked out and go from there."

She fell against my chest and started to cry. "I can't have a baby. I don't understand what's happening. I'm pregnant?"

I held her, one hand on her belly, one hand rubbing her back, "I know it's a lot to wrap your head around, but I promise you everything is going to be fine."

"When did I become such a crybaby?"

Luckily, she couldn't see I was smiling, which I didn't think she'd appreciate at this particular moment. "Welcome to pregnancy hormones."

That set off a new round of tears, "You are not helping."

I held her against me and reveled in the fact that she was in my arms and was all mine.

Chapter 57

Alex

A month had gone by, and still, my memory hadn't come back. I kept having bouts of Déjà vu, but I didn't know if what was coming was memories or just thoughts in my head.

Whenever I went out, no matter where I went, people stared at me. Some of them came up to me and asked if I was Alex Walker. Then, more often than not, they'd ask if they could take a picture with me.

I had no idea how they knew who I was or why they were asking for a picture with me. It freaked me out so much, I rarely left the ranch these days and was starting to feel like a prisoner.

On top of that, I was getting angrier that no one would tell me anything. It was obvious my memory wasn't going to come back, and I wanted to know at least *some* details about the last few years of my life. I wanted everyone to stop looking at me with pity or like I was some sort of freak, wanted them to stop watching every word they said around me.

I was also frustrated beyond belief that Cole kissed me, touched me, slept next to me every night, but still refused to take things any farther. I didn't understand why and his explanation that he felt he'd be taking advantage of me just wasn't reasonable anymore. I'd never been sexually frustrated before. It was the worst thing I think I ever felt.

I had a feeling he'd changed his mind about us and didn't want to say anything because I was pregnant *and* had lost my memory. Which could be why tonight I was seriously irritated and once again asked him to tell me *something* about my life.

He looked at me and sighed, "Come and sit down, Alex."

"I don't want to sit down; I want someone to tell me something about the last two years of my life. Obviously, a lot changed. I could somehow afford this house, or I wouldn't have built it. For some reason, Brooks kidnapped me...twice, but I don't know anything about that or why he did it.

"Wherever I go, people look at me like they know me, and I have no idea who they are. I've caught people taking my picture; people ask me if they can take a picture with me. Strangers know my name. It's creepy, and I have no idea why they're doing it or how they know me. It's my life; I deserve to know."

"The doctor said telling you things could set you back. Telling you could make things worse."

The fact that he was so calm only pissed me off more. "How could a setback be worse than *this*? And what if knowing is what triggers the memories to return? The doctor also said I might never get my memory back. Is everyone just going to hide those years from me forever?

I never get to know because all of you decided I don't get to know?

"I'm supposed to just put my life on hold and sit hidden inside until I remember or until Brooks kidnaps me again? No. This is *my* life. You might have bossed me around before, but no more."

"I don't boss you around." He smiled at me, "as if anyone could."

I wasn't amused. I was angry, frustrated, and annoyed. I crossed my arms over my chest and stared at him, "Tell me about my life or go."

Cole walked over and stood in front of me, taking my hands in his, "It's not that I don't want to tell you, but the doctor said it could harm you. I'm not trying to be mean or bossy, and I can't imagine what this feels like to you, but I would never do anything that might hurt you. I'm sorry I can't tell you."

I jerked my hands out of his, "Then go."

"Alex...."

"No. Tell me or go; those are your choices."

"Even if it pisses you off, I'm not going to do anything that might hurt you. I'll go...for now, but don't expect me to stay away, Alex."

Cole reluctantly left, and I didn't know what to do. I was mad, sad, terrified. I called Gabe; he wouldn't tell me anything. Then I called uncle Mal, and he wouldn't tell me anything either.

I searched the house but didn't find anything. I went to the ranch house and searched it but didn't find anything there either. Wherever they'd hidden everything, I couldn't find it.

That was when I got the idea to treat it like a mystery and wrote down all the things I did know. But they'd all been so good at keeping the information from me it didn't lead me anywhere or make anything click in my head.

The next afternoon, I got a call from a local store that sells western wear, saddles and tack telling me my order was in. I didn't know what order, so I went to pick it up, thinking it might be a new clue.

When I got there, they showed me a Stetson Cattleman cowboy hat. It was dark grey with a thin black hat band, too big for me, but it looked like it would fit Cole.

It was expensive. I couldn't figure out why I'd pay so much for a hat, especially since Cole told me I'd only just started teaching him to ride.

The cost of the hat was the clue that led me to the bank, where I asked for the balance of my accounts and almost fell over from shock when they gave me the numbers. I made them confirm the amounts were accurate... twice.

I drove home and went for a swim. I couldn't stop thinking about the money. Where did it come from? I was still thinking about that when I started remembering people wanting to take my picture. Why? No one asked about taking my picture before, and no one actually took my picture before. *Why do people know who I am?*

An idea hit me, and I felt stupid for not thinking of it before. I might have thought about it if everyone wasn't distracting me, or I wasn't filled to the brim with pregnancy hormones.

I went to my computer, sat down, and typed my own name into the search bar. I didn't know what I expected to find, but it sure as hell wasn't what I saw.

There were pictures, videos, and magazine articles, and lots of them. Some of the pictures didn't even look like me, I was wearing makeup and clothes and shoes I would never wear, just like the photo Cole showed me. From what I was looking at, it appeared I was a somewhat famous singer. *What. The. Fuck. I'm a fucking singer? How the hell did that happen?*

I started clicking on some of the videos. I started with Treasure You because I remembered Gabe asking me to sing it. In fact, that was the last thing I remembered from my old life.

It was a beautiful song, and I had to admit I sounded pretty damn good singing it. That caused flashes of being on stage and singing, but no concrete memories.

There was so much information, I wasn't spending a lot of time on any one thing, I was jumping from one thing to another. I'd been looking at the search results for about half an hour when I watched the video for the song Vixen and started getting flashes of Cole.

Cole calling me vixen. Touching him and telling him I was his stripper vixen. Talking to Gabe and Chance and telling them Cole called me vixen. Being in a recording studio.

But the images in my head were like trying to recall a dream, like wisps of smoke in my head that I couldn't grab on to.

Then I clicked on a magazine article:

"With her powerful vocals, Alex Walker stole the show when she delivered a high-spirited performance at the annual 'not-for-profit' fundraiser.

"Stunning in a Raffi original, Walker's performance included musician/songwriter Gabriel Carmichael on piano and rousing performances of Walker's hits Treasure You and Fatal Love, as well as the haunting debut performance of I Wish You Could Stay.

"But it was Walker's handsome mystery man that sparked romance buzz when the steamy couple shared a sizzling dance and were seen leaving the benefit together. By her side most of the night, the mystery man is rumored to be a family friend of Walker's."

The article included two photos. The first was me on stage, a microphone at my mouth, in the middle of a stride, pointing out at the audience.

The other was Cole and I dancing. I had him by the tie; we were smiling at each other, our heads close together, his hands spanned low on my hips. When I saw the picture of myself dancing with Cole, what felt like memories started flashing in my head.

When I clicked on the video of, I Wish You Could Stay, the memories didn't come slowly, but so fast I couldn't possibly process all of them, as if two and a half years of memories were being uploaded into my brain at lightning speed.

Once the bombardment of images stopped, I had a nasty headache. But even with the pounding in my head, the memories were still there. I sat stunned and started crying; then I was laughing and crying at the same time.

I jumped up and took a shower, packed a bag, and got in the car. I knew exactly where I was going and exactly how to get there. I couldn't get there fast enough, and I smiled the whole way.

The house was dark, but I knocked on the door and waited. When no one answered, I knocked again, a little louder. The lights finally came on, and Cole opened the door.

He seemed surprised then concerned to see me, "Alex? What's wrong?"

"You called me your girlfriend, why did you do that?"

He seemed confused, and scrubbed his hand over his face, "Because you're my girlfriend."

If it was possible, my smile got wider. I'm not sure I've ever smiled this big in my whole life, "I am? You really mean it?"

"Yes, I mean it."

"Can I come in?"

He opened the door wider, with a shake of his head, "Of course. Sorry."

I stepped inside, and he closed the door behind me. He just stood there, looking confused, staring at me.

I handed him the box I was holding, "I brought you a present."

He took it, frowning at me.

"Open it," I told him, smiling and nodding.

He opened the box and looked down at the cowboy hat. I took it out and put it on his head, "It fits. Looks good on you."

He set the empty box on the counter and looked at me for a moment with his brows drawn together, "I didn't bring you here after the hospital," he murmured.

My smile was huge, "No, you didn't, cowboy."

He smiled, and it lit up his entire face, "You just called me cowboy."

I smiled back at him and nodded, "I did."

"You remember."

"I remember. I remember every moment, every magnificent kiss, every glorious inch of your perfect body, and I remember having the most fantastic sex with you!"

He grabbed me and hugged me, picking me up off the ground and spinning me around, holding me tight, "How?"

I peppered his face with kisses before I answered, "Google."

"Google?"

"Yep. It was all right there."

He set me on my feet and I took his hand, "C'mon, cowboy, we've got some catching up to do, and this time, you're the one that's going to wear the hat."

He tipped his hat at me and spoke in a thick southern drawl, "Yes, ma'am."

We were both smiling huge as we headed for the bedroom.

Chapter 58

Cole

It had been a week since Alex regained her memory. I'd called my dad and told him I had met someone I was serious about.

Yesterday, he showed up unannounced for a surprise visit and instantly fell in love with Alex. After a couple of hours, they acted like they'd known each other for years.

With my dad here, we'd invited the team and the Commander for dinner. We were in the rec room of the ranch house, the team, the Commander, my dad, Popeye, Falcon and Carl all milling around when we heard someone yell, "Jellybean Walker!" from the door.

We all turned around, and Alex smiled and took off running, "Gonzo!" She threw herself into him, and he hugged her and spun her around.

"Holy shit, that's Gonzo Gonzales," Jax said, staring.

Gonzo was a legendary SEAL, now retired, who was rumored to be able to get information on anyone and was the go-to man for off the books 'problem solving'.

Some of the rumors said he worked for the CIA now; others said the Defense Intelligence Agency, but no one was sure who, if anyone, he worked for.

Alex hugged him tightly, “Where have you been? I’ve missed you.” She pulled back and looked at him, gently touching a scar on his face, “What happened?”

“Little mishap with a blade, I’m okay. Chicks dig scars.” Alex laughed and hugged him again.

I stood watching them, my hands fisted at my sides, watching the way they interacted with each other, wondering what history was between them that they seemed so overly familiar with each other, especially since Gonzo had a solid reputation as a loner.

The Commander came and stood next to me and spoke so only I could hear him, “Alex’s brother died on an op that went sideways on her nineteenth birthday.”

My head jerked in his direction, “Jesus.”

“Mad Dog was already sick but didn’t tell her. He died a year later, a few days before her twenty first birthday, and Alex just snapped. That’s why she doesn’t celebrate her birthday.”

“After Mad Dog’s funeral, she disappeared. Gonzo was the one that tracked her down and dragged her back. She was not the Alex you know today. Not the Alex any of us knew. She was drinking a lot, angry and in so much pain. She was vicious and mean, pushing everyone away from her.

“There’s a cabin on the far side of the property. Gonzo took her there and kept her there. He stayed with her for months, put up with everything she threw at him, took the brunt of her rage, and helped her through it. It created a bond between them. She’s like a little sister to him, and he’s like a brother to her.”

I nodded, and my hands un-fisted. I couldn’t imagine what that must have been like for her. My heart ached for her, but I still didn't like the way Gonzo was touching her or the fact that he still hadn't let go of her and set her on her feet.

He finally set her down, and Alex grabbed his hand, "C'mon, I want you to meet everyone."

Alex walked straight for me, dropping Gonzo's hand, putting her arm around me and leaning against me, "Gonzo, this is Cole 'Reaper' Montgomery. Cole, this is my brother from another mother, Raphael 'Gonzo' Gonzales."

Gonzo looked at me, "I remember you. You went on a mission with us when you were still on green team."

I nodded and shook the hand he offered.

Alex introduced him to my dad and the rest of the team, and afterward, Gonzo turned and took Alex's hands, "I came to tell you the Brooks Kennedy problem has been solved. John didn't think it would be a good idea for any of Reaper's team to track him down. He sent me so the team wouldn't be involved. That bastard won't be coming after you again."

"You killed him?" Alex asked.

Gonzo smirked, "Slowly and *very* painfully."

"Are you okay?"

He smiled at her, "I'm just fine, happy to do it."

Alex hugged him, "Thank you, Gonzo."

"My pleasure. Now get an old friend a beer, will you? I want to talk to Reaper."

Alex looked between us and poked Gonzo in the chest, a move I was sure no one else would be able to get away with.

"Be nice," she cautioned.

After Alex walked away, Gonzo turned and looked at me, "She looks different. Happy."

"She is happy. We're happy."

"She better stay that way." He looked me over, "So, you're the one? I'm only gonna say this once, you better be good to her, treat her right. If you hurt her or cheat on her, don't protect her or break her heart, I'll kill you."

I understood he cared about her but was pissed he thought I might harm her, and that anger was evident in my voice, "She's mine. I'm not letting her go. I'll do everything in my power to make her happy. I'll never cheat on her, and I'd rather cut off my own arm than hurt her."

He stared at me before he smiled and nodded, "You're a lucky man; she's a special woman."

Alex came back with the beer, and Gonzo kissed her on the cheek, "Happy for you, Mi Amor." Then he went and sat down with everyone else.

We hadn't told anyone about the pregnancy, although it was getting harder to hide her baby bump, which Alex thought was growing at an alarming rate. But the bigger she got, the prouder I seemed to be.

I stood behind her, my arms around her, my hands rubbing her belly, one of my favorite past times these days and leaned down and whispered in her ear, "I never thought about pregnant women before, but seeing you like this, knowing my baby is growing inside you is the biggest turn on. I can't wait until you're big and round. The caveman side of me is extremely proud of my cock."

Alex huffed out a laugh and leaned her head back so she could see me, "There's something so wrong with you, and you're proud of your cock no matter what it's doing," she whispered back, smiling.

Smiling, Midas interrupted us, "Is there something you two want to tell us?"

"Why do you keep rubbing her belly, Reaper?" Boomer asked.

Smoke smiled at us, "Yeah, Reaper, what's so fascinating about Alex's stomach these days?"

Alex craned her neck and looked at me, "I think we're busted; you might as well tell them."

I smiled a smile I knew lit up my whole face, "Alex is pregnant."

"Apparently, we were just too distracted for condoms," Alex offered by way of explanation.

The Commander abruptly stood, "Alexandra Harlow Walker, get your ass over here."

I stiffened, and the rest of the team looked stunned at the Commander's gruff tone. Alex smiled and didn't hesitate, walking toward him. When she'd almost reached him, he broke out in a huge smile and spread his arms wide, and Alex walked right into them, and he hugged her tight.

Alex smiled up at him, "Guess you guys are finally getting that grandkid you've been bugging me about. You're gonna be a grandpa."

The Commander smiled back at her, "I wish your dad was here for this."

"Me too."

The Commander let her go, and my dad was next to hug her.

"I'm gonna be a grandpa!" The Commander crowed, throwing his arms in the air.

"Me too!" my dad said, smacking the Commander on the back, the two of them looking like kids on Christmas morning.

The team laughed, and everyone got up to congratulate us.

Chapter 59

Alex

The next day, after Cole got home from work, we went for a walk.

As the sun was setting, Cole pulled me into him, one hand on the nape of my neck, the other on my back, looking at me with an intense expression on his face, "I've seen and done a lot of really bad things. I thought I was a man who didn't deserve love, so I never let a woman get close to me.

“Then you came along, and it was like walking out of the dark and into the sunshine. I wanted to stay away from you, I tried to stay away from you, but you're a force I couldn't resist.

"I didn't feel alive until I met you. I've been hiding, shielding myself behind walls to keep from feeling anything. But you snuck in, and once you got in, there was no way to go back.

“You set me free, showed me how to live, taught me how to feel. You make me smile, make me happy. You're my happiness, Alex."

Tears were rolling down my face, "What's happening?" I whispered.

"You own me, heart and soul. You're everything I don't deserve, but I feel like I can't breathe without you. Without you, I'm back in the dark, and now that I've lived in the sun, I don't want to be in the dark anymore.

"We made a baby together. It scares the shit out of me, but I feel happy about it. I love you, Alex Walker. It's how I've felt for a long time, but I just couldn't admit it."

"Say that again," I whispered.

Cole took my hands in his, "I love you." He dropped to one knee, and I gasped. "I love you and want to marry you. I want to marry the hell out of you. I want us forever. I want to spend the rest of my life loving you and our kids. You're mine, and I'm yours, marry me and let me love you forever."

I threw myself at him, and he stood up with me in his arms. Tears were streaming down my face, "I love you too, Cole, so much it scares me. I knew it the moment I laid eyes on you. Are you sure you want to marry me? This isn't just because I'm pregnant, is it?"

He looked at me, emotion swirling in in his blue eyes, "I've never been more sure of anything in my life."

I laughed through my tears, remembering I said the same thing to him on our first night together.

"Then yes, cowboy, I'll marry you."

Cole reached in his pocket and kissed my hand before he put a ring on my finger and kissed the crap out of me. When he pulled away, I was smiling, and he dropped to his knees in front of me, his hands on my belly.

I put my hands on his head, and he kissed my stomach, "Your mom said yes."

I laughed and cried at the same time.

I looked at the ring. Set in platinum, it was channel set French-cut diamonds that went all the way around the band.

“I measured your finger while you were in the hospital. It’s from the 1930s. I thought you might like something vintage and knew you wouldn’t want anything that could snag.”

“It’s so beautiful. You did good, cowboy.”

"Marry me tomorrow?"

I laughed and wiped my face, still trying to breathe properly, "We'll need to plan a little more than that. How about next Saturday, here at the ranch?"

"Yeah?"

"Yeah. I think we can pull that off.”

“We can do anything as long as we’re together.”

Chapter 60

Alex

On Saturday, I stood wearing my dad's trident as my something old and something borrowed. Gabe was acting as my maid of honor, Chance and Gonzo acting as my bridesmaids, the three of them looking handsome in their tux'.

The entire team was wearing their dress whites, standing next to Cole. Their medals jangling on their chests every time they moved. The lineup was unconventional but completely and totally us.

My dress was simple but beautiful and hid the fact that I was pregnant. I was standing next to Uncle Mal, who was about to walk me down the aisle.

"Ready, sweetheart?"

I looked up at him, smiling wide, "Hell yes. Let's go get me a husband."

We were both smiling as we headed toward my future.

Cole watched me walking toward him, never taking his eyes off me. For someone who had vowed never to be in a relationship, he should look nervous, should look scared that he was about to tie himself to me, but he looked happy and relaxed. Excited. The love he felt obvious in his eyes, and I was sure I was reflecting that love back at him.

When I reached him, Uncle Mal kissed my cheek and told me he loved me, then looked at Cole, “It’s my duty to tell you how happy we are about this, but if you hurt our girl, we’ll kill you.”

Cole just smiled at him and nodded. I moved to stand in front of him, a beautiful smile on his face as he took my hands in his and I faced him.

I had never seen him in his dress uniform. My voice was low, only for his ears, "Holy shit, you are smokin' hot in that uniform, Mr. Montgomery. We are so having sex while you’re wearing that."

Cole pulled me into him, his hands resting on my ass, my arms immediately going around his neck, "You are a smokin' hot bride, Mrs. Montgomery, and I will fuck you any way you want me to."

We smiled at each other, and he kissed me.

"Hey, you're not married yet," Uncle John yelled from the audience.

We broke apart and laughed as we stood ready to become husband and wife.

Chapter 61

Cole

Six and a half months later

We were on the plane, on our way back from a mission. I was anxious to get home since Alex was ready to pop any day.

I saw the Commander walking my way, he was smiling at me, and I knew from the look on his face there was news.

At that same time, I received a video message. I shook my head, not wanting to hear the news of what I'd missed.

Ignoring Mal, I turned my attention to my phone and Alex's beautiful face filled the screen.

"Hi, baby. So, you won't be distracted, you won't get this until the mission is done. I'm in labor. I'm sorry I couldn't wait for you, although I'm not really running this show.

"Don't worry, and don't be upset. Look on the bright side, you'll miss all my screaming and all the mess, and you won't have to see me in pain, which I know you'd hate.

“To be honest, if I could, I'd change places with you right now. I'm scared, but I totally got this; after all, I am Alex Montgomery, badass Navy SEAL wife. I love you, Cole. I love you so much. We'll see you soon.”

She smiled and blew me a kiss.

My fingers touched the screen as if I could feel her. I hated that she was scared, and I wasn’t there, that I was going to miss this. I looked at the message and saw that it had only been sent about an hour ago. There was no other news, so it was still possible that I wouldn’t be too late.

The Commander was standing next to me, and the rest of the team was looking at us, wondering what was going on.

"Alex is in labor," the Commander announced.

The team cheered but started voicing concerns because Alex wasn’t supposed to be due for several more weeks. I was pacing, wanting to know what was going on, wanting to be there for my wife.

My phone dinged with a text from John:

“I'm on my way to the hospital and doing everything to clear the way to get you there in time. Cars will be ready and waiting to take you all to the hospital when you land.”

The text was new, so I still held out hope I might make it in time.

A few hours later, I burst through the door of her hospital room and was at her side, kissing her as if we were the only two people in the world.

Her hair was in two braids, wisps of hair sticking to her forehead from sweat.

She was crying, hanging on to me, "Are you whole? Is everyone okay?"

It was the same question she asked every time we returned from a mission, and I knew she needed to hear it before she could relax, "We're all fine."

"You got here just in time."

As if to prove her point, a huge contraction hit her.

*****

My dad, the team and the Commander were waiting. John, Doug, Gabe, Chance, Ryan, Popeye, Carl and even Gonzo had also shown up.

John caused a serious stir by arriving unannounced. Because the President of the United States was here, the hospital gave the group a private waiting room that was being guarded by the Secret Service.

About forty-five minutes after we arrived, wearing scrubs and a huge smile, I walked down the hall toward them. I could see Boomer looking through the window of the door. They didn't wait for me to get to them; opening the door, they streamed into the hallway.

Smoke was on my left holding a pink teddy bear, Jax on my right holding a blue teddy bear. I stopped in front of them, looking at all of them, then reached out toward Smoke and took the pink teddy bear from him, and everyone cheered.

There were hugs and backslapping. I smiled wider and reached toward Jax, taking the blue teddy bear from him. For such a large group, there was absolute silence before a huge cheer went up.

"Twins?" my dad asked, shocked.

Still smiling, I nodded, "Twins. We've known for most of the pregnancy, but Alex thought it would be fun to surprise everyone."

"Well, it worked," Boomer said.

"How's Alex? The babies?" Gabe asked.

"She's amazing. Tired. I have no idea how she just did that. I have a whole new appreciation for my wife. And our daughter and son are perfect."

I couldn't wipe the smile off my face if my life depended on it.

Gabe smiled, "Can we see her? Them?"

"The hospital staff said just a couple people at a time, but Alex said fuck that, bring them all in."

Smoke chuckled, "Sounds like Alex."

Everyone laughed, and we started walking toward her room.

I was through the door first. Alex was holding a baby in each arm, and it was the most beautiful and emotional sight I'd ever seen.

Midas, Boomer and Jax took out their phones and snapped pictures. I sat on the bed by Alex's side and gently took our son from her and held him.

"Everyone, I'd like you to meet the newest Montgomery's," Alex said. She looked at Gabe, "Weighing in at six pounds three ounces; this is our daughter, Gabrielle Charlie. She looked at my dad and smiled, "And weighing in at six pounds five ounces; this is our son, Cade Wyatt."

Alex handed our daughter to Gabe, who had tears running down his face, and I handed our son to my dad, whose own eyes were shiny with tears as he looked at his grandson in awe.

There were oohs and ahs, and badass SEALs baby talking, as our twins were being passed around so everyone could hold them.

I knew they were in good hands, so at the moment, I only had eyes for my wife.

I leaned down and kissed her, "I love you, Mrs. Montgomery."

"I love you more, Mr. Montgomery."

"Not possible."

She smiled wide at me, "Tie?"

I nodded, smiling back at her, "Tie."

I didn't know it was possible to love this much. The love I felt for Alex and these two babies was staggering, and I saw that same emotion shining in Alex's eyes.

We smiled at each other, and I leaned over and kissed my beautiful wife again, reveling in the fact that we were a family.

EPILOGUE

Smoke

Six months later

It was Friday evening, and the team had gone to Alex and Reaper's for dinner; when we got the call we were being spun up very early tomorrow morning.

I was packed and ready, sitting outside on my patio getting into the right headspace. I was enjoying the peace and quiet when I heard my neighbor come out of her house and into her backyard.

She'd been living next door to me for almost seven months, and I'd wanted to meet her since the first time I saw her.

Something about her pulled at me, and I wanted to get to know her. She stood about five foot six and had the sexiest curves I'd ever seen.

Her hair was light blonde, almost white, shoulder length and curly. So curly, it bounced around her head whenever she moved. I wanted to put my hands in that hair. She had big blue eyes and a mouth that was meant to be kissed.

But something was off with her. She was a hermit, rarely leaving her house, and when she did, she always looked around before she came out. She was skittish and normally only left her house to walk her dog, a big, young black lab.

I wondered if she was hiding from someone, and if that was the case, I didn't want to scare her, so I was trying to go slow. I did manage to get a wave out of her before she ran away the other day, so I was making progress.

The only other thing I knew about her was that she was an artist. I knew that because most of her clothes were paint splattered, and I could see into the room she used from my kitchen window. I couldn't see details, but she sat in front of an easel painting almost every night.

Tonight, when she came out into her backyard, she was on the phone, talking to someone she obviously didn't like. I assumed she didn't know I was sitting here and could hear her side of the conversation.

"Okay, fine, you're sorry. Now stop calling and texting me. It's over."

"Twenty-three texts and twelve voicemails just today, Lonnie. You need to stop. You need to leave me alone."

"Ask me how many fucks I give. Go ahead, ask. I don't know what you're smoking, but I don't want anything to do with you ever again."

I almost laughed at her spunk. I was glad to hear her standing up for herself but had to wonder if 'Lonnie' was the reason she acted so afraid whenever she emerged from her house. It sounded like he was stalking her, and that concerned me.

"I don't care; goodbye Lonnie, don't contact me again."

After she hung up, I could hear her talking to herself, "Ahhh. As if I'd go anywhere near you after what you did, jerk face. Please don't let him find me, please, please, please.

"We're fine, everything's fine, miracles happen all the time, right, Hank? Miracles better happen because we really need one, buddy."

Hank must be her dog.

"You know the worst part about some jerk stealing all your money? Well, besides our electricity about to be turned off or that we really need food, and we'll probably be living in the car next month? There's no alcohol. Right now, I'd take a good stiff drink over electricity. I really would. If ever there was a time to get plastered, I think this is it."

The dog barked, and she laughed. "I see you agree. You're a smart one, Hank. C'mon, buddy, let's go back inside."

I wanted to help her, but how could I do that without coming off as a complete weirdo, especially when I didn't even know her name?

*****

We were on the plane as we headed out for our mission. Jax and Midas were talking while Boomer and Bruiser were sleeping. Reaper was sitting alone, and I went and sat down next to him.

"Alex told me your dad is coming in next week," I said to him after sitting down.

"Yeah. She wants to build a small barn with an apartment over it next to our house. Since dad's in construction, she was thinking she could talk him into building it and get him to stay awhile. It's part of her plan to build him a house and talk him into moving here."

"She wants to build him a house?"

Reaper grinned at me, "If she had her way, she'd build houses for dad and the whole team. She set aside two hundred acres to build a village. She likes having the family close."

"If she really feels the need, she can build me a house."

Reaper turned and smiled at me, "But that would take you away from your new neighbor."

"Speaking of, I overheard her on the phone last night; I think someone's harassing her. That could explain why she rarely leaves her house and is nervous as hell when she does."

"Harassing her? Harassing her how? Any idea who it is?"

"I think it's her ex-boyfriend. He sounds like a real asshole. I heard her say he'd sent twenty-three texts and left twelve voicemails in one day. She told him it was over, he needed to leave her alone and to stop contacting her. After she hung up, she was chanting, don't let him find me."

"Fuck. She needs to shut that shit down; it sounds like he's stalking her."

It wasn't surprising Reaper would react with anger.

I nodded, "Yeah, after everything that went down with Alex, we know how fast that shit goes sideways."

"What is it with these dickheads that just can't take no for an answer?" He asked, but I knew the question was rhetorical.

"That's not all of it. I think he stole her money, and she's having financial issues."

"What makes you think that?"

"After she told the jerk not to call her anymore and hung up, she was talking to her dog about someone stealing her money and not having food, her electricity about to be turned off and living in her car next month."

Reaper sounded as concerned as I was, "Fuck, Smoke. What are you going to do?"

"I don't know. I want to help her, but how do I do that? But I can't just walk over there and say, 'hi, I live next door, here's some groceries and by the way can I help you out with your rent and electric bill?' That makes me sound like a crazy person."

"If you could, *would* you bring her groceries and pay her rent and electric bill?"

"Yeah, I think I would."

"You really like this woman."

He wasn't asking; he stated it as a fact. It didn't surprise me since we were all as close as brothers, and I'd spoken of my neighbor many times before.

"I've never even talked to her, but there's something about her. Something that makes me want to get to know her. She's so adorable. She's sexy as hell, and I just want to put my hands in that crazy curly hair."

"Don't you think that would be easier if you actually met her?" Reaper asked with a laugh.

"You're enjoying this, aren't you?" I grumbled.

Reaper smiled wide, "A little bit, yeah."

*****

Will Smoke meet his neighbor? Is trouble lurking? Is his neighbor in danger? Find out what happens between Smoke and Hali in book two, *The SEAL and the Artist.*

Made in the USA
Middletown, DE
06 January 2023